MAGIC & MANNERS

Curtsies & Consequences, Book Two

Melissa Constantine

Contents

Dedication

*For Amy and Michelle,
I regret to inform you
that after almost 30 years
of friendship,
you're stuck with me.*

Chapter One

Diana

When her ship finally docked in Tull Harbor, Diana knew three things about the would-be finance she'd come to visit. One, he was incredibly handsome. Two, there was the distinct possibility that he drank too much. And three, that if he didn't show his face in the next five minutes, she was absolutely never going to forgive him.

Diana had pictured being greeted by the royal household. Prince Travers in his regalia, flanked by an army of servants lined up to take her trunks and traveling cases to sleek, lacquered carriages. Handsome men in the ornate teal livery of the Corvin family riding black horses beside them as they made their way up the coast to Tull Castle. A pennant or two waving in the breeze.

Perhaps it had been foolish – or naïve – imagining a grand welcome. The docks were a busy commercial district, crowded with ramshackle warehouses, used crab traps, and man-sized coils of rope. There wasn't exactly room for a royal procession. But, someone should have been here to meet her ship. The plans had been in place for months, yet there wasn't a prince in sight. Nor were there any carriages. Not even a dodgy-looking gardener with an ancient buckboard to take her belongings.

And, if the humiliation of being stranded didn't kill her, the overwhelming smell might. It was as if every fish in the Known Kingdoms had decided to die off all at once. Diana clutched a handkerchief to nose to cover the cloying miasma of rot.

"My Lady," said the Captain, hat in hand, "we're due to set sail again in an hour. We've got to get your belongings offloaded."

Diana flushed, and worry surged in her chest. "Of course. My staff are ready to assist."

The Captain gave her an apologetic look, the tips of his ears reddening. "Plenty of folks store their luggage with the Harbormaster while they sort out their transportation."

It was all too easy to imagine what her mother would have done if she were here. She'd pull herself up to her six-foot height, point imperiously at the Captain, and demand he delay his departure until the Prince arrived. Diana was tempted. If there was ever a time to channel the glorious confidence of the Countess of Wills, surely it was now.

But it wasn't the Captain's fault Travers was a reprobate. In their short acquaintance, the prince had shown a blithe disregard for proper etiquette. She'd tried to remember that while her mother planned their summer. Travers wasn't likely to have changed in the three months since she'd last seen him. She'd wanted to come to Tull with her eyes open. But she supposed she'd been caught up in the fantasy of it all. An official royal visit to an island known for its beauty, temperate climate, and abundance of polite society was a dream.

The rotting fish, however, were quickly turning it into a nightmare. Almost as soon as the white cliffs of Tull were in sight, the captain had sent out men in rowboats to clear a path through what appeared to be hundreds of thousands of small – and very dead – silvery fish. As omens went, that was bad.

Having no one here to greet her was worse.

"What do we do, My Lady?" her lady's maid, Maryann, asked.

Maryann suffered severe seasickness during their two-week journey from Wills, heaving into a chamber pot several times a day. Diana hoped that arriving on land would put her back to rights, but their luck thus far wasn't great.

Diana passed her one of her handkerchiefs. "I'm going to talk to the Harbormaster, and we'll see if we can send word to the castle. I'm sure there's been some innocent mistake."

Maryann shot her a weary look as she tied the cloth around her mouth and nose. Diana didn't blame her for being skeptical. Maryann knew all about Travers and his habits and had ventured to suggest that the visit wasn't a good idea. Being stranded on the dock was simply proof.

Diana had to trust that there had been some miscommunication with Lady Passwood, Travers' aunt and chatelaine, who had written with the date she should arrive. Surely the great lady had told her nephew when the ship would dock and Travers had forgotten.

Or been too drunk to remember.

Since they were clearly not in the kind of district in which hire carriages lolled around waiting for fares, she needed to do something before a tower of trunks grew around her. After all, what kind of impression would she make as the possible future Princess of Tull if she stood around helpless? Or worse, get crushed by her luggage five minutes after arriving?

Diana took one last bracing breath through her handkerchief, stuffed the material in her pocket, and squared her shoulders. "You and Alice wait for me here while Jonah and Bill get the trunks, " she said.

Maryann, whose eyes hadn't quite settled on a single disturbing image around them, nodded.

The Harbormaster's office was in a lop-sided red building, smaller than the entrance hall at Wills Castle. Diana knocked once, sharply, and let herself in. The office was one large room, with about as much organization as the surrounding neighborhood. Crab traps – bits of broken shells still clinging to wires – being the principal decoration.

A man in a wrinkled teal uniform sat at a large desk. He didn't glance up as Diana approached.

"Sir, I am in need of assistance," Diana said loudly.

"This is a shipping business, not a charity operation," he said, shuffling papers in a way that told Diana he was doing his best to look busy.

"I am Lady Diana Yarborough," she said. "If you would be so good as to look at me when I am speaking."

Hundreds of miles away, Diana could picture her mother smiling.

With a peevish expression, the man behind the desk looked up. His eyes were watery, and deep lines cut through his forehead. He wasn't much older than Diana, she decided, but whatever life he led, it was clearly harder than her own.

But it was not the time to demure. She needed to get herself, her staff, and her things out of the wharf district and up to Tull Castle.

"I need a message sent to the castle. The prince was supposed to have carriages here on my arrival."

"During the Quarter? Unlikely."

"I beg your pardon?"

The Harbormaster raised his eyebrows but otherwise declined to provide context. Diana felt as if he were speaking in code, and she was missing a critical cypher. "I am here on an official royal visit," she said carefully.

The man's laugh was like a short bark from a skinny dog. "Royals aren't on this part of the island during the Quarter."

"I have my invitation," she said, realizing that the Duchess's letter was in her traveling case, currently buried under her unmentionables. She wasn't about to riffle through them looking for it, and certainly not for this man.

She unclenched her jaw and tried to imitate her mother's voice. "Furthermore, I am a Lady. I require your assistance. Decency would demand you attempt to help me."

"I can't leave my post," said the man, as if explaining something to a child. "If I'm not here, the ships can come and go as they please."

"Can you at least direct me to where I might find transportation?"

The man remained silent. Diana did her best to keep her irritation in check, but she was afraid her flushed face might give her away. Being pale and redheaded was a disadvantage when faced with this kind of insolence.

"You are an employee of the crown, are you not?"

The Harbormaster nodded.

"I should hate to tell my host, the Prince, that I met such reluctance among his staff," Diana chose her words carefully. Threatening the man's job didn't feel good, and so she'd hoped a subtle implication would be enough.

Thankfully, the Harbormaster, while irritating, wasn't stupid. He sighed and pushed himself up from his desk. The uniform he wore was similar to the Tullish sailors that roamed over the docks, only less fitting. It was a guess, but she suspected that the man had simply put on the uniform of the last person to hold the job – a much larger man – rather than get his own.

"And what do you propose I do?" he asked.

"Do you have a vehicle I can borrow? I would like to get my staff on their way to the castle."

"Do I look like the type to keep a fancy carriage?"

"A cart would do," she said, refusing to break eye contact.

His sigh was legendary. He could win awards for it. "It's a single pony cart. But it is supposed to be used for official business only."

"I am as official as they come," she said. And then added as sincere a smile as she could manage. "Out back, is it?"

"Don't be sending my Penelope back hungry and overworked. She's a good girl."

"Penelope will be rewarded generously. I will make sure of it. And when our business is concluded, I am sure the Prince will send along a lovely thank you for you as well."

He shrugged. "Penelope likes carrots."

"Undoubtedly," she said, exiting through the door behind his desk.

***

The recalcitrant Harbormaster hadn't been lying. Penelope was only a pony, and the cart wasn't big enough for more than her two footmen. Her things would have to be stored until they had adequate means to get them out of the wharf district. Still, borrowing Penelope was better than waiting around to be robbed.

Diana gave the old pony a few pets and promised her a ton of carrots as she untied the animal's lead. "You're a pretty girl," she cooed. "You just come with me."

If horses could be said to have a dubious expression, the old girl did, but she allowed Diana to attach her reins and lead her out to where the four members of her staff waited.

"Bill," she said to her lead footman, "This lovely creature is to be our helper. She's got a small cart out back. I thought perhaps you and Jonah could take her up to the castle to help us make better arrangements."

"If we're up to the castle, My Lady, where will the rest of you stay?" he asked between placing kisses on the pony's nose.

"I am sure there is an inn where we can wait," she said. Although the surrounding area didn't look promising, surely the sailors had to spend their coins somewhere.

"There's a tavern up the street," Her younger maid, Alice, said. "While you were inside, one of the riffraff whistled at Maryann and me to join him at the Goose and Grouse."

"I'm sure that's a perfectly charming establishment," Diana muttered as Bill and her second footman got to work loading the pony cart with a few of the trunks carrying the more valuable items she'd brought, and moving the rest of her trunks into the disgruntled Harbormaster's office.

Diana, Alice, and Maryann found the Goose and Grouse just out of sight of the Princess Vogel, and as expected it was disgusting. But needs must. A lady and her servants couldn't very well stand around on the docks waiting for rescue. They might as well place a target on their backs.

Diana chose a booth in the far corner, away from the bar, while Maryann went to get them whatever passed for drinks. The tabletop in the booth was sticky with old ale, but Diana had better things to worry about. While Maryann was paying the tab, Alice used a spare handkerchief to scrub away some of the fresher puddles.

"This is not how I expected today to go," Maryann said, setting down three tankards.

Diana murmured her assent. Nothing on this voyage had gone as expected. First, her mother was to accompany her to Tull, but, just before they sailed, the Countess had come down with a nasty illness. Her cough and fever had gotten so bad, so quickly, that a healer was summoned, and then a traveling witch. Mother was going to be fine, but the witch had suggested that travel was ill-advised for several more weeks. Given that all of the arrangements had been made for the visit, there was nothing to do but continue without her.

With a surge of guilt, Diana remembered the freedom she felt on stepping on the deck of the Princess Vogel without her mother. She'd never traveled without the Countess, and it had felt exciting to be going to visit her possible future home by herself.

That effervescent feeling lasted exactly three days — until the sloop hit a massive storm. Diana wasn't prone to sea sickness, but Alice had been queasy, and Maryann downright miserable. Bill and Jonah weren't as bad off as the two maids but were in no shape to help tend to her. Diana didn't like to think of herself as helpless, but in those few days, tossed around on the sea like fallen crane petals on the wind, she'd missed the Countess so fiercely she wondered if she was cut out to ever leave home.

And now she was sitting in a seedy tavern, drinking ale that at best she'd describe as Fairie's piss. Awful, but perhaps if she drank it anyway something better would happen.

"My Lady, did Maryann tell you her big news?" Alice asked with a mischievous gleam in her eye.

"You have news?" Diana asked. Considering they'd spent the last two weeks cooped up on a ship it seemed odd that Maryann would have any secrets.

Maryann blushed. Like Diana, she had the classic paleness of the Northern Territories, so her skin turned a bright pink. "Bill proposed," she said hesitantly.

"That's wonderful," Diana said, glad for some happy news. "You'll make a lovely bride."

Alice, young as she was, seemed somehow happier for her fellow maid than Maryann was herself. Or perhaps that was just the effect of the lingering seasickness and the bad smell that wasn't quite absent from the pub.

"They're going to get married when they get back to Wills!" Alice said. "And I shall get to drink champagne at their reception."

Diana smiled. "Well, champagne is always a good idea. I'm happy for you, Maryann. Bill is a good man."

"Thank you, My Lady," Maryann said, pushing her tankard away. "I can't seem to shake this sickness. I thought a bit of water would help, but..."

"It's been a rough trip," Diana said. "Hopefully, once we reach the castle, your stomach will settle."

"And then you can plan your wedding!" Alice said. "Oh, I am so jealous. I would love to have a wedding."

"You'll need a fiancé first," Maryann said softly. Alice didn't hear that, bubbling along about getting the chance to wear a fancy dress.

"Have you decided if you'll keep working once you marry?" Diana asked.

Maryann had been her maid for two years. For the first time, Diana realized that if she did decide to marry Travers, she'd be moving to Tull. Most of her servants would likely stay in the north. Maryann had a big family and wouldn't want to move.

"I'm not sure yet," Maryann admitted. "I suppose it will depend on how soon we have children."

Diana rubbed her upper arms, suddenly cold. *Maryann was already thinking about children?* She was a year younger than Diana. Marriage was one thing – starting a family was entirely another. Not wishing to dampen Maryann's happy news with her own fears, she shifted the conversation. "I hope you will invite me to the wedding. I would love to see you so happy."

Maryann blushed. "That's kind of you, My Lady."

"But you shall have your wedding to plan!" Alice said, blue eyes wide, as if she just realized the entire purpose of their trip.

"Not yet," Diana said. "Prince Travers and I have not officially agreed to the engagement. This summer is about exploring that possibility."

A possibility that looked less and less likely the more time they had to wait in the Goose and Grouse.

They were ignored by most of the patrons in the tavern. Diana did her best to focus on the conversation with her maids, rather than dwell on the disappointment the day had brought. Maryann shared a few wedding plans she and Bill had discussed. They would likely have a small ceremony at the edge of the crane fields on her parent's farm.

"It's silly, but I thought if we could do it during the golden hour, just before sunset, we wouldn't have to spend much on decoration."

It sounded lovely, and a much different wedding than Diana was likely to have. The Countess wasn't going to want a small affair. Not for her only daughter.

"My sister Josie will want to be maid of honor, but I can't help but think she'll make a cake of it," Maryann laughed, a hopeful sign that her nausea was subsiding. "She can't even match her stockings most days."

A pang of envy temporarily displaced the worry in Diana's chest. She had no siblings, let alone scatterbrained ones. Although her parents had wanted a houseful, it wasn't to be. That was part of why it was so important for Diana to make a good match. Her family was far too small to continue to prosper.

The bar to the tavern opened, letting in a gust of bilgy air and a stream of sunlight that bit into Diana's vision. Three backlit figures walked up to the bar, and as Diana's eye adjusted to the change in light, Alice let out an audible gasp.

Maryann tried to shush her, but Alice wasn't deterred. "Have you ever seen that?"

The three Fairies who'd walked into the Goose and Grouse didn't acknowledge Alice's rudeness. The male and two females wore high-collared coats, despite the warm weather, and walked in gliding steps straight up to the bar.

"My mum says that if you see Fairies, something bad is going to happen," Alice said in a harsh whisper.

"Don't be silly, Alice," Maryann chided her. "They have as much right to be here as we do. Probably more so."

And yet, her lady's maid made a little crooked symbol with her middle and index fingers to ward off any potential curses.

At the bar, the Fairies were given three tankards. Diana had read every book she could get her hands on about Fairies, both Light and Dark Court, and none of them had ever mentioned any Fairies popping into a tavern for a drink. Most of them were keen to point out that Fairies didn't eat at all.

Tull was closer to the Unknown Kingdoms, where the population was heavy with Fairies, so she supposed it might not be unusual here. But the three standing at the bar were attracting their fair share of attention. Both of the women had brilliantly colored hair, one shocking pink and one sky blue. Both had dusty, tan skin and looked enough like twins that must have at least been sisters, while the tall, male Fairie had a milky, pale complexion that looked almost sickly. And though she couldn't be sure, she suspected his leather coat might be hiding a pair of wings.

"What do you think they're doing here?" Alice asked.

"Drinking," Diana said.

Which was all the three were doing, as far as she could tell. They weren't talking to each other. They stood at the bar, each of them with a tankard, sipping like it was a job instead of something enjoyable.

Given the flavor of the ale, Diana couldn't blame them.

After a pregnant moment where it seemed every patron in the Goose and Grouse was watching the Fairies, an older man emerged from the tavern's back room. He signaled to the Fairies with an imperious gesture. All three put down their tankards and walked stiffly toward him, where the door was shut firmly behind them.

Alice's mouth hung open. Even Maryann who was trying to be more circumspect, looked agog.

Diana couldn't blame them. Her curiosity was just as piqued.

There was no time to dwell on it, however, because Bill and Jonah were the next people to make their way into the tavern. Both men looked stricken as they approached the table. Bill clutched his hat in his hands.

"Is something wrong?" Diana asked, her gut knowing the answer before the next words were out of Bill's mouth.

"The Prince's family is not at the castle," Bill said.

Diana felt her stomach drop even further. "What?"

Bill glanced at Jonah, who took a step back as if excusing himself.

"No one seems to know you were to arrive today," Bill said. "And the butler says Lady Passwood, the chatelaine, is visiting a lord and lady on the other side of the island until the end of the month."

No, no, she had a letter from Lady Passwood to her mother, assuring her that today was the perfect day for them to arrive at Tull Castle. *It was in writing.*

"Perhaps they assumed we would be delayed," Diana said, although the feeling of being badly played like a cheap violin was settling rapidly into her chest. She was aware that Prince's aunt wasn't her biggest supporter, but to not be at home when company was expected?

"There's something else," Bill admitted.

What could possibly be worse? Diana wasn't sure she wanted to know.

"The whole place is torn apart. Not even the staff are staying at the castle while some work goes on."

Chapter Two

Diana

Finding a place to stay hadn't been terribly difficult. Every hotel in Tull seemed to have availability. Diana had chosen the best of them. If she couldn't stay in a castle, she wasn't going to hide in anything less than a luxury hotel. Diana knew her mother would approve. The Countess of Wills didn't do anything by half.

The Rutledge Hotel was a lovely, white-washed stone building perched on the edge of a cliff overlooking the sea. Diana had taken the nicest rooms for her and her staff. Her bedroom had a private balcony, which looked out over the water to Tull Castle. That couldn't be helped, she supposed. At least if the family did return, she wouldn't have to wait for word. She'd be able to see tiny little carriages approaching from miles away.

The hotel was surrounded by lemon groves on two sides, which filled the air with a sweet, citrus scent. Or it did, so long as the wind didn't shift and send the smell of dead fish wafting up the coast.

Maryann summed it best, her pert nose scrunched from the unpleasant smell. "It's like someone forgot to tell this island that it was supposed to be nice."

Diana couldn't help but agree. The visuals might have made for magnificent paintings, but the smell was downright awful.

Regardless, Diana was determined to course correct. And she would do that by taking stock. Several of her trunks had made it up to her room, but she needed to catalog everything to make sure nothing was lost. Her new wardrobe alone was twelve trunks.

Mother had employed an army of seamstresses to create new garments for her, almost from the moment the arrangements had been put in place, Diana would have thought the clothes she brought last spring to the Festival of the Flower were fine enough, but apparently, being the maybe-fiancé of a prince required changing her clothes several times a day, every day, for the rest of her natural life.

As the prince in question wasn't around yet, Diana couldn't confirm.

"Have you seen the blue trunk?" Diana asked. "The one with the gold straps?" She fought off a moment of panic that it might have gone missing.

"I think it's still downstairs," Maryann said, opening one of the clothing trunks and shaking out the wrinkles from a day gown.

"I'm going to go find it." The blue trunk had some of the most important things Diana had brought with her from home and she was loath to leave it to chance.

"My Lady, perhaps..." Maryann said, hesitantly, "Let me go look for it. You should write to your mother."

Oh, most definitely not. It was too early to bring in the cavalry. "No, I'll go. I need to do something productive."

Maryann's hands twisted. Diana felt just as unsettled, but no good would come of dwelling on it. Best to direct the maid's attention elsewhere. "Leave the clothing, it can surely wait. Why don't you find Bill and spend a little time together?"

Maryann blushed furiously. Diana suspected she was torn - do the right thing and remind her mistress that she really ought to write to her mother, or spend some alone time with her new fiancé after two full weeks at sea?

In the end, love won. Which was just fine by Diana. She headed to the hotel's reception area to see what had become of her blue trunk.

The Rutledge was a beautiful hotel, with modern black and white floor marble floors, and brightly polished brass chandeliers lit with dozens of enchanted Zephyr lamps. A double-sided spiral staircase surrounded the front desk like a crown, and the paintings on the walls were a series of seascapes in pastel colors. Really, it was beautiful.

And oddly empty.

It was summer. Tull was renowned for being the place to go boating, sea bathing, or walk along the boardwalks and eat salt-water taffy purchased from little shops.

Or so all the guidebooks she'd read in preparation for her trip had promised.

In any case, a hotel like the Rutledge should be overflowing with royals and other wealthy families. So why did it feel like there were at best a handful of guests? The entrance hall was strangely vacant, save the stacks of her luggage and one of the hotel's doormen, snoozing on a stool in a patch of sunlight, streaming in through mullioned windows.

The blue trunk wasn't in the stack in the front storage room. She needed that trunk. It contained what she had determined was her best chance of making a favorable impression during her time in Tull. She would use the contents to create something beautiful, a unique blend of her northern roots and her new life in the south. Something that regardless of her decision about Travers would create a sensation.

"Sir," she called to the sleeping man, "I require your assistance."

The man jerked awake. "Can't a man sleep?"

His voice, even sleep-weary, was familiar, and a prickle of awareness swept over her.

No, no, it couldn't be. Not here. What was he doing in Tull? Diana stared at the man, mute with shock. His dark blond hair was scrapped back into a half-hearted queue, and he wore a thick beard that was in bad need of a trim. Why was he sleeping in a public place? It was indecent. Uneasy, Diana asked, "Are you an employee of this hotel?"

He scoffed. "What gave you that idea?"

She pointed to the filigree patch on his jacket, the insignia of the Rutledge Hotel.

He looked down at it as if it were some deeply foreign object. "Must have got cold," he said, shrugging it off, and tossing it over the stool he'd just vacated.

Of all the people to be at a hotel, a thousand miles from where she'd last seen him.

He grinned at her like a cat who caught a canary. "I knew you enjoyed our kiss, but to follow me to Tull? Naughty girl." He had the audacity to roll back his shirt sleeves, exposing strong forearms.

Diana tried to look away. He was doing it deliberately, trying to draw her attention. Well, she wouldn't give it. "First of all, it was barely a kiss. It was an accident."

She had meant to kiss him on the cheek. A simple thank you for what she'd assumed was a sleeping man, recovering from a mysterious illness. He was the one who turned out to be awake and kissed her! "And furthermore..." Diana realized a beat too late that she'd fallen right into his trap, her dreaded blush heating her face again.

Sir Jordaan Van Dine let out an infuriating laugh, a low grumble of a sound that nonetheless worked its way down her spine.

Chapter Three

Jordaan

Fairies be, she was magnificent. The look of shock on her face would keep him warm for a winter. A flush ran through her freckles, and her mouth hung open, just a bit. There was a delicate little line just in the middle of her forehead. All in all, the confusion was adorable on her.

"What are you doing here, Sir Jordaan?" she asked, her voice a little breathless.

"Well, I was taking a nap."

"I mean in this hotel? In all of Tull, actually. You're supposed to be in Dunlock."

"That was months ago. A man can only sleep in someone else's castle for so long before he wears out his welcome."

"You..." She shook her head, the untamed frizz in her thick copper hair catching the last of the day's sunlight.

"Relax, Lady DeeDee, I'm here recovering."

She narrowed her eyes. "You very well know my name."

Jordaan yawned and stretched. "Maybe I do, maybe I don't."

She held up a hand as if words failed her. He wanted to laugh, just to see if he could make her any more angry. But she turned and walked toward the ridiculously large tower of trunks that had been clogging up the entrance hall. He followed her, eager to see just how far he could push her.

"Please tell me that this monstrosity isn't yours," he said.

"I am here for a royal visit, of course these are some of my things."

"Some? Fairies take me, what can all this possibly be?" He flipped the lid on one of the top trunks in the pile, exposing what looked like a pile of frilly white fabric.

Diana's large brown eyes went wide and she scrambled to shut the trunk. "If you would be so kind as not to expose my undergarments to the entire hotel."

"There's literally no one else here," he said, gesturing to the empty lobby.

"Be that as it may, these are my private things."

"Scandalous," he said drily.

She blushed to a shade he wasn't sure was possible on a human. It was too easy to rile her, but that didn't mean it wasn't fun. He leaned against the pile of trunks, yawning once again. The damned sleeping sickness was inconvenient. He'd been traveling with the witch, Caris Mourne, as she looked for a cure, but so far, he still needed a near-constant dosage of her potions. And as much as he wanted to keep standing here, needling Diana, he was going to have to excuse himself soon or he wouldn't be able to stay awake.

"If you're done acting like a child," she said. He could tell she was gearing up for a lecture, but she was interrupted by the opening of the front door and the arrival of three Fairies in long, dark jackets.

Two of the Fairies, the women, were small and had the sharp, pointed features common in Light Court Fairies. The male was considerably taller, and wore a grim expression, making his face appear like spoiled milk. The three of the Fairies didn't so much as make eye contact as they passed by them and the tower of trunks, but the sense of tension they brought into the hotel was palpable.

The Fairies seemed to know where they were headed, as they didn't so much as pause to look around. They headed for the front desk and then around the back of it into the manager's office. The door closed behind them, and a fission of some kind of magic sparked bright pink around the frame.

Diana gasped. "What the everlasting...?"

Jordaan feigned shock. "Language!"

But she didn't have the sense to blush this time. "That's the second time today I've seen them."

"Fairies showing up in public places? It's weird but not unheard of..."

She shushed him. She actually shushed him like he was a noisy toddler!

"What was that?" he asked.

But Diana was already moving toward the front desk, ignoring his manufactured outrage. Which is probably why he followed after her. Aside from the fact that she shouldn't be eavesdropping on Fairies. That was a good way to end up spending eternity as the back half of a goat.

"Delilah, this is not a great idea," he said, once again unable to stop a yawn.

She spun around so quickly that he ran into her. Which wasn't a bad thing. Diana Yarborough was all lush curves. He didn't have much time to enjoy that fact, as she quickly pushed him off with a little impatient shove. "Do me a favor and shut up, Johnny," she said in a harsh whisper. "I want to find out what's happening."

He put a hand on her arm to stop her from going any closer to the office door. "Trust me, you don't want to get caught listening to Fairie business. All around bad."

The redhead actually rolled her eyes as she shook off his hold. "Twice today, I've seen those Fairies march into buildings and disappear behind locked doors. Don't you think that's weird?"

Jordaan got a sick feeling in his chest. He hadn't dealt with Fairies directly, but he knew – that way trouble lies. "Denise, let it go."

"Please be quiet, James," she hissed as she pressed her ear against the office door.

He definitely needed to get himself up to his room. He needed more of the anti-sleep medication. His limbs and his eyelids were already beginning to feel heavy.

"Darla..."

"Jack?"

Jordaan had to admit, the name thing was getting old fast. "Do us a favor?"

"Hmm?" She said, still straining to hear whatever was none of her business.

"Don't let my head hit anything sharp," he said, just as his legs gave out underneath him.

He was mildly certain he heard her shriek before he passed out.

***

In the months since the sleeping sickness had started to affect him, Jordaan had woken up in some less-than-ideal places. Tavern floors, water closets, and once curled between the seats of a beached rowboat. Generally, he was roused by the witch, Caris Mourne, forcing some kind of concoction down his throat.

Waking up to Lady Diana leaning over him was by far his favorite. Even if she was calling him Justin and poking him in the chest. "We have to stop meeting like this," he croaked.

She exhaled in relief. "Oh, thank the Fairies. I thought you were dead."

"Not dead," Jordaan said, struggling to sit up.

"Are you all right?" she asked. She pressed a bare hand to his forehead as if taking his temperature.

"I'm prone to falling into a deep sleep at all hours of the day, but other than that I'm fine."

She moved her hand to the back of his neck. "I don't think you have a fever," she said.

Not that he minded her touch one bit - but he wasn't an invalid. "I'm fine. I promise."

She withdrew her hand, tugging a neat green leather glove back on. "Well, I'm glad. Those trunks are hard enough to get out of his lobby, I couldn't imagine getting a body out as well."

"You are so charming," he muttered. The door to the manager's office was open, with no sign of the Fairies who'd entered it. "Where did they go?"

She stood up. "They left after I screamed. I sent the hotel employee they were with to find Caris Mourne."

He groaned. He wasn't in the mood for the witch's quirky little reminders about taking the potions she made for him at the appropriate times.

He rubbed his eyes with his palms until he saw stars. "Thank you."

"Do you need help standing up?"

He raised an eyebrow. "Why would you think that?"

"You're a knight, Sir Jordaan. And a lady is standing while you're still sitting on the floor."

"Where?"

"Excuse me?"

"A lady, where?"

"You're exceptionally rude, do you know that?"

Jordaan leaned back against the cool marble tile of the hotel floor. He meant to get up. He did. It was just that his body wasn't exactly cooperating. But he'd be damned to the Fairie Wastelands if he was going to take Lady Diana's help. "Don't forget I'm also an impertinent scallywag." He yawned, shutting his eyes against the light which seemed suddenly too bright. It was possible that sparing with her was more interaction than he'd had with anyone in weeks.

"I prefer to think of him as a charming pest," he heard Caris Mourne say.

"And my savior arrives," Jordaan said.

The witch's footsteps echoed through the lobby, and her distinct scent of fresh-cut grass grew closer. In the last few months, he'd come to know her presence by sound and smell, because when she approached, his eyes were often shut. Actually, it wasn't a bad way to get to know anyone. Diana, for example, seemed to always wear a subtle, floral perfume that gave him indecent thoughts.

"Ma'am," Diana said to the witch. "He fell, out of nowhere."

"He does that a lot."

"I have a condition!"

"Of course, Sir Jordaan. If you would be so kind as to sit up. I have a dose of the stimulant potion for you."

"Joy." He sat up, trying to take a deep breath, though his lungs weren't cooperating. "All right, give it."

A small vial of brilliantly blue liquid was dropped into his open hand. He grimaced. The blue was absolutely the worst. He would belch for an hour afterward. He uncorked the vial and knocked back the potion before the sour taste could linger too long on his tongue.

Nasty as it was, the effect was immediate. He felt it zing through his blood, waking up his sluggish body bit by bit. "Thank you, My Lady," he said, remembering his manners.

"You're welcome, Sir Jordaan." The witch turned to Diana. "I keep telling him to carry a dose with him, but he is reluctant."

"The vials leak! I ruined two perfectly good tunics." Jordaan wasn't sure why he felt the need to defend himself, only that Diana had an arch, amused expression that jabbed at him.

"It is good to see you again, My Lady," Diana said, curtseying to the witch.

"Are you staying at The Rutledge?"

"For now. I'm visiting Prince Travers for the summer."

"Well, then I hope to see you around. Please feel free to ignore my patient. He tends to get underfoot."

"I am a grown man, not a child!"

Diana bit back a laugh, which was a shame. He suspected that her laugh would be worth hearing.

"If you'll excuse me. Before Sir Jordaan had his episode I was on the search for a particular piece of luggage and I would like to resume the hunt."

He noticed she left out the part where she attempted to spy on a pair of Fairies.

"Did it happen to be a small blue piece, with gold trim?" Caris Mourne asked. "It was mistakenly delivered to my suite. I'll send a porter down with it." Diana's shoulders dropped as though she'd been carrying a heavy load she was grateful to finally put down. "Thank you."

"Is that where you're keeping all the drawings you made of me during the Festival of the Flower?" Jordaan couldn't help but ask.

"Yes. I distribute them along the Royal Route to warn people about you," Diana said, with a final curtsy.

Chapter Four

Xavier

There were stranger ways to start the day, but finding a crown prince face down in a puddle was definitely high on the list.

"Travers. Trav. Get up." Xavier nudged him with his boot. "Come on, man."

Travers didn't so much as twitch. Xav knelt down and rolled him over so that the prince wouldn't drown in an inch of water. It wasn't an elegant move, and the process displaced most of the puddle onto his clothing.

"Trav! Seriously. Wake up."

Travers snored.

Fine, he would resort to more extreme measures. Xav stuck a finger in his mouth, gathering a bunch of spit, and then plunged the finger into Travers's ear. The effect was nearly immediate. Travers yelped and moved away as if he'd been shocked.

"What in the..."

Xav wiped his finger on his trousers. "You ever need to get a brother out of your space, you go with the wet willy."

"That is disgusting."

"Says the man who looks like he was dragged through a swamp. When I left you last night you were safely in the Goose and Grouse. How the hell did you end up out here?"

Travers rubbed a hand through his black hair, his dark eyes squinting against the burgeoning sunlight. "I don't know. There was wine, women, song... possibly some illegal gambling. That's as far as my memory goes."

"You're a mess. Come on, let's get some breakfast."

"That's the only useful thing you've suggested in days."

"Occasionally I have a decent thought."

Travers pulled himself up off the ground, and the two of them made their way toward the wharf, where there was a small bakery that sold hand pies, mainly to sailors coming off the ships. They were hot, cheap, and great for sopping up alcohol rolling around in the stomach. Coffee would also help. Xav was nursing a hangover that felt like Travers looked.

"Where did you go last night?" Travers asked.

"You don't want details."

"So you had fun with that sailor then?"

Xav shrugged. He didn't kiss and tell.

Travers didn't press. For all his faults, he was the kind of friend who knew when to keep his mouth shut.

The waterfront wasn't a pretty place. In other years, it might have skated by with the little charm it earned with waves lapping against the shore and the gentle call of the seabirds, but not during the Quarter Year. Xav had learned the hard way on arriving in Tull two weeks ago about the brutal fish die-off that took place every fourth summer. The smell had been nauseatingly bad. Xav had tried to convince himself he'd gotten used to it in the past few days, but he was on the verge of admitting defeat. It was awful and was only getting worse. He understood why Travers could go incognito in his own territory. Royals likely didn't stick around when the island smelled like literal death. Of the few people they passed on their way to the pie shop, all of them were dock workers, sailors, or laborers going about their day.

Mina's Pies was a welcome respite, calling to them inside with scents of butter and cinnamon. They gratefully grabbed an empty table in the back. There was no such thing as a menu. As soon as they sat, the proprietress came over with two mugs of coffee.

"Morning, boys," she said with a cheery sing-song. "Another late night?"

"Something like that," Travers muttered.

"We'll get some pies out to you in a minute. Best thing for getting you going in the morning."

"Thanks, Mina," Xav said.

The pie shop owner gave them one of her bigger grins, before disappearing into the kitchen.

"You think she knows who we are?" Travers asked.

Xav didn't think so. Two princes turning up every day looking like gutter rats was a situation bound to be good gossip. And gossip like that would draw a much bigger crowd to Mina's shop. The shop had a handful of tables with a view of the wharf, although not enough customers to fill them. Which was a shame, because Mina's pies were good - filled with fat apples, or spiced pumpkin, or whatever she felt like cooking. When the plate of pastry was delivered, they ate in silence. Travers looked worse than Xav had seen him since they started traveling together in late spring. While they'd both been indulging in a variety of vices, Travers had gone so much farther. He was running from something, but Xav hadn't asked too many questions. He had his own secrets to keep. Still, he was glad they'd arrived in Tull. Maybe being home would help Travers get cleaned up.

Literally and figuratively.

It had definitely been a while since the crown prince had a bath. Spending last night outdoors didn't help. The two of them seemed to be competing to make themselves into the biggest wretch this summer.

Mornings like this, recovering from too much to drink, were all too common. This morning was no different than three dozen others, although this time Xavier was well aware he was probably projecting. Maybe Travers didn't need to go home, but he certainly did. He wasn't sure when he'd realized it; sometime in the last few days between pints of ale and another chorus of some bawdy ballad. But he felt an undeniable pull to sober up, put on a clean shirt, and set sail for Dunlock.

He simply had no idea how to bring it up.

The pie shop was quiet and peaceful.

A little too peaceful.

He was going to say something to Travers, but the prince's face had gone pale, sweat gathering in the slick, black hair at his temples. He looked ill, rather than just bottle-weary.

"You don't look good," he said cautiously.

Travers put his head down on the tabletop, using his folded arms for a pillow. "'Emfine," he said, slurring his words.

"We can take breakfast back to the Inn."

Travers waved his hand to say no, and let out a groan as if the minimum effort he put into the conversation was taxing.

Xav got up and ventured to the front counter. "Can I have some water?" he asked. "My friend is a bit under the weather."

Mina raised an eyebrow, clearly skeptical. "Sick, is he?"

Xav blushed. They'd been coming most mornings since they arrived in Tull, and despite not knowing their names, the baker wasn't blind to the way they'd appeared in her shop the last two weeks. She fetched a chilled bottle of water and a couple of glasses, smirking as she handed them over.

Xav thanked her and slid over an extra coin for her trouble.

He poured Travers a cup. The prince grasped at the air a dozen times before he was finally able to take it. As the liquid dribbled down his chin, the door to the bakery opened, and three people in long, dark coats strode up to the counter. Xav was distracted from his task of tending to his friend at the site of them.

It was the heat of a Tull summer, and yet each of them wore their coats buttoned up to their necks. They stood at the counter in a V-formation, the man standing a step forward from the two women, one of whom had shocking pink hair. She had an identical, pixy-like face to the other woman, whose short-cropped hair was baby blue. The man stood a head taller than both women and had a glare that could cut glass. Fairies, Xav realized. He tried to nudge Travers into looking, but his friend only moaned and then made a pillow of his arms.

"Can I help you?" Mina asked the Fairies.

"We seek Prince Travers," the man said to her in a brusk, dismissive way.

Xav was startled to hear Travers's name from the Fairie. What reason could magical beings be looking for him?

"You won't find a prince here, Sir. We cater to drunks and sailors."

The male Fairie tightened his expression. "You will tell us where to find the Prince," he said, turning his cold blue eyes out to the small collection of tables. Interestingly, his gaze seemed to slip over them, as easily as water flowing over a round stone. "We believe he is here."

Mina scoffed. "I know you Fairie-types don't eat, but this is a bakery, not a castle. We don't keep Princes lying around in the back with the flour."

No, princes got tables by the window. Xav hoped Travers wasn't inclined to pop his head up. Hungover as he was, that wasn't likely, but not impossible. He had a feeling it wasn't a good idea for Travers to greet anyone, much less Fairies, in the state he was in.

"You will not speak to Smit of the Light Court so disrespectfully," the pink-haired Fairie said with a vicious tone.

"I don't care who he is," Mina said. "I serve pie here. Savory, sweet, whatever you like, but not royals."

Xavier tried to remember if he'd ever read or learned anything about a Fairie called Smit. His memory was a blank space, with only the vestiges of last night's debauchery around the edges. If he were sober, perhaps something might stand out to him, but likely it was a name he'd never heard before. Which could mean Smit was high up in the Fairie Courts. The higher the fae, the more the Fairies kept to themselves.

"You will produce the Prince!" shouted the pink-haired woman. She was a bit like an angry cat, Xav thought, all hiss and spite.

Travers groaned. "Tell her to shut up, would you?" he mumbled.

His words didn't draw the eyes of the Fairies. In fact, they might as well have not been there at all for all the Fairies knew.

It was speculation, but Xav was sure they couldn't see him.

The pie shop smelled heavily of cinnamon. That wasn't unusual, but a heavy scent of cinnamon was also indicative of certain types of magic. Light Court magic.

But why would members of the Light Court have used an enchantment that prevented them from seeing the very person they were looking for? It was a conundrum that made Xav's head hurt far beyond the bottle of whiskey he'd drunk last night.

"Do you see this?" Xav turned to Travers, but the prince was unconscious. Again. There should be a rule against rousing the same friend more than once a day. "Trav! Hey!" Xav said, trying to keep his voice low. "Wake up."

He grabbed Travers by his lapels. The prince's head flopped back like a limp rag doll. Xav stuck his fingers in Travers's water glass and flicked some of the liquid at his face. It roused him, at least to wince and try and wipe away the droplets.

Travers groaned, and his eyes opened, only for Xav to realize his mistake. Drool had gathered at the corners of Traver's mouth. He knew what was coming. Honestly, he'd be less surprised if the bakery's doors had blown off.

"Don't even think about it," Xav said in warning, but the words were barely out of his mouth when Travers heaved, covering him in half-eaten pie, and what might have been the entirety of the Goose and Grouse's ale stores.

"What in Fairie Hells?" Mina gasped. "You can't be doing that here!"

She bustled out from behind the counter, completely ignoring the three Fairies, who stood in their formation, each of them with their hands clasped, unconcerned with the chaos of a vomiting prince.

Mina threw a towel at Xav. "Who do you think you are, coming into my shop and doing that? Men who can't hold their liquor don't get pie."

"I apologize on my friend's behalf. He had a rough night." Xav said, trying his best to get the sick off his shirt front.

"Rough night?" Mina said with a huff. "Fella, that's a rough week and a half. It'll take me an hour to get this stink out."

"He's been depressed," Xav said. "He's going through some things."

Mina's expression softened. "Yes, well, do you have someplace you can take him? In his condition, he needs a healer."

Oh, they had a place. "Yes, I can... I can get him home."

"Get some good plain food for him, and plenty of water. And don't let him drink. Not if you ever want to be in my pie shop again."

Xav reached into his pocket and took out the remainder of his ready coin. "For your trouble," he said. Mina accepted the coins, thrusting them into her apron pocket. Xav knew he'd have to visit a bank to get some more funds, a thought that filled him with dread. His father would get notice of the draft. Xav had taken more money from his account in the last three months than what was needed to run Dunlock Castle for a year. He could practically feel his father's disappointment from here.

Having cleaned himself and Travers as best he could, Xav got the prince to his feet. Travers immediately slumped against him, dead weight. Hopefully, Travers had some money on him for a hack, otherwise, it would be a long walk to Tull Castle.

Leaving the shop they passed so closely to the Fairies that Travers's leg brushed against Smit's long coat. No look of recognition passed in the Fairie's expression.

***

The housekeeper screamed. The butler went white as a ghost. Thankfully, The head groom pulled Travers from the back of the borrowed pony cart by his coat – rather like a puppy being picked up by its mother – and dunked the prince in the horse trough a handful of times until he woke up sputtering and fighting.

"What in the Fairie Hells?" Travers gasped.

Xav kept his answer to the household staff vague. "The Prince and I ran into some trouble by the wharf."

"I'm fine," Travers said, but then turned to retch over his shoes.

"Did that trouble happen in the sewers?" asked the head groom with a skeptical eye on the filthy, dripping prince.

"Near enough," Xav said.

"You're supposed to be with Lady Passwood," the housekeeper. Her voice was fretful, which matched the way she wrung her hands. "At Vella House."

"Mallory Vella hates me more than any other person in the world," Travers said with a hiccup. "Why would I subject myself to that?"

Xav took note of the name. He'd heard it on more than one occasion. Usually when Travers was the sleepy kind of drunk and feeling particularly sorry for himself.

"Your Highness," began the butler, a little bald man with a congenial kind of roundness to him, "you see, you weren't expected home for several more days."

Travers's confusion was visible even with the mud on his face the water in the horse trough hadn't managed to remove. "Why should it bloody matter?"

"Um," the butler hesitated.

"Yes, you see..." the housekeeper said.

"Lady Passwood ordered some renovations," the butler said quietly. "As you wouldn't be returning until..."

"My aunt is a menace," Travers gasped.

He retched again, in great soul-shaking heaves. Xav was unable to save his shoes as he kept his friend from collapsing into the dirt.

Chapter Five

Mallory

Not for the first time, Mallory observed, there was an art to being a royal. And as artists went, Lady Passwood was a true master.

She'd been in residence less than a week, and already had the attention and respect of the entire staff. Even the newer servants who had never been subject to one of her visits before seemed to hang on her every word. Mallory's maid, Trudy, was currently lapping up the good Duchess's instruction on the newest, most fashionable hairstyles. Worse, she was taking notes in a little book, like a schoolgirl.

Mallory shuttered to think of the subtle torture she'd undergo in the name of "Waterfall braids," and "an elegant, side-swept chignon," whatever that was.

It wasn't just the staff that had fallen under Lady Passwood's sway. Her parents thought the sun rose and set on the woman. Baron and Baroness Vella considered her their oldest, best friend in the entire world.

They didn't seem to mind one bit when she came to stay and took over the entire running of the house. Her mother welcomed it.

"It makes her happy to run things," Mother had said when Mallory complained. "And who am I to stop a Duchess from being happy?"

Mallory had to wonder if the kind of control she exerted did make the woman happy. It seemed as if she were trying to hold the whole world up on her shoulders. That had to be tiring. She'd almost asked Lady Passwood at dinner last night, but her father had stopped any impertinent questions she might ask by making prolonged, and significant, eye contact and shaking his head ever so slightly.

"You see?" Lady Passwood said to Trudy. "Lady Mallory has a very oval-shaped face."

"Yes, I suppose," Trudy said, drawing a shaking oval in her notebook.

"Let me show you, to be sure," Lady Passwood said.

Mallory was unable to protest before Lady Passwood swept her hair away from her face, holding the majority of it away from her neck. She gestured to Mallory's jawline, "You see the curve here?"

"Yes, yes," Trudy nodded excitedly.

"Excuse me, would you stop?" Mallory asked. She would have liked to leave the room altogether, but her chair was parked in the sitting room, and she hadn't the strength to reach down and release the break herself. She would need Trudy to do that, and the girl was too enamored of the great lady teaching her about Mallory's face shape.

"Hush, my darling, I'm showing her for your own good. You can't leave this mass of hair as it is. Eventually, it will get caught in the wheels of your chair and then where would you be?"

Mallory rolled her eyes. Yes, technically it was true. Her hair was much too long, well past her waist. But it was shiny and healthy and she'd grown it and cared for it all herself. Unlike her legs, her hair worked 100% of the time. She didn't need new hairstyles, because she liked it the way it was. Who cared if it was fashionable to put it up in complicated towers of curls? She preferred to wear it down. Even if that did mean she ended up sitting on it from time to time.

"I don't have the patience to have my hair done," Mallory said.

Lady Passwood smiled. It was a soft smile that said, "What are you going to do, run away?"

Which of course she couldn't, even on her good days.

Mallory wanted to throw something.

Unfortunately, throwing things was yet another thing her body wasn't willing to do at the moment. It was simply one of those days where she had more than her fair share of limitations.

"Let's get you some tea," Lady Passwood said, knowing she'd won this round of sparring with her Fairie goddaughter.

The Duchess sent Trudy to the kitchens to have the tea brought up, leaving the two of them alone.

"I prefer coffee," Mallory said.

The idea was immediately dismissed. "Coffee leaves you with terrible breath."

"So?"

"So you will hardly attract a spouse with bad breath."

Mallory had no response. She wasn't going to find a spouse. The rich and the royal didn't want a Baron's daughter with a middling dowry who often needed a wheeled chair to get around. "That is an awful reason to avoid the superior drink."

Lady Passwood was unconvinced. She settled herself on the settee, her great pink skirts arranged artfully around her like a fussy china doll. Really, she was beautiful, in the way that older women could be. And Mallory supposed it was the way she carried herself with confidence that made a person ignore the small wrinkles at the edge of her eyes and bits of gray in her black hair.

"Tea is not just a drink," the lady said. "It is an event."

"Tea *time* is an event. And as I have had far more lemonade than tea during tea time, your assertion is false."

"Children are given lemonade," Lady Passwood said. "You are no longer a child. You are one of the most beautiful, eligible young women in the Known Kingdoms, and it is my job as your Fairie godmother to find you the husband or wife you deserve."

"You are entirely biased," Mallory said, "as you've known me my entire life."

The Duchess didn't seem to think that was an issue at all. She forged ahead. "Yes. I am. But I also have excellent taste. And therefore I have decided that it is my mission to help you. I've spoken to your parents about it and they agree. It is time you were out in society, and I will shepherd you through it until such time as you find your true love."

Mallory groaned. True love was a myth of the highest order.

"What if I don't want one? What if I just want to get old and crotchety and have eight thousand cats?"

Lady Passwood's response was a succinct, "No."

"Those cats could be my true love!"

"You're allergic, dearest."

Chapter Six

Diana

Diana brushed a damp lock of hair back from her face. She needed to get up, have a bath, and get ready for bed, but she was moments away from a breakthrough. She could feel it.

She dabbed her wrist with her newest concoction. The top note was right, the sweet, plummy scent of Tull's Exe Crane. But then it all went wrong far too fast. Instead of a pleasant middle note of citrus, and the final, subtle waft of the Wills crane, her skin had a rather... unpleasant moldy smell. She had been so careful with the ingredients, measuring out the drops of the refined essence into the alcohol and oil mixture.

Why weren't the scents emerging as they ought? She flipped through the book on perfume making, trying to see if she'd missed anything.

But no, the order, the amounts, she'd measured them all precisely. And each of the vials of the various crane extracts smelled wonderful on their own.

"My Lady?" came Maryann's thoughtful inquiry. "Did you get any sleep last night?"

"Huh?" Diana grabbed a clean handkerchief and wiped the unfortunate mixture from her skin with some cool water. "What time is it?"

"Near seven."

In the morning?

"I suppose not, I've been working."

"I can tell," Maryann said, clearly trying to hold her breath.

Diana looked around; her vision momentarily blurred as she realized that the sun was streaming in through the suite's large windows. She hadn't meant to work all night. She'd only wanted to see if she could get a start on the new perfume she wanted to create. But then, there had been failure after failure. The book said it might take considerable time to get the ingredients to work together, but Diana was impatient.

Perhaps it was silly, but she felt as if she could create a new scent that mingled the Wills crane with the ones from Tull, she'd make a good impression on the people here. One based on her accomplishments, not just that she came with an enormous dowry and a title.

"Let's get you cleaned up," Maryann said gently. She took the vial of would-be perfume from Diana and helped her to her feet. "I'll have Alice handle putting these things away."

Diana looked at the mess she'd made. The carpet was littered with small brown bottles and glass droppers. She'd have to find some way to dispose of all the rejects, or else the entire hotel might be subject to them. Although, it would do a fair bit to cover the fish smell. Even high on a bluff, the Rutledge wasn't immune to the stink.

"I'm so close to getting it right," Diana said, yawning.

"Of course," Maryann said, leading her to the attached bathing room. "Maybe a hot bath and some breakfast will be just the thing to give you a fresh start."

Which was a nice way of saying, "Please wash, so the rest of us don't suffer."

Maryann fiddled with the taps over the tub. Wills Castle had many luxuries, but running water wasn't one of them. Her father hadn't yet seen the need to install them when they had an army of servants who could fetch and carry buckets. There were pumps in the kitchen, and in the washroom, but nothing so refined as the system that drew heated water up to the third floor. Diana had loved having piped in water at Dunlock during the Festival of the Flower, and she was glad to see that The Rutledge was likewise equipped.

When the tub was filled with warm, soapy water, Maryann helped her out of her perfume-soaked dress.

"I'll have to send this out for cleaning," she said, taking the mass of green and pink striped fabric in her arms. "And possibly mine as well."

"Sorry," Diana said, sliding under the bubbles.

Maryann left her alone to soak, and Diana let the warmth sink under her skin. She had to be doing something wrong with the perfume. All the books she'd read on the subject had said the same things. Make the mediums, add the scents in order, and ta-da, a new perfume.

She should have known it wouldn't be that easy.

Nothing ever was.

This trip, for instance, should have been easy. Her mother had made all of the arrangements with Lady Passwood. They had arranged the ship, the exact dates when the weather was known to be exceptionally fine, and assured Diana that she would be welcomed at Tull Castle.

And yet, here she was in a nearly-empty hotel, without her mother, and without any idea of when she could expect to move to the castle. If at all, given the slight.

She should write to her mother as Maryann had suggested yesterday. But how would she even begin to explain it in a way that wouldn't make the Countess worry? Until Diana could be assured that her mother had recovered from her illness, she didn't want her to worry about anything.

Maryann returned to help her wash her hair. Instead of one of the fashionable, high-waisted day-dresses that filled her mountain of trunks, the maid brought over a sensible flannel nightgown. "I thought you had best try to get some sleep," she said. "For a few hours anyway."

As she was in danger of falling asleep in the bath, Diana didn't object. When she'd pruned up to her liking, she got out and gladly donned the nightgown.

"It's going to be warm today," Maryann said, turning back the covers on the large four-poster bed. "I could leave the windows open."

"Please. The air can't be any worse than the mess I made."

***

Diana didn't believe much in the idea that dreams were prophetic. She was too practical for that. But when she awoke several hours later, the remnants of a nightmare clung to her like spiderwebs. She couldn't remember the exact order of things, but there had been a spinning wheel clacking, soft and repetitive, as a servant in a white cap spun copper-colored thread. It had been pleasant, — until it wasn't. Fear had crept up behind her like an advancing shadow. She'd run from it through a series of staircases and long, stone corridors.

Was she supposed to be afraid of something? She couldn't imagine what. And yet, her legs ached as if indeed she had run miles and miles.

Although maybe that was sitting on the floor all night playing chemist.

Alice brought her a pot of tea and a tray of pastry from the hotel kitchens, for which Diana was grateful. She preferred to start her days with breakfast and was suspicious of anyone who said they didn't like to eat in the mornings.

How sad must their days be if they couldn't take twenty minutes to eat an apple pastry while still in their nightclothes?

"Did you sleep okay, My Lady?" Alice asked, refilling her teacup.

"Bad dreams," Diana admitted. "I can't seem to shake them."

"Try some cold water. My mum also says anything can be fixed with water. A good cry. A swim in the sea, or a cold glass to take your troubles away."

As advice went, that wasn't bad. "Your mother sounds like a smart woman."

"That's what my da always says he loves about her. Other women might have been richer, or more beautiful, but beauty fades and money gets spent. Smarts are forever."

Diana smiled. She'd like to be known for her brains, rather than her money. Diana dismissed the idea of being known for her beauty. She was too tall, her feet too big, and her hair was too far on the orange side of red. Not to mention that she was incredibly fond of cake. She'd never be as thin as the women depicted in the fashion plates her mother poured over each month, but that was just fine by Diana. She liked her body.

She just wasn't the type that anyone was going to fall in love with at first sight. Not Princes or even poor knights. Those men, in particular, tended to like the small, waifish blondes with questionable behavior.

Diana drained her tea, shaking off her momentary melancholy. She had tried not to dwell on everything that happened in the spring. She'd spent most of the Festival of the Flower imagining herself in love with one of her oldest friends, Sir Robert Lycette. Her head had been filled with a hundred scenarios about how they might end up together. Too bad he was busy falling in love with someone else. All her hopes had come to nothing, and she'd been left feeling heartbroken and foolish.

"Would you like me to fetch you that water, My Lady?" Alice asked. "There's a spring near here where the hotel gets some fancy mineral water."

"I'll go myself," Diana said. "I think I could use a walk. Can you ask Jonah to meet me in the entrance hall in half an hour or so?"

Alice curtsied and hurried off to find the footman while Maryann helped Diana with her dress.

"Alice is sweet on Jonah," Maryann said. "But I don't think he's as enchanted with her."

"They're both very young," Diana pointed out. "I doubt anything will come of it."

"I just worry she's setting herself up for heartbreak."

Diana's own heart thumped in her chest. Perhaps she would make sure Alice had little interaction with Jonah going forward – for her own good.

Not that absence had made her own disappointment in love any easier to deal with.

***

The front desk clerk assured Diana that the best place to get water from the spring wasn't to head into the orchard and visit the source, but to visit a place called Stuart's Pump Room, to see and be seen.

Diana didn't care much about being seen as of yet, but she was mildly curious about the mineral water. She had Jonah accompany her as she walked the mile into town. Diana had always been relaxed with her servants — it seemed silly to ignore people who were always hovering about waiting on you — but Jonah wasn't chatty. He'd walked a pace behind her as she made her way to Stuart's, which was on the high street running through the fashionable part of town.

Or, at least it appeared to be the fashionable end of town. Gone were the warehouses and crab traps that had populated the waterfront. The buildings here were neat, well-maintained, and very, very beige. The same light stone seemed to have made all of them.

Still, there were a handful of shops, including a dressmaker's that had some rather lovely gowns on display in the window. Not that she was ever likely to need more clothes, but it was good to know her mother hadn't been wrong in her choices for Diana's visitation wardrobe. The clothes she'd brought were equal to what she saw at the dressmaker.

The building that housed Stuart's had twenty steps up to the front door, as if somehow forcing patrons to walk up so many stairs gave them a sense of occasion.

Diana gave her name to a man at the entry, who announced her presence in a booming voice, along with the tap of a heavy wooden staff on the floor. Caught off guard as all eyes in the room turned toward her, Diana tried to descend the steps down into the ballroom without falling.

The pump room got its name from a frightfully large iron contraption that was built in the middle of a ballroom. It was at least eight feet tall and had a number of gears that turned together to bring water up from an underground stream. The water was then pushed through a series of long, skinny pipes that wrapped around the pump. When a glass of mineral water was requested, a man with a very bushy mustache would fill a crystal goblet from a gold spigot attached to the end of one of the pipes.

"Madame," said the man with the mustache. "I do hope you enjoy."

"Thank you," Diana said, taking the glass.

Although the man had assured her when she'd asked that the water was filtered inside the pump, the liquid she was given had a gray tinge. It also smelled of sulfur.

Diana was starting to realize that maybe the reason she'd had no luck with her perfume yet was that Tull was simply too smelly of a place. Even the water had a bad odor.

Still, others in the room were drinking it. The thing to do seemed to be to find a friend, clasp arms, and walk around and around the pump as you drank. Having no acquaintance, Diana lingered by the windows, watching people as they requested mineral water with eager expressions, only to look aghast at what they were served.

The water itself wasn't ... well, wasn't good by any stretch of the imagination but it wasn't awful. If she held her nose she could ignore the smell. The taste, however, was mind over matter. It was a bit too earthy for Diana's palate.

She had just passed her half-full cup to a passing footman when the announcer at the door tapped a heavy wooden staff on the floor to draw everyone's attention. Diana realized why all eyes had turned when she arrived. Because the entryway was above the ballroom, when the door announcer smacked his staff against the floor, it boomed throughout the space. She couldn't help but glance up to see the cause of the commotion.

"Now entering the pump room, Sir Jordaan Van Dine of Margate."

Chapter Seven

Jordaan

The gold he'd slipped the front desk clerk to find out where she'd gone was money well spent. He spotted Diana right away, standing by the windows with the afternoon sun creating a halo around her. She was also taller than most of the women in the room, which he appreciated. Short women were damned hard to find in a crowd.

Although it wouldn't have been hard to spot Diana among this particular crowd. Most of the royal families had fled Tull this summer, so the room was filled with the wives and daughters of the middle class who normally wouldn't be granted attendance at a venue like this one. The announcer must have thanked his lucky stars when Diana came in, royal from head to toe.

When he caught her eye he gave her a wink and strolled right past her to the pump. As he expected, she was far too curious to simply leave when he walked in. Admittedly, Jordaan didn't know her well, but he guessed that she was going to want to know why he was there, and what he was up to. He had trouble keeping the satisfied smirk off his face as she came up behind him.

"Another glass, My Lady?" asked the attendant hopefully.

Diana hesitated, "Um, I..."

"She will have another!" Jordaan said, handing over an extra coin. "My treat."

Even her scowl was sexy.

The attendant handed her a goblet that she was too polite to refuse.

He tipped a small vial of stimulant potion into his own before chugging it down. Neither the water nor the potion were any better for being combined, but they couldn't get any worse.

"How can you do that?" she asked.

The two of them were forced to move away from the pump because of the number of people in the ballroom, and they fell into step, circling the room because that was the only option.

"A man can do anything if he has to," he said.

"Well, I suppose that's true." She sniffed at the suspect liquid in her glass. "This is…"

"Revolting?"

Diana grimaced as she attempted another sip. "Downright repulsive."

"The witch has me coming here about once a week. Thinks the mineral content will improve my chances of recovery."

"Has it?"

"I'm upright. That's an improvement over a month ago."

Her expression softened to something like pity, and Jordaan regretted bringing it up.

"Anyway, why are you taking the magical waters, Lady Desiree?"

"Obviously, I am immersing myself in the culture of Tull, Sir Jessica."

"Oh that's good, have you been saving that one?"

She smiled, "I have. It's all that blond hair it just says, *Jessica.*'"

He was months overdue for a haircut, but he'd been a little busy falling asleep at inconvenient times. He'd gathered it all back with a bit of leather lacing he'd taken from one of his training gauntlets, but more of it was escaping than was contained. "Most Jessicas you know have a beard?"

"I'm from the far north, so, all of them."

Thankfully he'd already finished his drink, else he'd have spit it out. Not that the joke was all that revolutionary, but that she said it all. Lady Diana having a sense of humor was a surprise.

"Perhaps I'll visit the barber today," he said.

"I wouldn't."

He raised an eyebrow. "Do you have an opinion here?"

She shrugged one elegant shoulder. "Scruffy suits you."

Jordaan felt his day get immeasurably better.

He should have known it wasn't going to last.

The announcer's staff boomed, followed by his voice echoing through the room. "Now entering the Pump Room, Prince Travers Daniel Corvin of Tull, and Prince Xavier Moorelow of Dunlock."

***

The flurry of gossip began immediately, the crowd unable to contain their excitement as not one but two princes made their way down the stairs. Jordaan had no particular opinion about Xavier Moorelow – he knew him as a friend of a friend – but if he was hanging around with Travers? Jordaan had serious doubts about his judgment.

He'd had the misfortune to serve his squire training alongside Travers for more than a year before the prince had inherited his throne. And while it had been sad when Travers lost his father so long, no one was sorry to see him go.

And that miserable wretch was going to marry Diana?

Not that Jordaan had any claim on her, but that made him want to punch a wall.

The two princes entered the ballroom, the crowd parting for them in a series of clumsy curtsies and awkward bows. Jordaan knew Travers saw her, but the jackass barely acknowledged her as he made his way to the pump. Xavier, at least, had the decency to look embarrassed as they passed, his face flushing with heat.

"You're going to marry that ass?" Jordaan asked under his breath.

She blushed. "It's a possibility."

"You can do better."

"Than a prince?"

"A rat would be an upgrade," he said, just as the two men approached them.

"Good to see you, Diana," Xavier said. "It's been ages."

She reached out and briefly squeezed his hand. "I can't believe we didn't have time to catch up during the Festival. That whole time was insane."

"That's one way of putting it," he said.

Jordaan felt Travers giving him the side-eye. "Have we met?" The Prince asked.

So that's the way he wanted to play it? Fine then. Jordaan could be petty with the best of them. "Looking a bit rough, there Trav. Did you strap your ale goggles on last night?"

The prince didn't appreciate his obvious hangover being pointed out. His expression narrowed. He turned to Diana, bowing with barely any of his body. "A pleasure, Lady Diana."

She curtsied like a champion. How any woman could dip that low and not twist an ankle was a miracle, but Diana made it look easy. "It's good to see you, Your Highness. You've met Sir Jordaan before, I believe?"

Travers's only acknowledgment was a glare. Jordaan didn't doubt that if he weren't holding the glass of mineral water Travers would have stuck both his hands in his pockets and sulked.

"Are you and the Countess in Tull for the summer?" Xavier asked.

Diana's cheeks flared with two spots of cherry red. "Just me. My mother took ill before our planned visit to Tull Castle."

He noticed that she was careful about her phrasing. She wasn't visiting the pompous prince; she was visiting the castle. *Interesting.*

"Nothing too serious, I hope?" Xavier asked.

"Just a bad cold, thankfully."

Travers snorted. "I doubt something so ordinary as a cold would take down the Iron Countess."

The change in Diana was subtle, but he could swear she drew herself up taller until she ever so slightly towered over Travers. "Indeed," she said with a sticky sweet tone. "I could only hope to be half as strong as my mother one day."

Never insult the Countess. Lady Diana was definitely a mama's girl.

Travers drained his cup. "I need another."

He flagged down a footman and dropped a large gold coin on his tray, far more than the cost. "Hurry," he said.

"You like your drinks to smell like rotten eggs that much?" Jordaan asked.

"Yes," Travers said tonelessly.

There was probably some nonsense about the waters being good for a hangover. Because Travers was most definitely on the backside of a bender. For a man with naturally tan skin, he was colorless. His eyes were unfocused, and exhaustion came off him in waves. Xavier wasn't much better, though he seemed to be faking it with more aplomb.

He jumped in to cover Travers in excuses. "We're sent by the castle healer for the curative properties. It's supposed to be good for you."

Diana gasped, reaching for Xavier's hand once again. "Xav, are you alright?"

"I'm fine," he assured her.

She didn't look convinced. A pit opened in Jordaan's stomach. She couldn't possibly have feelings for a second prince, could she? *No. No. Not possible.*

"Nothing serious," Xavier assured her.

The footman returned with Travers's second glass, and a pile of smaller gold coins in change, which the prince waved away. Even though the content of the cup was an opaque gray, he knocked it back in one long guzzle.

Jordaan swallowed a wave of revulsion. He'd drunk plenty of the stuff himself in the weeks he'd been in Tull, but he usually had something to add to it that helped him explain the taste.

"I hope you're both well," Diana said to the two princes.

"Fine," Travers said, without making eye contact.

"I was told you were visiting a family on the other side of the island."

Travers kept a vacant expression. Silence, heavy as lead, filled the space between them until Xavier jumped in to smooth things over.

"We've been traveling. We just arrived in Tull... recently."

"So you haven't been with your aunt?" Diana asked Travers.

Jordaan could see the gears in Diana's mind turning. She was practically vibrating with all the questions about to burst out of her.

"Why would I?" Travers asked.

Jordaan had a feeling it was a good thing Diana had given up her glass, or else its contents would have ended up all over the Prince of Tull.

"Ah, Diana, perhaps..." Xavier said.

"No, Xav," Diana said, "I don't need you to make excuses for him."

Fairies-damn, even her anger was beautiful.

She curtsied again, ever perfect. "If you will excuse me, I believe I am done here."

Jordaan wanted to applaud, but he had a feeling she was very close to her breaking point.

Her exit was blocked by a scrum of people, all of whom seemed to be running for the stairs. Patrons were rushing away from the pump, pushing against others and causing a scrum, as smoke was quickly filling the room. Chatter around them rose to a fever pitch, which was only abated when the announcer's staff boomed. "The pump room is closed."

No, the pump room wasn't just closed. It was on fire. The giant monstrosity in the center of the room was giving off a shower of rainbow-colored sparks. As the sparks hit the wooden floorboards, they ignited. Men and women alike screamed, dodging the flames. The air was thick with acrid gray-blue smoke, and there was a mad rush for the stairs.

They needed to get out. All four of them were being pushed and pulled with the sway of the bodies and were in danger of being trampled if they didn't move.

Jordaan shouted to Travers and Xavier to follow him. He threw an arm around Diana's shoulders, sheltering her from the surging crowd.

"We won't be able to get up those stairs," she said.

"I know another way."

They fought through the mass of people toward the opposite end of the room. There was no obvious door, but Jordaan had seen plenty of the pump attendants go in and out through one hidden in the paneling. The hidden seam wasn't easy to find, especially as his vision was clouded by the smoke. He banged on it until the latch gave, and the door swung open.

From the adjacent room, there was a door at street level and they were able to escape into the fresh air. The day was unusually bright after the dimness in the pump room. All around them, patrons were running into the street, several from the door they'd left open. Smoke was pouring out of the building's high windows. In the distance the wail of a fire bell peeled, summoning help.

"What happened?" Diana asked. "One minute it was...and then... then."

Jordaan kept his arm around her, although they were a safe distance from the fire. He should have let go, he knew that, but he suspected she might need the support. She was shaking ever so slightly.

"You're okay... I promise. You're okay. You're magnificent. Have I told you that?"

Diana's eyes went wide.

Chapter Eight

Xavier

Travers walked away. He said nothing, absolutely nothing. He made an impolite bow to Diana and then took off. Xavier didn't have time to analyze what had just happened, only to make his excuse to Diana and Sir Jordaan.

"I'm sorry, I think… I need to go help him, are you two all right?"

"Fine," Sir Jordaan said. He kept his arm around Diana. Xav knew that if she wasn't in a state of shock, she'd probably have put the knight in his place, but she was too stunned to say anything. Xav promised himself he'd make it up to her, somehow, and then turned to catch up with Travers.

In the three months they'd traveled together, Xavier had gotten used to his friend's silence. The prince was prone to a thousand-yard stare. But Xav expected him to say something. Where he was going, Xav had no idea, they just made their way through the neat streets of the historic district, and into the sprawling area of the wharf, where they'd spent the last few weeks.

"Fairies be, what was that?" Xav asked.

Nothing. Travers kept going. He walked with purpose, so Xav followed.

"Were you hurt?"

Travers huffed but didn't speak.

Help for the fire was rushing in from all directions, and so they were mostly ignored as they headed from the trouble.

"So we're getting a drink like nothing happened? Excellent. Fantastic plan." Xav said as they made it back to the Goose and Grouse. Travers held the door open, and they slipped into the murky interior.

Speaking wasn't required, one bitter ale. Xav grabbed two pints from the bar and brought them to the table. Usually, Travers could down a pint in seconds, but he simply wrapped his hands around the glass, staring at it as if he expected it to explode.

They sat there for an excruciating moment that seemed to stretch into the next week.

"We should have stayed," Xavier said, trying to be careful. "There's probably people hurt, and they know we were there."

Travers just shook his head.

Xav was at a loss. They'd been traveling together for months, and yet, he wasn't sure he knew Travers at all. Granted, he hadn't been in the best of circumstances when they left Dunlock after the Festival of the Flower. Travers had said, "Screw it all, let's go get drunk," and it seemed like a good idea. He and the Prince of Tull hadn't been more than casual acquaintances prior. But the idea of having company without having to explain himself and his heartbreak after breaking up with his first boyfriend felt freeing. Necessary even.

He hadn't wanted to pour his heart out to a friend. He just wanted to forget. And the best way to do that was to run away.

It took him a little too long to realize that Travers was also running from something.

They'd had a lot of fun, to be sure. Late nights in the taverns along the Prime Road in Spire. A short jaunt through the dance halls in Zinnj's capital. Even a week on a pleasure ship that sailed the waters between Wentshill and Corlea. Travers was always the first one to buy a drink, throw his arm around a stranger, and start a song.

The first one to lose himself in the bottom of a wine barrel and wake up with a raging hangover too.

"I don't think you can ignore what happened today."

Travers shrugged, the only indication that he'd heard what Xav had said.

"You realize you could have died. We all could have."

Travers looked him in the eye for the first time in days. "It's the Fairies," he said.

"What?""

The Fairies, they want me dead."

No, that didn't make any sense. "What are you talking about? Which ones?"

"All of them."

***

As dramatic declarations went, the idea that Travers was under siege from every Fairie in existence was pretty high up on the scale. But his friend seemed to believe it.

Xavier wasn't buying it.

Fairies rarely concerned themselves with humans. They might be more visible in Tull, given its proximity to the Unknown Kingdoms, but that didn't — by any means — change their approach to humanity. They accepted offerings and prayers, as was their due. Unless something was incredibly intriguing, they were very much hands-off.

Travers wasn't the most dynamic person, it was unlikely his assertion was true.

Thus, Xav answered his friend with the one thing that could be said in their present situation. "Get your head out of your ass, Trav."

Travers blinked, his eyes clearer than they'd been in months. "I just told you..."

"Yes, and you are so full of it your eyes are brown. What is really going on?"

"The Fairies are trying to kill me!"

"Fairies do not kill. They wait and let us die of natural causes because they have three to five times our lifespan."

Travers's eyes bulged with indignation. "They're following me. You might have noticed the number of accidents that have been happening around me? When I fell off the pleasure cruise and had to be fished out of the water?"

"You were highly intoxicated."

"When I tripped in that bar in Spire and crashed through the wall to the storeroom."

"Same answer."

"The Pump Room?" Travers prompted.

"Faulty equipment?"

"For the last eight months, I have been hounded by accidents and misfortune."

"Bad days happen. What evidence do you have that Fairies are involved at all? It could just be that you're stupid and make bad decisions."

Travers's normally calm facade was in tatters. He pounded his mug of ale against the tabletop. "Because they told me it would happen!"

"Who, Trav? Who told you anything?"

Travers chugged the rest of his ale, swallowing hard and then using his ungloved hand to wipe his mouth. "Last winter, a contingent from the Light Court of the Fairies came to visit Tull. They brought a copy of an old covenant with them."

"How old?"

"A thousand years."

Xav leaned over the table to hear Travers's increasingly whispered voice.

"Payment is due. And Tull doesn't have the money."

"What payment?" Fairies didn't use money. They didn't care enough to create commerce. So what could they want that Travers couldn't provide?

"My territory. All of it. They want Tull back for themselves."

Chapter Nine

Diana

Diana's breath came out in short huffs, her heart beating furiously.

"Jonah," Diana gasped, realizing who she didn't see among the crowd.

"Not really the time," Jordaan murmured.

"Not you!" Diana said, pulling away from him. "The footman who came with me. He was in the servants' hall."

"What did he look like?"

Diana drew a blank. She knew Jonah. She did. But his face wasn't coming to her. "He's short. And um..." Her breath came in hard spurts as panic welled up in her chest. "His ... his hair is ... what if he's hurt? I'm responsible. I'm..."

Jordaan gently put his hands on her shoulders. "Take a deep breath. Nice and slow."

He took a big gulp of air, demonstrating.

Diana attempted to follow, but her lungs felt as if they were taking flight.

"Slow breath," he said in a low voice. "You're tough. You're not scared."

Oh, she was scared all right. They'd been so close to the flames. Several of the sparks had burned through the outer layer of her skirt, leaving singe holes in the lush fabric.

"You are the daughter of the Countess of Wills. And you are just as strong."

She was. The Countess wouldn't buckle and she wouldn't either. She nodded. "Jonah Berry. He's about 25, um, light brown hair. Brown eyes. Sharp features."

"Good. He was in the servants' hall? When did you see him last?"

"About an hour ago."

"I'm going to go look for him. You stay here. Help if you can," he said.

She could help. She was unhurt, while others clearly were.

"Jordaan, be careful," she called after him. "Please."

His mouth lifted in a half-smile at her before he jogged toward the building. Flames were still licking at the windows from the inside, and Diana felt a moment of panic watching him get closer.

Several people had come to help from nearby, and begun organizing the victims based on their injuries. An older woman in a heavy black skirt, a white cap, and an enveloping apron was giving orders to whoever would take them, and she pointed Diana toward a water bucket to pass out drinks. "Take some yourself if you were in that smoke."

Diana got to work, ladling scoops of the clear water into whatever vessels were available. When the bucket ran dry, she ran with it to one of the town pumps at the end of the street, and brought it back full, her arms straining with the effort. A great deal of the water sloped onto her dress, but the majority got into the hands of people who needed it, so she ignored it.

She would never forgive herself if Jonah didn't emerge from the fire. Jordaan either. If his potion wore off while he was searching for Jonah he might be in real trouble. The fear and the guilt kept her working, handing out water and tearing strips off her petticoat for makeshift bandages.

The volunteer fire brigade arrived with an army of buckets, but there was no saving Stuart's Pump Room. The light-colored facade was licked with ribbons of soot, and all of the windows were broken. Regardless, the men and women of the bucket line got to business putting out the flames. It seemed to Diana that the whole scene went on for hours, bucket after bucket, but in reality, the fire was out within a few minutes of their arrival. Smoke continued to curl into the bright blue sky, but no sparks or hint of fire was left.

She spotted Jordaan pushing past the fire captain and entering the building. She was too far away to hear what they were saying, but it was clear the knight wouldn't take no for an answer when the other man tried to stop him from running into danger. The same sense of panic she'd felt while the fire was still raging returned watching him go into the damaged Pump Room. It clawed at her, vicious as a trapped animal.

She found she couldn't look for fear she would see something she didn't want to see, so she kept busy. The woman organizing the helpers forced her to stop and take a drink.

"You'll not help anyone if you go down," she said, holding out a ladle-full.

Diana drank gratefully. The water was warm, and like the mineral water from Stuart's a bit earthy, but it was clean and took away the feeling of shards of glass in her throat, however temporarily. "Thank you."

The woman eyed her. "You're not from around here, are you?"

Diana shook her head, too tired to discern any implied rudeness in the question. "I'm visiting from Wills in Corlea."

"During the Quarter? Brave girl. Have another, Love."

Diana drank a second ladle. The mineral water from the Pump Room had nothing on the public water supply. She could feel it spreading through her, filling the small places where the fire had burned away.

"What does that mean? People keep saying it, but…"

The woman laughed. "Tull's best kept secret. You've noticed the fish?"

"I can even smell them now."

The woman's mouth lifted in a smirk. "Happens every four years. Whoever you're here to visit did you no favors asking you to come now."

Diana had no more capacity for shock.

"Your young man went back into the building," said the woman in a statement, not a question.

"He's not mine," Diana said. "Just a friend."

"Friend who ran into a burned place for something you misplaced?"

A wiggle of unease went down Diana's back. "A someone, not something."

"Hmm," said the woman, taking back the ladle. "You've been a help. I suggest you go find that handsome knight of yours."

Diana nodded and gave thanks once again for the woman's help. She made her way up to the barrier that the fire brigade had put up between the front of the building and the street. She asked if anyone had seen Sir Jordaan emerge, but no one seemed to have any idea what was happening on the far side of the barrier.

"We're moving anyone injured to the Rutledge," one of the volunteers shouted. "Anyone hurt, follow me."

A line of carts and carriages waited at the far end of the street for the injured to climb in, or be placed on. The announcement cleared the street and gave Diana a better view of the remains of the Pump Room. It still stood, but it didn't by any means look safe. If the structure wasn't surrounded on both sides by other buildings that hadn't caught fire, she was sure it would have already collapsed.

Jordaan had been in there too long. Panic rose in her without something to occupy her. Her heart beat out of control, thumping in her chest as if she had run from Wills.

Finally, there was a cry of, "Someone is coming out," and a raucous cheer carried through the crowd. Diana held her breath as Jordaan emerged from the building, his arms wrapped around two people. A maid in a disheveled blue dress, half-conscious at best, and Jonah, shirtless, covered in soot. Two men broke the barrier to help. Jordaan looked the worse for wear. His tunic was gray and torn, as if he'd caught it on something sharp. His eyes were unfocused and there was at least one cut causing blood to run down his face and into his shaggy beard.

Relief swamped her. He was okay. Jonah was alive. Hurt, clearly, but alive. She wasn't sure how she was going to be able to properly say thank you to Jordaan. He, however, didn't look like he was going to stay on his feet much longer. His eyes were unfocused, and as he handed off the injured, his body began to sway. He was going to drop if someone didn't help him. Diana ducked under the barrier and ran to him. She threw her arms around him to keep him steady.

"Why Lady Diana, who knew you were so concerned," he said with a yawn.

"Where's your next dose of potion?" she asked. She locked one arm around him. It wasn't a romantic hold, it was practical, but she was all too aware that she was standing in front of dozens and dozens of people in physical contact with him.

"Around my neck."

He reached into the collar of his tunic and pulled out a thin black cord, suspended from which was a small glass vial. Diana took it, unfastening the small vessel from the cord, and taking out the stopper before holding it up to his mouth.

He tipped his head back, swallowing with a grim expression. "Always a treat."

"Better that than faint in front of your new fan base," she said, putting her arm around him once more as they walked toward the waiting carriages.

"I don't faint!"

"Well, what do you call it when you drop like a stone?"

He grumbled but had no answer.

Several volunteers rushed over to help, and Jordaan was assisted into one of the carriages headed for the Rutledge.

"Are you hurt, Miss?" one of the volunteers asked.

Diana started to say no, but Jordaan insisted she join him. "You have got to go back to the Rutledge anyway," he said when she protested.

Well, that was true. And since her escort was currently unconscious, she climbed beside Jordaan.

Although the hotel was less than a mile from the town, squeezed in next to Sir Jordaan on the lumpy rear-facing carriage seat, Diana could have sworn the ride lasted for an hour.

Chapter Ten

Mallory

Lady Diana Yarborough recently had three gowns in the fan-front style made by a seamstress in Zinnj. One from green silk, one in blue crane, and one in fine cream wool.

Mallory rolled her eyes, but as the magazine of fashion plates wasn't itself sentient, it couldn't respond.

Lady Passwood, flipping through a similar stack of magazines across the room, wasn't so unencumbered. "Dearest, really," she said, without looking up.

"It's complete nonsense."

"Fashion plates are how we learn what to expect of the competition."

"These women and I are hardly in competition," Mallory said.

Taking her meaning for the complete opposite of what she intended, Lady Passwood smiled. "I couldn't agree more. You far outshine them."

Mallory suppressed the urge to roll her eyes again. It was extremely difficult. "They all seem to love this Lady Diana character."

"Her mother likely sent notices to all the editors. Crass, really."

Hmm. Mallory took note of the dismissive tone, reminding herself not to cross the good lady.

"Have you found anything you like?" Lady Passwood asked.

Mallory had set a few pictures aside and indicated the pile. She wasn't enamored of the full skirts and high waists of the current styles. She wasn't sure they suited her height, so she'd gone toward ones that sat more naturally above the hips. They weren't the ensembles that the magazines declared to be "a la mode" but they would be better for her figure.

Not that anyone would see if she was confined to her chair. Her strength had been negligent in the last few days. The healer who came to see her had recommended she get out in the sunshine, but Mallory hadn't had the wherewithal to ask anyone to help her outside and had no desire to do so during the Quarter. Vella House was well away from the worst of it, but not immune from the smell. She was feeling so lethargic, she had no hope for the glorious debut that Lady P was planning.

Such was the way with her condition. Some days she was fine, but for other periods her body just wouldn't cooperate. She needed her chair or a cane.

Lady Passwood sorted through the pictures, shaking her head ever so slightly. "You need more color," she said.

"I like black."

"You're looking for a spouse, not mourning the King. What colors do you like?"

"Black."

Lady Passwood's only answer included a pair of spectacularly raised eyebrows. "Based on your complexion, I'd say jewel tones. Magenta, Teal, anything vibrant."

"Do I have any choice in the matter?"

"No. But I will have some black trim placed on your riding habit."

"I do not ride."

"You will. I've sent a letter to the stablemaster at Corlea Palace. He'll know which leather smith to use for an adaptable set of horse tack."

In other words, Mallory was going to learn to ride whether she wanted to or not.

Mallory picked up another magazine from the stack, not for the content, but to distract herself from the urge to stab her Fairie Godmother with the nearest fork.

Her eyes fell on yet another article on Lady Diana. This one was not so much about her clothing as her plans for it.

The young lady will debut her wardrobe when she arrives in Tull on the 7th of the month for an extended summer visit. According to sources within the household of County Wills, the lady met Prince Travers during the Festival of the Flower this spring. Despite the turmoil surrounding that fateful event, the two young people made a connection, and have a wish to explore it with more time together, which led to the invitation. The Fashion Fete does not doubt that given Lady Diana's impeccable choices, she will make a lasting impression on the Island.

Mallory bit the inside of her cheek to keep from laughing. The 7th of this month? Not only was she subject to Travers, the wretch, but she arrived during the worst of the Quarter? Poor girl.

And besides, if this important royal was visiting Tull, what was Lady Passwood doing at Vella House? She was chatelain to Prince Travers, the drunken wastrel. The duchess should have been in attendance at the castle for a royal visit. Both as de facto chaperone and hostess.

How much did she dislike Lady Diana to be fifty miles away at the time of the young woman's arrival? And when, exactly, could Mallory meet her? Because anyone Lady P disliked that much was likely a delightful person.

"Lady Passwood, when was the last time you heard from your nephew?"

Lady Passwood's eyes narrowed. "Is there a reason you ask, dearest?"

Mallory shook her head. "No, no reason. I think I may have just read something about him expecting a visitor to Tull Castle."

The lady brushed off the inquiry as if it were nonsense, eyes looking anywhere but at Mallory. "Next month sometime. No one important, I assure you."

Interesting. Lady Passwood wasn't a very good liar. Mallory tucked that information away for later. She had no doubt her Fairie Godmother was up to something.

***

Polly refused to lend Mallory her black ball gown, the one with the short train. "I made my debut in that gown. And we are not some poor family that has to hand down the good dresses."

"Pol, she wants me to wear pink!"

"Pink is all wrong for you. Lady P would never," her older sister said.

"She swore magenta was my color. That's pink."

Polly shook her head. "No, it isn't. It's a much darker shade closer to purple. And she's right, that would look great on you."

"I just need to have a dress that I actually like with me. Instead of all the things she's planning on buying."

Polly was unsympathetic. "You're going to have your coming out at a castle! Why are you freaking out? Lady P will dress you up and tell you exactly what to say. You literally can't go wrong."

"Exactly. I'll be nothing but her puppet. You at least got to do all of this with Mother."

Polly groaned. "Don't remind me."

"Mother is not so bad."

"Mother was so busy gossiping with her friends, that it took me ages to get introductions. At my own debut! Thankfully, Lady Astley took pity on me and introduced me to her nephew so I had someone to dance with for the opening set."

"Why would you have to be introduced to someone you already know? The whole system is silly."

Polly shrugged. "It is what it is, Mally."

Polly had met her fiancé, Henry, by the end of that night, so Mallory had to suppose it wasn't all bad. Even if Henry Gaitlin had large ears and weird hair, he was nice.

And exceedingly rich, even though he was a third son.

Polly pushed Mallory's chair through the garden, which had enough blooms to mask the fishy smell coming from the coast. Summer had settled into the flower beds, which were bursting with black and teal Exe cranes. A proper Tullian summer garden. Unlike most cranes that bloomed in the early spring, their long, tweedy stems doping with the weight of their petals, the exe were summer flowers. They stood tall, their blossoms reaching for the sun.

Mallory couldn't blame them. She'd do the same if she could. The healer had been right. The sun was making her feel better. It might be time to admit that as a person she was little better than a houseplant.

"You've been in the chair for days," Polly said, stopping next to one of the benches that dotted the garden. "Usually you're up and around by now."

Mallory had no answer as to why this particular spell was so long. Perhaps it was a sign of some greater aspect to her disability, but she hadn't wanted to push her thoughts in that direction.

"Maybe you should ask Mother and Father to call a witch. A healer doesn't seem to be enough."

Mallory had to wonder if her sister considered this condition something healable. It wasn't. It was just how she was made. "I doubt there's anything a witch can do that a healer who has known me my entire life hasn't figured out."

Polly bit her lip as if she were weighing out her words. "I heard Caris Mourne is staying at the Rutledge."

"So? A witch like that is not going to see me."

Polly sighed. "Mally, you know I love you, but you're entirely too cynical."

Mallory frowned. "I'm practical. It's what you adore about me."

"Among many things. But you've always just accepted your fate. And yet there's so much we don't know. You might be..."

"Don't you dare say normal."

"I would never. What I mean is that there is a small, but not inconsequential, possibility that you are holding yourself back. Chair or no chair. You deserve better than rolling around this house being miserable."

"I am not miserable."

"You are misery itself."

Polly fixed her with a look that said she was older by an entire year and would brook no argument. She smoothed the blue skirt of her dress unnecessarily.

"Well, what do you think I should do?"

"I think you should go to Tull Castle. Let Lady P dress you in the best fabrics, and teach you how to be charming so that when you make your debut in the fall, you don't scare off all of your potential partners.

"I'm already charming."

"You're snarky and too smart for your own good. Neither of those things is charming."

A couple of grounds staff pass by with wheelbarrows full of fresh bulbs to plant for next year. They tipped their caps but continued to the far side of the garden. When they were out of sight, Mallory groaned. "Do I really have to spend the rest of the summer with Lady P? She drives me crazy."

"I'm so sorry, Mally," Polly said with exasperation, "your life is so hard. You have a Fairie godmother who adores you and wants you to be happy. The injustice!"

"Stuff it, Pollyanna."

Polly just smiled, and stood up, pushing Mallory's chair back toward the house. "Have you thought about not complaining? It is just a thought but it might make your life immeasurably easier."

Chapter Eleven

Diana

The Rutledge's lobby was filled with people from the scene of the fire. Volunteers were setting up chairs and makeshift beds in the ballroom, all while the hotel manager ran around trying to stop them from making too much of a mess.

Diana wanted nothing more than to retreat to her suite and forget all about what had just happened, but there was too much to do, too many people who still needed help. Alice pulled her aside and helped her into a clean and more practical dress so that she didn't disgrace herself, but otherwise, Diana stayed on her feet.

Sir Jordaan's dose of the stimulant potion had worn off by the time they arrived, and he was brought to his room. Although she was worried about him and grateful for all he'd done to save Jonah's life, she needed to be away from him.

He wasn't the man she should be thinking about.

She was in Tull on an official, royal visit. One that would determine her future. Not to suddenly find an infuriating man attractive.

Because he was infuriating. On a level she had never encountered in another person.

What did it matter if his eyes were a warm brown, or that his shoulders were delightfully broad?

Fairies be, she was in trouble.

Caris Mourne was helping with the triage, assessing the injured for what they'd need to get back on their feet. She passed out potions from a large, multi-tiered case. Generally pink for those suffering from smoke inhalation, or red for those who had more serious injuries.

Diana knew the potions likely had names connected to their uses, but there was something comforting about being reductive. If something simple like pink or red could cure so many people, then perhaps the effects of the fire wouldn't be so bad.

Or perhaps she was fooling herself.

She'd been up all night trying to make her silly perfume, then the fire, and now trying to be at all useful. She ached with tiredness.

"Lady Diana," Caris Mourne said. "Would you be so good as to help me for a moment?"

The greatest witch in the Known Kingdoms was asking her for a favor? Diana gladly gave up on rolling bandages. "What can I do, My Lady?"

"In my room, there is a small hinged box. Would you fetch it for me? You'll find the door unlocked."

"Of course," Diana said, dropping a hasty curtsey.

She took the stairs from the lobby two at a time, her tiredness momentarily gone.

Caris Mourne was on the second floor, at the opposite end of the hotel then her suite. Unlike the white-paneled doors that marked the rest of the hotel's rooms, her door was a heavy oak, with an iron handle.

Diana hesitated a moment. She might have been wrong, but it looked like the same door that had been at the Dunlock Witch's Tower. Which was impossible. Witches didn't carry around their doors with them, did they?

That had not been in any of Diana's books.

And she'd read a lot of books on witches, especially as a child when she'd imagined magic a part of her future.

It was a large space, with great glass-less, floor-to-ceiling windows open to the fresh air.

It was the same room with the massive stone hearth that she'd been in while visiting the witch in Dunlock. It was as if, to be spared the inconvenience of packing, she'd simply wrapped the Dunlock Witch's Tower in a bow and carried it with her.

Again, that should have been impossible.

And yet, Diana knew that no part of the Rutledge had a Witch's Tower attached. It was nearly a perfect rectangle. The only rounded part of the entire building was the columned portico over the front door.

Diana's estimation of the witch's skill rose. Clearly, Caris Mourne had more power than anyone understood.

Diana located the box. It was small, not longer than her forearm, and sat on an oak table to the left of the fireplace. It had the kind of uneven, rough exterior that said it was likely very old.

It was heavier than Diana would have guessed. She picked it up and almost immediately dropped it.

Feeling like a fool she bent down to pick it up, only to be looking at a pair of orange shoes, rather than a small box.

Worse, there was someone in those shoes.

A tall, imposing someone with a shock of dark blue hair.

Diana wasn't sure if she screamed, or simply startled, before the wizard fixed her in his sharp gaze, and rolled his eyes. "Sending amateur witches to fetch me. Caris Mourne has gone too far."

***

Stunned, but realizing she couldn't waste a magical person's time, Diana curtsied and tried to quickly explain the fire. "There are dozens of people hurt. She could use your help."

The man adjusted his pointy orange cap and blew a breath. "Yes, yes, she never moves my box unless she needs me."

Diana dashed to the door to hold it open. "I'm sure she wouldn't have asked for you unless she was sure you were the best person for the job."

The wizard smirked. "She has you under her spell, eh?" he said with an exhale. "Is this what I am reduced to? A thousand years I've been alive, and I'm being fetched like a stale loaf of bread."

"I'm sure that is not the case."

The wizard shook his head, sending a cloud of fine, white lint into the air. "Well, lead the way."

"Of course," Diana said, still trying to parse out how a man lived inside the pages of a book. Granted it was large, but it wasn't as tall as a person.

Her mind felt unpleasantly fuzzy as they crossed from the Witch's Tower back into the hotel proper. She walked with a hurried step. "It's just this way," she said, to fill the silence.

"Yes, I assumed so," he said kindly.

The wizard was dressed in bright, screaming orange, including an elaborately braided coat. His shoes had a matching liquid shine and made no noise on the marble floor. In comparison, Diana was all too aware of how much her ankle boots squeaked. The sound seemed to echo, despite the chaos waiting for them at the bottom of the staircase. The number of people in the lobby seemed to have increased exponentially since she went to fetch the box, or rather, the person from the box.

He adjusted the front of his bright orange coat, smoothing out non-existent wrinkles as if he were looking to make a nice impression. "Yes, yes, a horrible mess," he said. "Tell me again what happened."

She did her best to give a hasty recap of how the pump fire started.

"Rainbow sparks, you said?" The wizard asked with genuine concern.

She nodded. "They came out fast, and the floor around the pump caught fire."

"I don't know anyone who works in fire magic," he said. "But I suppose that's neither here nor there."

Caris Mourne joined them in the lobby. All of the people she was tending seemed to have taken a toll on her, as she had the peaked look of someone who needed a good nap.

"William, thank you for joining us," the witch said. She dipped her head in the barest imitation of a bow, but the wizard seemed to take no offense.

"I come when summoned, no matter the inconvenience to me," he said.

"It is much appreciated. If you would be so good as to begin."

Diana wasn't sure what she had expected, but it wasn't for the man to disappear in a cloud of peach-colored smoke, or to reform just as quickly.

"That should do," he said, brushing a copious amount of fuzzy paper lint from his shoulders.

Around the room, the injured seemed to perk up as one. Curiosity burned in Diana's gut. She had no idea what had just happened, but she was desperate to find out. What kind of magic was at work here?

But it seemed she wasn't to find out. He turned to the witch. "I think we're done here."

"What, what did you do, exactly?" Diana wasn't sure if she asked out of curiosity or confusion, but either way, the words came out. She added a hasty, "Sir," to the end of her sentence to avoid any thought she was being rude.

"A calming spell, combined with a healing. All should be well within a few hours."

"That is remarkable," Diana said.

"It is," said the wizard. "Caris, a pleasure as always." He then turned to Diana. "Young Witch, I'm sure we'll meet again."

Young witch? Diana was about to say she was nothing of the kind, but the wizard had disappeared. Diana had no doubt the big leather box was back on its table, safely in the witch's tower.

"Ma'am," Diana said. "What just happened?"

Caris Mourne laughed. "A great many things I expect, but who is to say? Thank you for your assistance, Lady Diana."

Dismissed, Diana watched her idol turn back to the throngs of people waiting for assistance, blending into the crowd far more easily than her bright purple hair would suggest.

Chapter Twelve

Jordaan

Jordaan was startled as the Fairie, Jacobee, appeared in his room with a sudden pop.

"Caris sends her regards," they said, placing a tray of potions on his bedside table.

Jordaan struggled to sit up. "Three months, neither of you has learned to knock," he said, scrubbing his face with his hands.

The Fairie shrugged their thin shoulders. "Human concerns."

"Your wife is human."

"Is she? She's been awfully vague."

Jordaan felt an empty spot in his brain where logic should have been. The Fairie was unconcerned, however. They combined the contents of two of the vials, and passed them to him, with long, slim fingers.

"Thank you," he said, before drinking down the potions in three long swallows.

Jordaan wanted nothing more than to sink into the hotel's over-soft bed, but the Fairie had more to say. They tilted their head to the side, a long, pointed ear practically brushing their slim shoulder, and a swath of long black hair covering one eye. "Something bothers you."

"Wine, women, song, take your pick."

"A shame Caris has no potion for flippancy."

"Yes, a total shame. Isn't this potion supposed to make me less tired?"

"That is not the point of this one. Caris wants you to go through a memory exercise tomorrow to see if she can find the root of your problem, and this will prepare you for that. In the meantime, tell me, what bothers you, Young Knight?"

Jordaan swung his feet to the floor, reaching for his boots. It was fully dark outside the hotel's mullioned windows, which meant he'd slept the rest of the day since the fire. It might have been a few hours or a full day. "I'm bored. I'm tired of being tired. I want to see my friends. And Fairies Help Me, I'm desperate to get back to my post with the Duke of Lower Miser. I miss the ridiculous man."

"Restlessness, yes. Do you mind if I draw something for you?"

"Draw?"

"It's a particular talent of mine. Something I haven't done in some time, but I think you'll find it helpful."

Jordaan took some paper out of the hotel room's desk and passed it to Jacobee, who took a pencil from the pocket of their suit coat. They leaned the paper against the wall by the door. Their hand flew faster than Jordaan's eyes could comprehend. "When I first met my wife, drawing was often the only way I could parse out what she was feeling. You may have noticed she's bit.... quixotic."

"I suppose that's one way to put it."

"Human emotion is easy to feel but not often easily understood. Because she absorbs the energy of others, she's often feeling things that don't belong to her."

"You don't say?" Jordaan wasn't sure what he expected from the drawing that the Fairie gave him. But whatever it was, it was not an incredibly detailed picture of Lady Diana.

"Caris thinks highly of the young lady," Jacobee said. "As do you?"

"She's not for me." Jordaan had the sudden urge to push something. Preferably something that would break.

"Maybe not. But there is something in that picture meant for you. I suggest you keep it." There was another audible pop, and the Fairie was gone.

Jordaan looked at the small drawing, barely larger than the palm of his hand. Lady Diana had her arms extended as if attempting to stop advancing trouble. She stood in a room with rough stone walls and the dark encroaching. Behind her, partially blocked by the wide flare of her skirt, was an old-fashioned spinning wheel. Whatever that was supposed to mean, Jordaan couldn't say.

He wasn't sure how a drawing was supposed to make him feel better. If anything, his restlessness took on an unexpected intensity. He wasn't normally the type to brood. When he'd left home three years ago to train as a knight, he hadn't been emotional about it. Oh, he'd missed his family from time to time, but that was different. Van Dines were everywhere in the Known Kingdoms. If he even got the inkling that he missed any of them, all he had to do was show up at the house of one or another and get the longing for their aggressive happiness out of his system.

But this illness — whatever it was — seemed to have turned him into a nostalgic fool. He missed his siblings, and his nieces and nephews. He missed his apartments at Margate House with the view of the Trussan River. He even missed living in the knight's quarters on Lower Miser, where there was always a card game, a bottle of whiskey, and stories to swap. The life of an invalid wasn't something he'd recommend, even if it did keep him from overnight guard duty on the walls overlooking the Northern Sea.

But he'd take that if it meant being somewhere besides his own head.

The stars outside his window were thick as spilled milk. He was only on the second floor, but they seemed so close he could reach out and grab a handful. Caris Mourne had said that it would help if he could remember what happened to him, but like the stars, the memory was just out of his grasp. He'd been in the woods, helping Rob Lycette search for the princess. They'd been separated by the storm. He'd gone after the horses, and then... where there should have been memories there was nothing. It was all gone. One moment he'd been in the woods, and the next, he'd woken up with the witch leaning over him, telling him she couldn't undo a curse.

"Curses are puzzles," she said, as if he were supposed to know what that meant.

He'd been too out of it to have much to say. He was just tired. More tired than he'd ever been in his life. He'd been hungover more than his fair share, but never had he felt like he'd felt that first day of consciousness. Semi-consciousness. The first day and all that month, he'd been awake for less than an hour a day.

The witch had made progress, getting his doses of stimulant potion adjusted so that he was more or less alive most of the day. The stress of the fire, however, had drained him. He'd made it out of Stuart's by sheer will. He didn't want to think about how he might have collapsed if Lady Diana hadn't thought to help him.

He held up the drawing of her. The Fairie had managed to get her more or less correctly. The curve of her cheek, the gentle swoop of her chin. It was just a pencil sketch, but the detail was precise enough to get the slight frizz to her hair and the lushness of her lips.

She liked him. He knew she did. She wouldn't put up with him otherwise.

But he hadn't misspoken to the Fairie. She wasn't for him. Whether she married the wastrel prince or some other lucky son-of-a-bitch, it wasn't going to be him.

He wasn't a poor knight by any means. The Blythe crane flowers his family produced were used to make a fever reducer that was in demand all over the Known Kingdoms. But having money wasn't power. She was the sole heir to one of the most prosperous counties in Corlea. She needed power to keep it that way.

Fairies be, he was also damn tired of being morose.

There had to be a potion for that.

He'd go see the witch and ask.

It was either that, or go back to sleep, and he was damned tired of that too.

He ran a comb through his hair. Despite Diana's observation that he didn't need to change, he really should visit a barber. His beard was more than fashionable scruff, and his hair was long past his collar. There had been a time very recently when attempting to shave might find him falling asleep with a razor in his hand, and that was more dangerous than he liked to face.

The hotel halls were quiet, as he made his way to the far end of the hall, where Caris Mourne had inexplicably dropped her Witch's Tower, as easily as unpacking a suitcase. He'd stopped giving too much attention to the incongruity of an ancient, round stone tower accessible through the hallways of a modern hotel. He didn't have space for it.

He was about to knock on the heavy oak door when there was a subtle "meow" at his feet and the unmistakable slide of kitten fur along his ankle.

Said kitten, Veronica, was about the most beautiful creature alive, as far as Jordaan was concerned. He bent down and scooped her up. She happily rubbed her nose against his chest as he settled her in his arms.

"How'd you get out?" he asked.

Being a cat, she had no reply but continued to coo contentedly.

"You're a sneaky girl, you know that?"

Veronica's yellow eyes flashed something like offense.

"It's okay, I love you anyway. I do. You're the prettiest girl in the whole world."

She preened as he scratched under her chin and around her ears. People believed cats were standoffish, although Jordaan had never found that. They were simply selective, and he was lucky enough to be selected by most. Perhaps he was a cat whisperer?

He had to have talent somewhere.

Knighthood was a profession, but it didn't lend itself to the need for special talents. Mostly it required standing still, either while guarding against imaginary enemies or while royals processed here and there to impress one another.

If charming cats was his only talent, Jordaan would take it. Who needed drawing and languages and all that nonsense when there were perfectly lovely animals to be petted?

"I'm bored," he told the cat.

Veronica blinked.

If she could talk, she'd probably call him an insolent boy.

A bit like Lady Diana.

He needed to stop thinking about her. It couldn't be healthy.

He kissed the top of Veronica's head a few dozen times. "You don't need a royal, do you? No, you're a cat, why would you?"

"Of course, Darling."

Jordaan started, looking down at the sleepy kitten to make sure the voice hadn't come from her.

"You are taking precautions?" asked the voice.

Definitely not from Veronica.

Jordaan leaned closer to the door. He was fairly sure it was Jacobee's voice, now that he was confident the cat wasn't speaking.

The answering voice must have been Caris Mourne, but it was muddied by the thick door.

"You're taking longer to recover."

He shouldn't be listening. Not to a witch and a Fairie having some kind of lover's spat.

Well, he supposed it wasn't a fight, really, but there was tension. He could feel it through the stone walls.

Lady Diana's curiosity must be wearing off on him. That was the only reason he could explain leaning a bit closer to the door.

"We knew it wouldn't last forever," the witch said.

"I had hoped otherwise."

Whatever it was they were talking about, Jordaan realized it was serious. He was so used to a slightly unhinged silliness to the witch that it was a little disconcerting to hear her speak seriously.

"There is too much to do," said the witch, "we have no time to indulge."

"It is not indulging to worry about you."

Veronica meowed in protest because he'd stopped with his pets. He kissed her head one more time. "My apologies, pretty girl. I think I better go back to bed."

He put the cat down, hesitating only a moment as he heard one last chilling sentence.

"At some point, I will die, my Love. Everyone does."

Chapter Thirteen

Diana

Although Diana could feel the effects of the day like a lodestone around her neck, her mind was too busy for sleep. It seemed to swirl in a hundred directions; the fire, Travers's unceremonious exit, and especially Sir Jordaan. The last was especially troubling. She had a duty to Wills to see what might come of this visit, despite her less-than-royal welcome. So she did as she always did when she couldn't sleep — she dove into a project.

Unwilling to risk any more of her reserve of ingredients, she instead opted for re-reading the tome on perfume making she'd brought with her from Wills. There had to be something she was missing. She'd chosen this particular manual because, unlike many of the books she'd found on the subject, it used straightforward, practical language. Things like measurements and ratios.

It should have been simple. Follow the rules and create a new perfume.

Only it wasn't. The small vials of her previous efforts were evidence enough of that.

Perhaps she should have gotten her hands on one of the more flowery books on the subject, the ones that waxed rhapsodic on the beauty and mysteries of perfume making.

It wasn't that she didn't want beauty or romance or mystery. She did.

A little.

But from a purely pragmatic standpoint, she needed the fundamentals of making scents before she could get to the romance.

Back aching, and eyes strained, Diana stretched, and paced around her room. It was fully dark outside her window. Much later than she'd thought. She was in for another sleepless night if she didn't put the book down. And after the day she'd had, she wasn't sure her body could take it. Yet she couldn't simply fall asleep, not with the stress of the day still pent up inside of her.

The words swam on the page, and Diana rubbed her eyes trying to get them to sort themselves back into place. Perhaps she should ask Caris Mourn for a sleep potion to save her from herself?

Perhaps she could ask her about the issues she was having with the crane essences while she was at it.

Diana grabbed a shawl, despite the warm night. Given how empty the hotel was, she doubted she would see anyone, but it never hurt to take precautions against being seen in her nightdress.

The corridor hummed with silence as she made her way toward the witch's door. It was late to knock, especially uninvited, but she suspected that Caris Mourn was awake given that she was married to a dark Fairie. While there was no rule that members of that Fairie court were required to keep evening hours, Diana knew their powers were often stronger at night, and thus they usually only appeared with the moon.

A distant voice carried through the quiet as she crossed over to the other wing of the hotel. "No, you must go back," said the familiar voice.

Oh no.

There was no place to hide, no open doors she could duck into before Sir Jordaan rounded the corner.

"I love you, but I can't let you come with me," he said to a small black kitten at his feet.

A laugh bubbled out of Diana before she could stop herself.

Jordaan looked up. "I regret nothing, have you seen this magnificent animal?" He scooped up the kitten and scratched it under the chin. He held out the cat. "Care for a snuggle?"

"I'm not much of an animal person," she admitted, taking a small step back.

"Your loss," he said, placing a small kiss on the kitten's head.

"Where did you get a cat?

"She belongs to Caris Mourn, I think."

"She seems to like you quite a lot."

"Everyone does. I'm a delight," he said.

The image of the tall, blond knight cooing over the little creature was so odd, that Diana had no chance to stop her laugh. It came out big and boisterous, and she might have been afraid of waking other occupants of the hotel — if there were any.

Jordaan looked at her with what she could only describe as appreciation, and that was enough to make her pull it back. She didn't need his attention, nor did she want it.

He's just a complication.

"Don't stop on my account," he said, his voice a low timber. Diana drew her shawl tighter around herself.

"I'm on my way to see the witch. I need a sleeping draught."

"Uh, I wouldn't. Veronica and I were just there and it seems that there is something personal under discussion."

"Of what nature?"

Jordaan frowned at her. "What's that line about curiosity, Lady Diana?"

"You really want to be quoting the particular idiom in front of the love of your life?"

Jordaan put the cat at his feet. "Go on, before you get us both in trouble."

The cat seemed to understand and scampered back in the direction from which she and Jordaan had come.

"Any ill effects from the fire?" she asked.

"Not any more than a typical day."

"I didn't get a chance to thank you for..."

He waved off her next words. "It's nothing."

Diana rolled her eyes. "You ran into a burning building because I was worried about my footman. That's not nothing."

It was as if his whole body tensed at once, like a bowstring being drawn too far back. Which didn't make sense. She didn't think Jordaan had ever been tense about anything in his life.

"It was foolish. And I spent the rest of the day unconscious because of it."

She wanted to ask him so many questions. What had brought on the illness? What made it better or worse? Why was he up so late if he was subject to a sleeping sickness? But Jordaan wasn't going to answer them. She could see that. She might want to know, but he didn't want to talk about it.

"I guess I'll go back to my room." She turned to go, only to have Jordaan follow and fall into step with her.

"Why can't you sleep?"

There couldn't be any harm in telling him, could there? It wasn't like he was going to steal her idea and make perfume.

"I've been trying to do something and it's not going well."

He raised one shaggy blond eyebrow. "Something naughty I hope?"

"Don't be crass. No, I had an idea to make something. But I can't seem to get it right?"

Jordan relaxed, his shoulders slumping. "What is it? Maybe I am secretly an expert."

"In feminine perfume?"

They had arrived back at her door, and Jordaan leaned against the wall as if he no longer had the strength to hold himself upright. Perhaps she had kept him up too long. Given all that she didn't know about his illness, he might collapse at her feet.

"Why are you trying to make your own perfume?"

"It's ... I need to make a good impression here in Tull. Whether or not I marry Prince Travers, I need to be something other than an heiress."

Jordaan's expression softened. "You're more than that, a blind man could see it."

Alarm bells rang in Diana's head. She needed to extract herself before she did something foolish, like kiss him.

Because despite his general air of impertinence and her desire to keep her head clear about why she was there at all, Jordaan was there in front of her like chocolate cake — beautiful and tempting.

"I thought if I could make a perfume that combines the crane flowers from Tull and Wills, it would be a good way to connect with the people here."

"The princess with her own perfume?"

"You don't have to say it like that! It's a good idea."

"I didn't say it wasn't."

He locked eyes with her, and Diana repressed the urge to shiver. It wasn't an easy fight. Jordaan had locked his warm brown eyes on her and she wanted to run and shout and pull his hair just to make him stop. Or making him keep doing it.

She was no longer sure. She needed to get away. Fast.

"I'm going to bed."

"That's an even better idea."

She wanted to hit him for being so infuriating.

"Goodnight, Sir Jordaan," she said.

He pushed himself off the wall and bowed low. As he brought himself fully upright, Diana was once again reminded of how similar in height they were. He was at best an inch or so taller than her. She might even be taller in her heeled boots. And for some reason that was lovely. When she did kiss him, there would be no awkward bending, or standing on tiptoe. They would be well-matched.

Which was not something she should be thinking about at all.

She turned the knob on her door, hoping to make her escape before she made a fool of herself. Only the knob wouldn't turn. She frantically jiggled it trying to get it open. It wasn't locked, just jammed.

Jordaan chuckled and he reached over her, and gave one solid smack to the door, just above the knob, at which point it gave way.

"My door does the same," he said. "Goodnight, Lady Diana."

Any other words were lost as he walked away.

Chapter Fourteen

Jordaan

He should have kissed her. *Damn his morals.*

The witch handed him yet another opaque vial. The fifth one in an hour. "Drink quickly. The potion is more effective if it is not exposed to sunlight."

In these situations, he found it was best not to hesitate. In the last three months, Caris Mourne hadn't bothered to tell him anything about the medicines she was feeding him, and thus he took any warning seriously. He popped the cork and tipped the entire contents back in a few seconds.

Whatever the concoction was, it was thick and it was bitter. His stomach twisted in response. He winced and swallowed again, just to keep it all down. Maybe death would be better.

Caris Mourne held out a glass of water. "Trust me, there are worse potions in my arsenal."

"Something to look forward to," Jordaan said, dropping into a chair and gulping down the water. Any further quips he might have had died from the immediate effects crashing into him. His head swam as if he'd been drinking hard liquor for days.

"What is that?" He croaked.

"You don't want to know," she said and pressed her hand to his forehead. "Breathe in and out very slowly. Keep your mind as empty and unencumbered as you can."

Jordaan had never found his mind to be a particularly peaceful place, but he did his best to clear out the detritus. He pictured a large broom sweeping through a cluttered storeroom, pushing books and teacups and clouds of dust. The figure of Diana, looking kissable, stubbornly stood her ground as he swept. Reluctantly he turned away from that image, doing his best to follow Caris Mourne's instructions. When the room was as empty as he could get it, Jordaan imagined himself seated on a cool stone floor, back to a wall magically painted white.

"Breathe deep, from your gut," the witch said. "Fill up your chest and your stomach, and let the air out as slow as you can."

Jordaan did his best. The problem was his life wasn't an empty room. He could feel his ordinary thoughts knocking on the door, demanding entry.

"Clear your thoughts," Caris Mourne said with a more forceful tone as if she suspected he was slipping.

In his mind, he turned toward the white wall, blocking out the rest of the mental picture he'd built.

"Better. Now, as you let out your next deep breath, I want you to picture the day of your accident. How was the weather?"

"Fairies damned awful," he said, swiping at what felt like heavy rain on his cheek.

"And the light?"

"Dark. Middle of the day, and it's practically pitch black."

"Is it cold? Hot? How's the temperature?"

"Cool. Wet."

The witch made a little humming noise.

"Where are you standing?"

He was in the woods. He'd only left the open road moments ago, but somehow he'd run into a copse of trees and brush so dense it crowded in on him.

"Are you still with Sir Robert?"

"No. He left."

"Do you know where he went?"

Jordaan shook his head. "No, I went after the horses."

"What can you see?"

"Rain," he said.

"Look beyond the rain. Try to make out shapes."

His vision was cloudy. The rain on his face was unrelenting, and the cloud cover was so dense and dark that it was hard to make out anything.

"Focus. Tell me one clear thing."

Jordaan shrugged his shoulders trying to dislodge the feeling of being crushed. "There's nothing... a lot of gray."

"Gray comes in many forms. Something must stand out."

He squinted as if his virtual eyes needed the assist. "A tree. Large canopy. I'm heading toward it."

"Good, As you get closer, does it give you shelter?"

"Yes."

"Once you're there, what's around the tree? What's on the ground?"

"Roots. Big, knotty ones."

"Dirt? Leaves? What else?"

Jordaan knelt. There was something in the space between the roots. Something that seemed to shine amid all the colorlessness. "I don't know what it is," he said.

"Touch it."

Jordaan couldn't say if what he saw just then was real or not. He didn't know if he was in a memory or some Fairie-conjured version thereof, but his eyes found the bright thing and so he reached for it. "It's warm. It feels weird. Like liquid."

"What color is it?"

"Gold. Has its own kind of light."

He held up the unknown thing. It was no more than a few inches long, a glowing strand, no bigger around than a strand of horsehair. "It tickles a bit."

"How so?"

"It's alive. I feel a tingling in my arm."

"Does it hurt?"

"No, it's..." Jordaan wasn't sure he had words for the feeling. His whole body felt like it was vibrating, not just the unknown thing in his hand.

The picture in his mind shattered like broken glass. The sensation of falling hit him, and he clutched the arms of the chair he knew himself to be in to keep from plummeting to his death. He gasped, taking in great gulps of air to calm his racing heart. His eyes snapped to the witch, who looked mildly alarmed.

"What pushed you away?" she asked, once again pressing her small, dry hand to his forehead.

"I don't know, I don't..."

Caris Mourne bit her lip, but her look of worry was quickly dismissed. "You did about as well as I hoped." She took her hand away from his clammy forehead, wiping it discreetly on her trousers. "We'll need to try again in a few days."

"For what, exactly?"

"The whole reason we are here, Sir Jordaan. Whatever magic has affected you is locked deep, and it has several barriers surrounding it to keep you out. Only here in Tull are the conditions right to brew this potion and achieve the hypnotic state required to plumb the depths of your mind."

"I'm starting to wonder if falling asleep is so bad after all," he said, focusing on returning his breathing to normal.

"It's your body's way of protecting you. You could choose to live with it, but you are too young to be an invalid for long."

Not for the first time, Jordaan had to wonder if the witch could read thoughts. She seemed to have plucked the thought directly from the forefront of his mind.

His eyes had not quite adjusted to the sunlight after the darkness of the remembered forest. "Yes, silly me for being young and virile."

Caris Mourne was not in the mood for his irreverence. "I think we're done for today. "Go have something to eat, and try not to be a nuisance to Lady Diana."

"Any reason in particular?"

The witch paused, her purple eyebrows drawing together. "I like her, and I don't wish to see her annoyed. You tend to be petulant."

"Please, tell me how you really feel." To his shame, Jordaan could hear the sullenness in his voice.

The witch let out a long, hard sigh. "The young get more ridiculous every year. Go. I'll let you know when we try this again."

Chapter Fifteen

Mallory

The seamstress had a wicked way with straight pins. "Stop fidgeting," she said, managing to speak around the dangerous number between her lips.

Mallory grumbled. She wasn't fidgeting on purpose, but she hadn't stood up for such long periods in weeks. Her back and legs ached, and she felt the strain of trying to keep herself upright throughout her whole body. "I'll need my chair soon."

Lady Passwood was unimpressed. "Let her finish. Madame Howell has agreed to a rush order to create the clothing you need. The least we can do is let her complete her work today."

It wasn't a matter of simply bearing the pain. She might collapse if she couldn't sit down soon. Besides the fact that her body wouldn't hold up tonight, any travel thereafter was going to take another toll on her. Whatever Lady P had planned once they arrived at the castle wasn't going to go so well if she could barely function.

"I am nearly finished," Madame Howell said. "Most of the pieces you've requested only need minor alterations. I'll have to send the debut gown onto Tull Castle in a few days."

"Excellent. Mallory, dearest, stop slouching."

"I can't help it." Mallory knew she sounded petulant, but she was flagging. She'd started the day stronger than she'd felt in ages, but hours of wardrobe fittings had left her in misery.

The seamstress pinched a last bit of fabric at the waist between her fingers and stuck it with a half-dozen lethal-looking pins. "That's all for now," she said, helping Mallory to remove the inside-out garment.

Grateful, Mallory shucked off the layers of fabric and slunk into the nearest chair.

Lady P crossed the sitting room and pulled a small stool toward her. She picked up Mallory's all-but-useless legs and settled them on the stool. "Thank you, I know this is hard on you."

Mallory yawned. She felt as if she could sleep right there in the ornate, horsehair-cushioned chair. "I'm not sure I am up to being a debutante."

"You were born for it, Dearest. I believe that with my whole being."

Fantastic, add a bit of guilt to the exhaustion. "Why me? I don't feel as if I have done anything to deserve you as my champion, Lady Passwood."

Lady P gave her a soft, amused smile. "You are one of the children of my oldest friends. You didn't have to do anything to earn it."

Mallory didn't know how to answer that. "Are you sure you can't have my debut gown made in black?"

The Duchess chuckled. "Over my dead body, young lady."

The seamstress had gathered up all of her tools and summoned a footman to help her remove them from the sitting room. Lady P waited for her to leave before drawing a chair closer to Mallory. "I have a favor to ask of you."

"Of me?"

Lady P took a bracing breath. "When we get to Tull Castle, my nephew will be in residence. I believe it is time the two of you settled your disagreement."

Mallory gritted her teeth. What had happened between Prince Travers and herself was not a disagreement. It was the opening shots of a war.

Lady Passwood read her nonanswer. "You were children when you last met."

Mallory had her doubts. "It was four years ago. And he was old enough to know better."

She might have asked what their acrimony was about, but Mallory suspected Lady Passwood didn't want to know.

"Travers has matured. As have you."

Mallory huffed. "Maybe I haven't. Perhaps I am a perpetual child who holds a grudge?"

"You are not. You are a kind, loving person, and I need you to extend that kindness to Travers. He has struggled since my brother's death. He was not yet ready for the responsibility that was thrust upon him, and it has taken its toll."

Mallory could acknowledge that, but she wasn't sure she could forgive. He had hurt her badly. First by his carelessness and then by his indifference. She didn't consider herself a particularly hateful person, but the prince seemed to inspire just that.

"Please, Mallory, I am asking you to be kind to him. Not overly effusive, or artificial, just kind."

The words seemed to come of their own volition, bursting out of her before she could stop herself. "He said he'd never want me because I was broken."

Lady Passwood paled. She struggled for an excuse on Travers's behalf. None came to her. Mallory could see the moment when she gave up, the new resolve straightening her spine and helping her choose her words carefully. "You know you are not broken. You have never been. He was wrong to say such a thing. I suspect that his words came from a place of his insecurity."

"He was nasty and I am not sure I can let that go."

Lady P leaned over and kissed the top of her head. "You may not. You are within your right not to forgive him. However, for my sake, please try to tame down the open hostility."

***

Polly brought the black dress, minus the train, to her room. "If you ruin it, I will hunt you down and make you sorry," she said, dropping the wrapped dress into one of Mallory's open trunks.

Mallory hugged her. "You are the best, thank you."

"Lady P won't let you wear it for your debut. So don't even try."

Mallory nodded. "Of course not."

"Don't make me regret it, Mally. I don't want to be on her bad side."

Mallory nodded eagerly. "I know, I do. But look at what she wants me to wear. I'm going to look like a clown."

"You are not. You'll look beautiful as you always do. Lady P has impeccable taste."

Her sister's faith in the Duchess was entirely too strong.

Maids were bringing in piles of clothing, freshly delivered from the army that the seamstress had working on her behalf. Shirtwaists, billowing walking skirts, and day dresses in an array of brilliant teals, blues, and even the dreaded magenta.

"What will your debut gown be?" Polly asked, looking through the piles of clothing.

"It's a purple-ish thing, I think?"

Polly rolled her eyes. "Honestly, Mal."

There wasn't much Mallory needed to take with her that Lady P hadn't or wouldn't provide. She had a drawing case and some nice art paper she planned to take, and her hair brushes, which the maid would pack in the morning. She had already tucked a small portrait of her family, and a cozy sweater for when she was unaccountably cold in the middle of a warm afternoon, into her traveling case.

"What did you need for your debut?"

"Comfortable shoes."

"Seriously?"

Polly nodded. "There's a lot of standing around, curtseying, and making small talk. At the end of the night, my feet hurt."

"I thought I was dying during my fitting. I can't imagine how I'm supposed to do it."

Polly shrugged. "Rest a lot beforehand. Take care of yourself. Do what you can to feel strong."

"I wish it were that easy."

Polly crossed the room and hugged her. "If you need your chair that night, you need your chair. Even Lady P knows that."

"She wants me to size up the competition and be nice to the problem prince, so I don't think so."

Polly laughed. "What competition?"

"Someone named Lady Diana Yarborough. She's visiting Travers this summer. And Lady P is not a fan."

The smile on Polly's face broke wide. "Oh, now I'm sorry I'm not going! Someone Lady P doesn't like? I would kill to see that."

"My point is, she's so determined to make me the perfect debutant that I think she's missing some obvious things. Like the fact that sometimes, I can't walk."

Her older sister blinked. "Then make sure she knows. You're not shy, Mally. Fight for what you need."

She didn't want to fight, but what options did she have? "It's going to be a long trip to Tull Castle."

Polly tucked a lock of Mallory's hair behind her ear. "Bring a book."

Chapter Sixteen

Diana

Maryann balanced Diana's breakfast tray on top of a small, portable writing desk.

"You could have taken two trips," Diana said, softly so as not to appear ungrateful.

Maryann handed over the cup of steaming chocolate first, then lowered the remainder of the items she carried onto the bed.

"Honestly, my lady, I just wanted to get away from Alice. The girl hasn't stopped crying."

Diana bit her lip. "Over Jonah?"

"Over Jonah's activities during the fire."

"Oh. Oh, the poor girl."

Maryann said nothing, but Diana could see the impatience with Alice written on her face. The woman was happily engaged, Diana realized. She didn't know what it felt to be pining over a man who wasn't going to love her.

"She needs a little time," Diana said. "Let her have the day off. You and Bill can take tomorrow."

Maryann seemed satisfied with that compromise. She started clearing some of the books Diana had been reading off the bed so that there was enough room for both breakfast and writing that all-important letter to the Countess.

Which she should have done yesterday.

Or possibly the day before.

Maryann put the stack of books back into one of Diana's many traveling trunks and got to work tidying the room. Diana felt slightly guilty about having discarded things here and there last night, but she'd been so discombobulated after her encounter with Jordaan she had flung things about until she was tired enough to fall into a fitful sleep.

The hot chocolate was a bit too sweet for Diana's taste. She liked a slightly bitter brew that showed off the taste of the chocolate, but she was thankful for the boost the drink gave her all the same.

She stared at the blank page in front of her, unable to think of how she should open the letter to her mother.

Dear Mother, I seem to have landed here several days before I was expected, given that Lady Passwood was out of town and Tull Castle was undergoing renovation when I arrived, and thus unable to accommodate me. While I am ensconced in a lovely hotel, in the course of two days I was almost set on fire, lost one of my footmen to smoke inhalation, my junior maid to crying fits, and my good sense to an unlanded knight whom I nearly threw myself at last night.

It wasn't exactly the missive she had intended to write, in which she imagined assuring her mother of her triumphant arrival.

She finished off her drink and set the cup aside. Unable to think of a decent way to open her letter that wasn't glib or alarmist, she instead composed a short note asking Caris Mourn to take tea with her. As much as she didn't need the complication of Jordaan, she was glad she'd run into him last night. Attempting to visit a magical person unannounced or uninvited was bad form. Yes, she'd had a reason, but manners were manners, and she needed to remember hers. She's remembered to curtsey to the box's inhabitant, but had she done so to the witch at all? If she was going to be a princess, she needed to do better.

If she was going to be a princess.

Which, given that she'd seen Travers for all of a handful of awkward minutes, didn't seem as likely as it had when she'd left home.

Her letter to the witch was newly signed when the page disappeared into a puff of smoke. Diana stared at the portable desk. The page she'd just been writing on was gone. There was another puff of smoke, just enough to make Diana cough, and a reply to her letter, neatly folded and sealed with wax, sat where her writing had been.

The note was short but filled Diana with a pleasant anticipation.

I would be pleased to meet you in your suite at two p.m.

– C. M.

Well, that was lovely. The girl in her, the one she'd been once, holed up with Robby Lycette in the attic in the castle at Greater Miser, dreaming of all the things they would do with powers like Caris Mourne, was giddy. The most famous witch in the Known Kingdoms was coming to take tea with her!

Through the little spurt of happiness, Diana realized it was likely the first time in ages she'd thought of Robby and not had the funny little pang of longing in her chest. She'd carried it for years, always on the edge of hope that something might happen.

There was now the troublesome matter of Sir Jordaan, taking larger swaths of her attention than he deserved, but she hadn't known him long. Her interactions with him were a mere handful compared to the childhood she'd shared with Robby. She could reasonably conclude she wasn't in much danger of moping after him.

Much.

She brushed off the lingering image of him last night, his shirt sleeves rolled up, cuddling the little black cat.

Maryann helped her into a sage-green day gown that swished pleasantly when she walked. Diana had loved it from the moment she'd seen the mock-up in the seamstress shop. It was the nicest dress she'd brought with her, notwithstanding the gowns meant for evening events. It was the natural choice for tea with her idol. She wanted to look her best.

Maryann wanted her to finish her letter.

"Ma'am, I can't help but think you're stalling, not writing to your lady mother," she said, braiding sections of Diana's red locks into an elaborate style.

Diana rubbed at her chest, willing away the feeling of falling. "I am struggling with the letter. She was ill when I left and I don't want her to take on any more worry."

"I'm sure she's better by now."

Which meant she might very well be on a ship to Tull, and any letter Diana might send would pass her somewhere on the ocean. Somehow, that made her feel a tiny bit better. What was the point, after all, if the letter was just going to miss her anyway?

"I'm sure she's packing her bags as we speak," Diana said.

"And when she gets here she's going to wonder why we're not staying at the castle."

Well, yes, that was a small, pesky problem.

"We'll deal with that when and if it comes."

Diana ignored Maryann's obvious disapproval and set about preparing for her tea with Caris Mourne. She was able to order a lavish tea tray from the hotel kitchen and sent Bill and Maryann off to procure flowers for the table.

She'd made up her mind to ask the witch about the perfume issue. Perhaps creating a new scent wasn't unlike creating a potion, something that Caris Mourne was known for.

The rest of the morning ticked by at a glacial pace. Diana took to pacing to burn off excess energy. She didn't remember being so easily excitable. She needed to get herself under control and be calm. But she was about to have tea with the most famous, most powerful witch in the world!

She fussed over the table set-up and sent Maryann back to the hotel kitchens a dozen times for just the right selection of tea and pastry. She'd pulled out the delicate porcelain tea set embossed with chains of Wills cranes and gold swirls. The set was to have been a hostess gift for Lady Passwood, but given that she was feeling most decidedly unwelcome, Diana didn't feel bad about pulling it from among the many gifts the Countess had gathered for this trip.

She justified it to the specter of her mother by telling herself at least a dozen times that the hotel's tea sets were industrial and unworthy of hosting tea with the witch.

Promptly at the appointed time, there was a delicate knock on the door to her suite.

Diana was too stunned to drop into the customary curtsey.

Caris Mourne radiated beauty, her long purple hair shining with an ethereal light all of its own. And her skin was bright and radiant. In comparison, Diana felt as if the events of the past few days were branded onto her face, all of the missteps etched into the dark circles under her eyes, and evident in the ashen surface of her cheeks.

Even her clothing was stunning. Instead of her usual attire of wide-legged blue trousers, a fitted white shirt, and colorful suspenders, she wore a sleek, light purple suit with a wide-lapeled jacket and a skirt which made her look much taller than her petite stature.

"You're so beautiful," Diana said. She felt foolish for speaking so impulsively, but she couldn't help it.

Caris Mourne gave her a wan smile. "Why thank you. I rarely use magic on myself, so it is nice to know I haven't lost my touch."

Diana remembered her manners, bobbed a quick curtsey, and stepped aside to admit the witch to her rooms.

"Your suite is quite lovely. I can see why this hotel has such a good reputation."

Diana indicated the little table she and Maryann had moved a dozen times to find the best combination of view and complimentary lighting.

"I was quite surprised to see that you were continuing to stay in the Dunlock Witch's Tower," Diana said carefully. She was dying to know more about how Caris Mourne had accomplished that, and she doubted that information would be in any book.

"I found that I quite like Dunlock as a home base. It's centrally located, and the Moorelows are very good employers. And constantly packing and unpacking was becoming tedious."

"Of course," Diana said, mind spinning.

When they were seated, Diana poured out the fragrant, lemon tea that was a Tull specialty.

"It is so nice to be invited," Caris Mourne said, stirring a lump of sugar into her cup. "I am usually the one doing the serving."

"It's nice to have company. Although I've likely driven my staff quite batty getting ready."

Caris Mourne nodded, and for a flickering moment, Diana saw her glamor slip. Behind the magical facade, she was pale and tired. But there was no dwelling because the manufactured image was firmly in place before she could articulate it.

"Well it is appreciated," Caris Mourne said. "I am glad to spend some time with you. I have felt so since our time during the Festival."

Diana did her best not to show the emotion she felt, but on the inside she was running in circles, shouting with joy. Her hero wanted to know her. "I am so pleased to hear that."

"Tell me, Lady Diana, have you ever considered training as a witch?"

"Me?"

The witch nodded and said after a delicate sip of her tea. "You may have noticed yesterday that my friend William called you a young witch. He has a gift for finding untapped magical talent."

Diana put her cup down to prevent the tea from shaking out. "I have never shown much of a magical inclination."

"But you have shown exceptional curiosity, no? Always reading, trying to learn as much as you can?"

Well, yes, that was true. Almost a third of the trunks that Diana had brought with her from Wills contained her books. It was a risk to bring her whole collection, but she knew that if she did agree to marry Prince Travers, she was unlikely to return to Wills for some time, and she did not like to be without her library. "I do like to understand things, but is that enough?"

"It could be."

Diana's head spun. She kept herself from spiraling into an abyss of possibilities by serving the delicate lemon cake sent up from the hotel kitchens. They made small talk, about the preponderance of citrus-flavored things that seemed to dominate Tull's culinary taste.

"I find that one of the many things I've learned throughout my travels has been that taste is the most particular thing in each reason," Caris Mourne said. "Two territories may be nestled right next to one another and yet have completely different cuisines. It is almost as if borders came not from land divisions, but by the peculiar tastes of the people themselves."

"As if they'd organized themselves according to who likes anchovies versus who likes cake?"

"Exactly."

"I suppose I can only hope that Tull's lemons go well with Wills chicken stew."

Caris Mourne laughed in her rusty way, and as she did her glamor slipped again. Diana blinked and the image of a lined face with a bluish tint disappeared. "It is a thought worth exploring, isn't it? You might be surprised with what you find."

"To do that I'd have to spend time with Travers, and so far, he hasn't been inclined."

The witch reached for another slice of cake. "I suppose you ought to go find him then, hadn't you?"

Honestly, Diana hadn't considered that. She had come all this way to visit him. The least he could do was make the short journey from the castle to the hotel. But that hadn't happened so far. Diana tried to imagine how the Countess would handle the situation, and the conclusion was simple. She'd put on her finest dress and go to the castle. And she would plant herself there until she was impossible to ignore.

Caris Mourne sighed in happy pleasure as she bit into her cake. "Perhaps there is too much lemon, but this dessert is excellent."

Diana agreed. "Tull may be a confusing place, but they do make excellent baked goods."

Her last bite demolished, Caris Mourne stood. "Now, if you will excuse me, I have a meeting with Prince Brandon."

"The Prince is in Tull?"

Caris Mourne blinked. "No. Of course not."

Diana was too discombobulated to respond.

The witch bowed with the barest inclination of her head. "Thank you for the lovely hour, Lady Diana. I hope you will think over what we've talked about regarding your future. I see bright things for you."

Diana doubted she would think of anything else.

***

After a fitful night's sleep, Diana made up her mind. She would go to the castle. She would show up, and demand Prince Travers's attention. He had been unharmed enough to flee the Pump Room fire, and so it stood to reason that he was alive, well, and in residence.

Unfortunately, by mid-morning, it was obvious she was going to have to rethink her strategy.

Maryann had swayed on her feet a dozen times helping Diana dress. Her eyes, which had been clear earlier in the day, were watery with sickness. She clutched her handkerchief to her mouth, as if afraid to lose the contents of her stomach.

"I'm sorry my lady, I don't know what's come over me," she said.

"Did you eat something that didn't agree with you?"

Maryann hesitated. "Perhaps it was the lemon custard served in the staff dining hall," she said.

"Citrus and milk is never a good combination," Diana said sympathetically.

"You can't very well help if you're sick," Diana said. "Bill can accompany me to the castle while you rest."

Maryann's cheeks filled with color. "I don't think so, My Lady. He ate his weight in custard." The young woman looked green at the thought of the offending dessert.

Diana forced a smile. "That's fine. I can find another escort. You both need to rest."

She dismissed Maryann and promised to inquire for warm broth and spare bedpans to be sent to them both. With Alice still wrapped in her misery and Jonah in recovery after the fire, she was effectively without staff. And she could not appear at the castle alone.

Not if she wanted the visit to go well.

The clerk at the hotel's front desk was apologetic, but he had no one to spare.

"I'm sorry, My Lady, but we're short of staff this summer. We don't have enough help to keep the door staffed."

And that was true. It was why she'd mistaken Sir Jordaan for the doorman on her arrival. She'd expected a body in the space just inside the door and there was one. Only it happened to be one not employed by the hotel.

"You might suggest you ask the young knight who has been hanging around my lobby," the clerk suggested. "A knight would be an acceptable escort."

Diana flushed. Jordaan was the last person she needed to see. However, as the clerk said, he was an acceptable escort. "Do you happen to know where I might find him?"

The clerk looked as if he wanted to say something cutting, but instead directed her to the second floor. "He has been known to spend time in the sitting room."

Diana thanked him and headed for the nearest stairwell.

The second floor of the hotel was a long corridor of identical doors, all of which seemed to be empty. It wasn't hard to locate the sitting room. It was a larger door, unnumbered, and the only one that light seemed to stream through.

Diana let herself in, only to stop dead in her tracks.

The sitting room was a space for all of the occupants of the hotel, a room with a dozen chairs in clusters of three and four, punctuated by silly little tables not big enough for more than a wineglass after dinner. It was meant for groups of people to gather and talk, yet Jordaan seemed to have taken it over as some kind of personal sanctuary. The first thing she saw was a shirt and his knight's tunic in a heap on one of the overstuffed green armchairs.

The second thing she saw was Jordaan, flat on his back, with the small black kitten perched on his bare chest. The cat was purring contentedly as he lazily scratched at her head.

Diana couldn't stop her mouth from falling open. "This is a public space," she gasped.

"I know," Jordaan said. "But it is as hot as the Fairie Hells in this building."

"Then go outside!"

Jordaan kissed the little kitten, unconcerned. "You can look for another minute, but then I'm afraid I'll have to charge."

Diana couldn't stop the furious blush that rocketed up through her cheeks. "I didn't... I wouldn't have come if I knew you were lying around on display."

Jordaan laughed, and quickly displaced the kitten, reaching for his shirt. Diana found herself mesmerized by the way the muscles in his arms flexed as he pulled the garment over his head.

"I'm sorry," she said, her tongue heavy. "I was told I could find you here."

"And here I am," he said, turning on his all-too-aware-that-he-was-charming grin. "What can I do for you?"

"Both my maids and footmen are ill, and the hotel has no one to spare. I need someone to ride up to Tull Castle with me."

"Oh, excellent. Taking would-be brides to their neglectful intended is my specialty."

Diana bit back a sarcastic retort and took a short, calming breath. She couldn't arrive at Tull Castle alone. It wasn't done. And if she was going to take Caris Mourne's advice and spend time with Travers then she needed to be there. "Please," she said. "If I show up alone, that's one more reason for Travers's aunt, Lady Passwood, to think ill of me."

Jordaan raised an eyebrow. "Who wouldn't like you? You're bloody perfect."

Diana blushed all over again, despite the throw-away tone Jordaan had used. No one had ever said anything like that about her. *Ever.* How was any of this happening?

"Regardless..."

"Yes, it would be my honor," he said, adding a half bow.

He could still be making fun of her, but Diana was too flustered to parse out nuance. She dipped a sorry curtsey. "I'd like to leave at three."

"Undoubtedly. Three it is," he said.

Diana turned so sharply that she made herself dizzy. Which wasn't difficult because she was already feeling as if her world were off its axis.

As she left, Jordaan's voice followed her into the hall. "I meant it, Diana. If they don't think you're wonderful up at the castle, forget them. You deserve better."

If only it were that easy.

Chapter Seventeen

Jordaan

He'd said too much to Diana. Jordaan knew that. He saw the way she'd reacted to his words and realized that he was getting her hopes up. She was going to get ideas about him.

She was in Tull to be engaged to a miserable son of Fairie. Flirting with her like he had been was no more than stringing her along. But he hadn't been able to help it. She did deserve better than to be ignored by the prince and his aunt.

He'd chosen a lovely, gentle mare for Diana. He had no doubt she'd be regal, even on a slow old job horse. He suspected she belonged on a thoroughbred, but the hotel had a handful of choices, none of which was as magnificent as the woman herself.

His horse, Bull, danced about, ready to run. He owed him a good ride, but with the sleeping sickness, he hadn't been able to do any real rides for some time. Now that Caris Mourne had drawn him up a potion that kept him upright most of the day, he needed to get out more regularly. Eventually, he would need to return to service on Lower Miser, and he needed his skills to be sharp to keep his place there.

He didn't need the money, so much as a job that gave him purpose. Otherwise, he'd end up like his next oldest brother, Peter, drinking his way through the taverns of the Unknown Kingdoms at 40. Every time he was home, Jordaan saw how his parents lamented over Pete's wastrel ways. It broke their hearts. And he refused to add to it. His parents were considerably older than most parents – he'd arrived as an unexpected surprise 26 years after his oldest brother Oscar.

He finished his check of the horse tack and led both horses to the front of the hotel where he'd meet Diana. It was another over-warm day, with the smell of lemons from the nearby grove, not quite overpowering the rotten fish smell that came up from the water below. Blue skies, fluffy clouds, dead fish as far as the eyes could see. Such was a typical day in Tull. Apparently, the fish were being pulled from the waters to be used for fertilizer and the smell would be gone in a few days.

He wasn't sure it would make things better. Tull was beautiful, but it wasn't anything like home. Margate wasn't so far North, but it was more temperate than the island territory with its constant summer. He wasn't a warm-weather person. When his days as a knight were done, he'd get a big old house in some rainy, windy place.

And fill it with cats.

He was smiling to himself with that image when Diana exited the hotel. She quirked an eyebrow. "Imagining all the trouble you'll cause?" she asked.

"Undoubtedly," he said. He held out his hand to assist her into the pony's saddle.

"I do appreciate you putting aside your shenanigans for me."

"Oh you vastly underestimate my ability to create shenanigans then," he said, as he swung into Bull's saddle. "I'll have to try harder."

She blushed, the color spreading through the delightful freckles across her cheeks.

He realized that without even trying he'd gone too far again. He needed to curb this impulse to needle her. But how was he supposed to help it? She rode the sweet old pony like a queen. In a deep green riding habit that made her red hair glow a deep auburn, all she needed was a crown to complete the picture.

Chapter Eighteen

Diana

Caris Mourne's advice to take herself to Tull Castle felt a lot less practical the closer they got to their destination. What if Travers wouldn't see her? Diana had no idea what would happen and it was making her uneasy. Although the ride wasn't treacherous by any means, her anxiety spiked as they got closer. And Jordaan had been so unusually quiet since they'd left the Rutledge.

He kept a respectable distance between their horses. Exactly as a knight acting as a lady's escort ought to do. But in the time she'd known him, he hadn't ever been so taciturn. It was unnatural. Diana was tempted to ask him if he'd fallen asleep in the saddle.

She kept her mouth shut. They weren't friends. Not really. They had a handful of days of acquaintance, which wasn't much when she thought about it. What did she know about him other than that he could flirt like it was his job?

Other than the fact that he was handsome. And a knight. Not to mention the fact that he'd run into a burning building to save someone he didn't even know.

That was admirable. Swoon-worthy.

His affinity for cats was a little troubling.

Cats were cleaner than dogs, but Diana wasn't an animal person by any means. Her mother's affinity for small, wheezing pugs had always baffled her.

She shook her head, trying to clear out any thoughts about Jordaan's better qualities. None of them were enough to throw away the future she and her mother had planned.

She was in Tull to spend the summer getting to know Travers. So that is what she would do. The last few days be damned.

She was only slightly mortified to admit that she would feel better if Jordaan had kept up the flirtatious banter while they rode. He could have said something outrageous and she would have blushed and stammered and told him he was entirely too cheeky. And then she definitely would not have had to think about the fact that she was essentially showing up at a man's door to demand he pay attention to her.

Her mother would be mortified.

Still, needs must.

They rounded the last bend that took them up to the front approach of the castle, the view that she could see from her suite at the Rutledge. It was bigger than she imagined, the light white stone facade of the castle gleaming in the sunlight.

But it was the scene in the drive that made Diana pull on the reins and stop. The drive was full of carriages.

Shiny lacquered carriages attended by outrides on sleek black horses. A dozen servants were unloading boxes and trunks, taking them into the castle.

Fairies be, they had pennants. Teal and black pennants waved from the posts of the carriages.

"Something wrong, Lady Diana?"

Face burning, Diana could only shake her head. She had no idea what was happening. Jordaan used her real name and the royal family of Tull had pennants! Her pennants, that she'd imagined. It hadn't been a ridiculous idea to suppose she'd been welcomed with them. They had them. Diana needed to get away from the castle as soon as possible. Her surroundings were a blur as she urged the pony back to the main road. She needed to get back to the hotel. Because if she got to the hotel, she could go back to her suite, and no one there would know she'd just thought she could solve her problems by visiting a narcissist as if nothing had happened over the last four days.

Never in her life had she been treated so badly. Why would she be? She was a royal heiress. And she wasn't ugly by any means. So why was any of this happening?

The pony only made it so far from the castle before she balked, rearing up either from exhaustion or some road hazard. Diana's heart was pounding so loudly in her ears, that it took her a moment after she'd calmed the pony to see where the animal had stopped and get her bearings. She was somewhere between the castle and the port town. Too far from the lemon groves for the rotting fish smell to be mitigated. Away from the castle was all that mattered really.

She should have written to her mother. Or waited for her to recover before getting on the ship. Or never agreed to this preposterous visit in the first place.

She dismounted, noticing the pony was breathing heavily. "Thank you," she told her, voice quavering more than she would have liked. To keep tears at bay, she went to each of the beast's hooves, checking for stones.

"You're okay, girl," she said to the pony after making sure the horse wasn't showing signs of going lame, nor of having any ill effects of her escape from the courtyard. There was a small stream along the roadside, so Diana let the pony drink.

There was no place to sit with any dignity, so Diana stood, unsure of what to do next. She should go back to the hotel. Return the pony, go back to her suite, and throw away any of her attempts at making her perfume. Clearly, Wills and Tull cranes weren't meant to mix. It was like the Fairies had been giving her a sign all along.

After she got rid of her supplies, she would send word down to the port about passage on the next ship going North. If there were no boats scheduled to leave within the next few days, she'd take a carriage.

She would buy a carriage if she had to.

But she wasn't going to stay in Tull any longer. She was the daughter of the Countess of Wills, and she would not put up with this smelly, ridiculous place any longer.

Diana wasn't sure when she began pacing along the side of the bank, but her kid boots slipped into the soft earth. She reached the pony and then turned, nearly colliding with Jordaan.

Diana stood her ground, although she wasn't exactly sure what to do with her limbs. They felt oddly heavy.

"Are you all right?" he said when he was close enough to touch.

Diana nodded, unable to say anything. Jordaan's eyes were such a warm shade of brown. With his scruffy beard and his too-long hair, he looked a bit like a storybook lion. She wanted to burrow into him. Which she absolutely couldn't do, because even holding his hand would be out of bounds.

Jordaan didn't seem to understand that, because he left only an imperceptible gap between them. "What spooked you?"

He had beautiful lips. Kissable lips. She shook her head, trying to get the image out of kissing him out of her mind. Because he was a distraction. A flirt who didn't want her, the same as Travers. The same as Robby Lycette.

"They had pennants on their carriages."

Jordaan's brows knit together. "Fill me in, Drucilla?"

"I came for a royal visit. An official royal visit. I was invited!"

Her explanation didn't register, but Diana had no time to manage his feelings. Her own were ricocheting around the clearing at lightning speed.

"I have a letter saying that I should arrive on the seventh of this month. And no one bothered to show up to greet me. *At all.* I have been waiting at this hotel for four days for some indication, some acknowledgment..."

Diana had never been so discomposed. No, it hadn't been romantic, but she and Travers had formed an understanding last Spring. He'd picked her, and now he was ignoring her? And there were plenty of people at the castle. Even if the prince was a complete numpty, Lady Passwood shouldn't have created such a breach of protocol.

Which meant... she wasn't sure but she wasn't going to stand on the side of the road, chased away like a rat from the kitchens.

"Why do I not like the look on your face?" Jordaan asked.

"I have to go back. I have to knock on the door and tell them that I will not be treated like... like I'm disposable."

"You're not disposable," Jordaan said, capturing her arms in his hands. His touch was firm and sure, and far more intimate than it had the right to be.

Faire Hells, why did he look so damn gorgeous? It was unfair.

"I'll announce you," he said.

"What?"

"When we get to the castle, I'll announce your visit to the butler. We'll hand over your card and ask if the family is at home. That's how things are done when making an unexpected call. And before you say anything, I know you are expected. But there could be a perfectly reasonable explanation."

"I am so angry, I'm not sure I should."

Jordaan brushed a stray hair from her face. "You'll rally," he said, with a confidence in her she didn't feel. "You'll remember that you are Lady Diana Yarborough of Wills,

Daughter of one of the most admired royal women in the Known Kingdoms, and you will go and sort out this mess."

She could just lean a little closer and kiss those beautiful lips. But no, the silly, beautiful, unserious man was right. She was the daughter of the Countess of Wills and she would conduct herself in a calm, rational manner.

"And if they don't treat you like they should, you can do so much better."

"You are terrible, do you know that?"

One of Jordaan's eyebrows shot up. "Excuse me?"

"Oh you know!" she snapped. "You're so bloody beautiful it's hard to even think around you, and because of that, everything is falling apart."

"I *think* I should be offended?"

Diana cocked her head to the side, considering. He was entirely too good-looking for his own good, and apparently, she was wildly attracted to that. Which was *absolutely* not helpful.

"You will make someone very exasperated one day."

"But not you?" he said, his voice dropping an octave.

He was standing too close to her again. He smelled nice, like pine and lemon soap. She went to resume pacing, but he still had his hand on her arm. She had no business knowing that. She had an impression to make.

"Not me," she said, her voice slipping into whisper territory.

She wasn't sure why she was speaking so low, only that the conversation didn't seem to belong to anyone except the two of them. The grass and the trees didn't need to know.

"Shame."

Diana shook her head, her mouth too dry for words.

He turned back to his horse. "Are we going back to the castle?"

Yes, they absolutely were going back. Diana took a bracing breath and was immediately sorry. The rotten fish smell was particularly bad in the clearing.

But at least it stopped her thinking about Jordaan's lips.

Chapter Nineteen

Jordaan

Fairies be, he was in so much trouble.

Chapter Twenty

Mallory

Mallory had to give it to Lady P, she had excellent taste. The interior of Tull Castle was elegantly done. Thanks to larger windows, the rooms had considerably more light than they'd had on her last visit. With new wallpaper and a fresh coat of paint on the trim, every room she'd been in so far gleamed. Even the portraits and the sculpture complemented the new furniture.

Mallory stepped carefully through rooms along the upper corridor. What she admired in the renovation were the new floors. All of them were even and smooth, meaning that if needed her chair she could easily navigate from room to room. A mechanical lift had also been installed that connected all the three floors. It would be a pain to use because it required three people to turn the crank and pulley system, but it was there.

Mallory had the nagging sensation that the improvements had been done like that for her comfort. Which was silly because that meant Lady P was scheming a match with her idiot nephew. And that was never going to happen. She should have immediately hated every inch of the castle on principle, but actually, she didn't. The castle was beautiful and it was accessible, which felt good. It was a relief to be in a home that she could navigate mostly on her own, even if it was only temporary.

For Polly's sake, Mallory tried to absorb as many details as she could. If she didn't write her a long, rambling letter about everything from the scent of the dusting polish to the number of scullery maids, her sister would probably come screaming down from Vella House to complain. And then blame Mallory for taking her away from her fiancé.

The whole house was lovely, so there was no shortage of things to list out. She'd start with the number of dried bouquets and bowls of potpourri that graced every table. They should have been overpowering, but the smell of rotten fish from the water's edge was so strong in this part of the castle that she needed a handkerchief soaked in crane oil in hand every time the wind blew.

She had no destination in mind, only the idea that she should enjoy the relative quiet of the castle before Lady P took over her day with dress fittings and etiquette lessons and whatever else debutant training required. After a full day of travel, her body was tired, but her strength didn't seem to be failing her. The only thing that threatened to take her out was the absolute boredom of looking at endless hallways of new furnishings.

"Lady Diana Yarborough to see Prince Travers and Lady Passwood," said a male voice in the entrance hall below. "If you could please let the family know she is here."

No, it couldn't be. The Lady Diana?

Oh, Polly was going to love this twist. Mallory peered over the balusters to the floor below, to see an exceptionally tall young woman with reams of red hair. She was... pretty wasn't the word for it. Striking was better. *Maybe?* She was something. Mallory had often wished that she could command a room like Lady Diana seemed to do, all steel reserve and inescapable beauty.

Behind Lady Diana stood a burly blond knight in a yellow and blue tunic. She tried to remember what territory had those colors, but the knowledge escaped her. Wherever it was, a haircut wasn't required for the job. He looked like some kind of ancient warrior. And by the way he was looking at Lady Diana, his missions concerned her, and her alone.

The majordomo took the card the knight held out, and left the two of them standing there while he went to see if the Lady was "at home."

Mallory was tempted to continue to spy on them, but she knew Lady P, despite being in her apartments, would most definitely have told the majordomo to turn anyone away. If Mallory wanted to figure out exactly why Lady P seemed to hold a grudge against Lady Diana, she was going to need to get to know her.

She took the stairs two at a time down to the front entrance hall. "You're here!" Mallory chimed, giving her biggest, falsest smile. For half a moment, the young woman looked startled, before a smile spread across her freckled face.

"Indeed I am," she said, stepping forward to meet Mallory, and linking their arms. "I'm sorry I'm late, there seems to have been some confusion about my arrival."

Mallory turned a smug little smile to the majordomo, who had materialized out of the shadows, Lady Diana's card still in hand. "Why didn't you tell me my friend was here? I've been waiting to see her for ages."

She ushered Diana and the knight farther into the castle, calling back to the stunned majordomo, "We'll take tea in the Southern Room."

"Yes, my Lady, but..." the man began to protest.

"And some cake," Mallory said. "No proper tea without cake."

"Tea is for old women, bring me a whiskey," the knight told the majordomo as they entered the sitting room.

The Southern Room was flooded with sunlight, which lit up a swirl of dust. Lady P would be furious if word got out that her parlors were dusty. Mallory started to make a list of everyone she would tell.

"You're not here to rob the place are you?" Mallory asked as she took a seat.

"Only if I see something I like," the redhead said, causing the knight to snort.

This was clearly a kindred spirit. "Fair enough."

The redhead held out her hand, rather than curtsey. "Lady Diana Yarborough of Wills."

"Lady Mallory Vella."

Lady Diana had a firm handshake. Up close, she was so much taller than Mallory had expected. All the fashion plate write-ups had suggested she was as dainty as candy floss. But no, she and the knight were well-matched, height-wise. Mallory felt like a mouse among very large house cats.

"Sir Jordaan, not that anyone cares," said the knight. He flopped into a chair by the window, his feet finding the nearest surface to rest on.

"Ignore him, he's got terrible manners," Diana said.

"Then why do you keep him?"

"Honestly, I don't know."

"I am right here," Jordaan said. He tipped his head back as if he'd take a nap.

Diana waved him off, her clear eyes only lingering on the reclining knight just a heartbeat too long. *Interesting.*

"Thank you for the rescue. I had the horrible feeling that man was about to turn me away."

"Do you mind my asking why? I've been trying to avoid coming here, so you understand, I'm incredibly curious."

"I don't blame you," Diana said, a little huff as she sat across from Mallory. "I'm at a loss myself. I was supposed to be visiting for the summer, and yet..."

"No one was here when you arrived," Mallory filled in for her.

Diana nodded. "I've either made a ghastly error or something sinister is going on here."

This mystery got better by the second. Lady P had some serious explaining to do. "How so?"

Lady Diana's cheeks colored. Mallory suspected that as fair as her complexion, that happened to her a lot. She was thankful for her own more golden skin that offered at least a little protection against her riotous thoughts.

"I arrived days ago for a visit arranged by Lady Passwood."

Mallory didn't think much of the politics of royalty, but she knew a serious insult when she heard it. She was speechless at the idea because Lady P was a stickler for protocol. Allowing a guest to go unwelcomed was not a small breach. "I don't suppose you've recently drowned a basket of puppies or burned down an orphanage?"

Lady Diana shook her head. "Not my style."

"Don't sell yourself short, Danielle," Jordaan said with a yawn. "You're much more menacing than you give yourself credit for."

"Don't confuse mercenary for menacing, Gordon," the lady said without batting an eyelash.

"Cheater," he volleyed back. "You stick to J names, I'll stick to D names. Rules of the game."

Mallory bit back a laugh. A blind man could see these two were infatuated with one another. So why would she want to visit Lady P and the Idiot Prince? She should probably make her debut and find out if all royals were as obtuse as these two.

"There is no game. Please be quiet," Diana chided the knight.

There was an infuriating scratching noise at the door just before a parlor maid entered with a tea cart. Given how quickly it was prepared, Mallory did not doubt that Lady P had been informed, dictated the sparseness of the menu, and would have been on her way before the cart left the kitchen.

They were quiet as the maid prepped the teapot, turning the handles on the cups toward each occupant of the room. Four cups, which meant she'd be here before too much else was said.

Diana took one look at the tray and squared her shoulders. And sure enough, the maid had only just left when Lady Passwood herself entered.

"My darling, I heard you've had company," she said. Mallory saw the moment Lady P recognized their guest and the smooth way she held back any emotion that brought.

Diana rose and executed what was likely the most technically correct, deepest curtsey known to woman-kind. "Lady Passwood, it is good to see you," she said, her voice losing any trace of the familiarity with which she'd greeted Mallory.

The tension of the moment was palpable, as if all she had to do was reach into the air between Diana and Lady P and she'd hit something solid.

"Lady Diana, you are early," Lady P said. "We expected you in Tull next month."

Feigning innocence was a risky move. Mallory bit her lip eagerly waiting for Diana's response. She wasn't the only one. Sir Jordaan had risen to his feet, and he was intent on watching the interaction.

"My mother sends her regards. She was unable to travel with me due to an illness."

For a moment, Mallory was disappointed that Diana hadn't struck back, but it didn't take long to realize the genius of not responding directly to Lady Passwood's statement. She wasn't acknowledging the fib. Lady P would have to try something else.

"I trust your journey was uneventful?"

"Remarkably so. Lady Passwood, may I introduce my escort? This is Sir Jordaan Van Dine of Margate."

The Duchess made the barest of acknowledgment to the knight's bow. She turned her critical eye back to Diana. "He doesn't wear the tunic of Wills," she remarked.

"Sir Jordaan is indentured to Lower Miser and in Tull on personal business. He was kind enough to act as my escort today while members of my staff are unwell."

"So much illness from the North," Lady P said, carefully sitting herself on the settee nearest the tea table. She picked up the preparation for the tea where the maid had left off, checking on the brew, and inquiring about milk and sugar cube preferences.

"Lady Passwood," Mallory said when her tea — black, no sugar — was handed to her. "I believe Lady Diana will be a great help with my debut. I would like to consult with her about the party preparations."

Diana raised a skeptical eyebrow as she accepted her tea.

"Oh, I don't know that such a thing is necessary. I'm sure the lady has more things to occupy herself.."

"I would very much enjoy helping," Diana said, before taking a delicate sip of her tea. "But I assume Prince Travers and I may be very occupied as we get acquainted."

Diana's shot landed. Lady P was visibly uncomfortable with that idea. She shook it off, as she did most things, but all four of them seemed to know exactly what was said.

The two ladies were in an icy standoff, and the knight quietly seethed.

Polly was going to lose her mind when Mallory's letter arrived. This was more drama than the time their uncle Horace got drunk and fell off the roof while attempting the widow's walk at the top of Vella House.

Chapter Twenty-One

Diana

Maintaining an air of polite unconcern when she was boiling with incandescent rage was more difficult than Diana would have imagined. Her skin prickled and her muscles tensed as she did her damnedest to keep herself calm in the presence of Lady Passwood.

Finally, when the tension threatened to break them all, the Duchess stood. "Well, I suppose we'll have plenty of time to socialize with your extended visit. I'll leave you all to get to know one another better."

Diana rose and curtsied. She noticed Mallory struggling to stand before Lady Passwood turned to her and assured her there was no need to get up.

"I'll have one of the footmen bring your chair," she said.

No sooner was the lady gone, than Mallory turned to Diana, a big smile cutting across her delicate oval face. "You are my new best friend!" she said. "I've never seen anyone rattle Lady Passive Aggressive like that."

"I doubt I rattled her one bit," Diana said, letting out her first deep breath.

"You did. Trust me, I've known her my entire life and she never, ever retreats."

Across the room, Jordaan yawned and kicked up his feet. "I have to agree. Not that I know the Duchess, but that was masterful, Daisy."

Diana could only shake her head at him. She had done her best to channel her mother's steely resolve. She hoped the Countess would be proud. "I could use a drink," Diana admitted.

"Now that I can get behind," Jordaan said.

Mallory was apologetic, but there was no chance anyone in the castle was going to bring anything stronger than tea. "One of the downsides of being Lady Passwood's Fairie godchild," she said.

Jordaan groaned. Diana rolled her eyes at him. "I'll have a bottle sent to your rooms at the hotel."

Those all-too-gorgeous lips curled into a sneaky smile. "Good, give me something to dream about."

He yawned again, assuring them both that they could talk all the feminine nonsense they wished, he needed a nap.

"Does your misogyny itch? Because I imagine it must be a nasty rash."

"Get your mind out of the gutter, Della," Jordaan said, tucking his arms behind his head. "Thinking about my rashes."

Mallory laughed. "Your escort is extremely odd."

"I know," Diana assured her.

"I have to admit, I did not expect to be this entertained today. Perhaps this summer won't be so horrible."

Diana couldn't say the same herself. "Are you the only guest of Lady Passwood?"

Mallory nodded. "Prince Xavier from Dunlock is here with Travers. But as far as I know, I'm her only guest. At least until my debut."

"So Travers is here?"

Mallory's expression darkened. "Unfortunately so. Although why you would want him to be is beyond me."

Jordaan let out a decisive snort that Diana did her best to ignore. "The reason I came to visit was to consider an engagement to the Prince. We were supposed to get to know one another, but it seems..."

"Oh. Oh," Lady Mallory said. "That's..."

"Yes," Diana agreed, because what else was there to say?

"I'm sorry, sometimes I speak before I think."

Diana believed her. Granted their acquaintance wasn't above an hour, but Mallory didn't seem the malicious type, nor the type to fake the loathing she displayed for Travers.

They were interrupted by the arrival of a pair of footmen with a large, wheeled chair. They carried it into the room, placing it next to Lady Mallory.

"It's been a long day," she said as if there were any need to apologize.

Diana felt a spurt of pity she suspected that Mallory wouldn't appreciate. She pushed it down, knowing that it was likely rude to say anything at all, even if it might have been well-intentioned. Mallory stood on shaky legs, holding onto one of the footmen for support as she transferred from the settee to the chair.

"If you need rest, well, I know I've likely overstayed my welcome already."

"Oh no," Mallory said. "I want to see where this all goes."

But where any of it went next, Diana wasn't sure.

Jordaan, despite his intention of napping without interrupting, had been following the conversation. "Suppose you'd better go to talk to the terrible, no-good prince then, shouldn't you?"

Chapter Twenty-Two

Xavier

The archery range was enough of a distance from the castle that the central tower was only a small, gray point over the trees. Xavier notched his arrow, drew back the bow, and concentrated on the target ahead of him. The wind was blowing in the wrong direction, and so he waited for it to subside. His arm muscles threatened to spasm, but he held on. Something large flew overhead, casting a shadow on the field, yet another sign that it wasn't the right time.

"Shoot the damned thing," Travers said. "Some of us need to be put out of our misery."

Still, Xav waited. He narrowed his focus on the paper target, only seeing the brilliant red center. When he felt the tickle on his neck that told him the wind changed direction, he let the arrow loose. It flew straight into the bullseye.

Travers groaned, dug into the pocket of his trousers, and came up with a small bag of gold coins. Xav caught it before it hit the ground this time.

"Next time we play cards. I'm better at cards," Travers said.

He wasn't, but if needed to believe it, so be it. Given what he was dealing with, there was no reason Xav shouldn't be kind.

He'd take his money if Travers wanted to gamble, but he could be nice about it.

"Have we stayed away from the castle long enough for your lady love to be occupied elsewhere?" he asked.

Travers rolled his eyes. "Don't remind me of her presence. For everyone's sanity."

It was interesting that he hadn't denied the love part of that taunt. Xav gathered up the bows and retrieved his arrows from the target. He passed them off to a waiting footman, who would bring them back to the castle.

"Are you afraid of women?" he asked Travers, once the footman was out of sight.

"Excuse me? You've seen me with women."

"Ladies, then. Do they frighten you? Because I can't think of any other reason you're avoiding them."

"Who am I avoiding?"

"Diana. Lady Mallory. Your aunt. I'm sure there are more, just give me a moment."

"My aunt..."

"I'll admit I'm a little scared of her."

Lady Passwood had arrived at the castle in the morning, rousing them all from bed entirely too early, and demanding that he and Travers help with the unloading of goods she'd brought back with her. She'd come with a veritable fleet of carriages, some of which were only filled with trunks of new clothing, and one royal spitfire.

"I am not afraid of Lady Passwood."

Xav shrugged. Travers wasn't giving him much to go on. "I mean, you've ignored Lady Diana, who I will tell you is one of the kindest people I know. You're ducking away from Lady Mallory. You see how that looks, right?"

"Not wanting to be around them makes it look like I'm afraid of them?"

"Yes."

Travers rolled his eyes. His whole demeanor suggested he was agitated, strung so tightly he wouldn't need a bow to shoot arrows. He could do it under his own tension. "Until I figure out this thing with the Fairies, I'm not giving either of them the idea that I'm going to marry them."

Well, that was a fair point. Why risk either of the women thinking they were going to be a princess if Travers was about to lose the territory? But he didn't have to be a complete twat and outright ignore them. So Xav said so.

Travers' only response was a rude hand gesture.

Getting the prince to tell him the particulars of the covenant between his ancestors and the Light Court of the Fairies had been like pulling teeth without whiskey for the patient or the barber. Painful on both their parts. From what he knew, Travers had said that a convoy of Fairies had arrived in Tull at the dawn of the new year. They'd requested an audience, stated that they owned the territory, and been promptly shown to the door.

The problem was that the covenant was legitimate. It had been signed by the first prince of Tull, Crater Corvin. He'd bargained for the island and a portion of the mainland that was fertile enough to grow crops. In exchange for a dedicated temple, and continued veneration of the Fairies, the Corvins would rule for a thousand year. Which left Travers about to lose his throne.

If such a thing could even be enforced.

Laws in the Known Kingdoms concerning the Fairies had been written in the proceeding centuries. And none of them were kind to the other beings.

"My aunt can invite all of the eligible royals she wants, I don't have to entertain them. I'll keep out of sight, and they will eventually leave."

"I don't think that's going to work the way you think it will," Xav said. Three figures had just come over the hill by way of the castle. And if he wasn't wrong, the very people Travers believed he was avoiding so expertly. He waved. Diana, who was pushing Lady Mallory in a wheeled chair, waved back.

Sir Jordaan trailed behind them, looking as if his nap had been interrupted. Xav knew he'd developed some kind of sleeping sickness while in Dunlock during the Festival of the Flower, but he wasn't sure of the particulars, as he and Travers had left the castle shortly after Jordaan, Robert, and Princess Kira returned. As the accident or incident that brought on the sleeping sickness had happened in his home territory, Xav wondered if he should feel guilty.

He didn't. But he wondered.

As the trio approached, Travers hung his head in his hands. "Does the old woman have a finding spell on me?"

Xav chuckled and went to meet the visitors. Diana looked resplendent. She wore dark green, a color that seemed made for her pale complexion, and she carried herself well. So much for the little girl he'd known who tripped over her too-large feet and frequently had jam on the front of her dress.

Diana embraced him. "I'm so glad you're okay," she said. "After the fire..."

And for that, Xav did feel guilty. He should have called on her, but he'd been so wrapped up in Travers's issues, that he hadn't thought to track her down. "I'm sorry for that. The prince..."

Diana held up her hand. "I know he's the worst."

"He's right here," Travers snapped.

"Don't mind her," Sir Jordaan said. "She does it to me too."

"I've known her all of an hour, Sir Jordaan," said Lady Mallory, "but I suspect Lady Diana has your measure. His too," she said, pointing at Travers.

"Fair enough," Jordaan said. "Having delivered you safely to your chosen escorts, I'm going to go find the knight's quarters and lay down. Drucilla, send someone to fetch me when you want to go back to The Rutledge."

"Thank you," Diana said to him.

Xav could be wrong, but he was almost sure there was a bit of wistfulness in that thanks? Perhaps a look that lingered just a little too long on Jordaan as he took off for the knight's quarters? He looked to Lady Mallory, who was suppressing a giggle. As subtly as he could, he pointed between Diana and Sir Jordaan.

Lady Mallory answered by making a little heart with her hands.

Huh. Well, that might solve Travers's problem with one lady. But it was not going to solve his issue with Lady Mallory. Xav had decided he liked her. In their short acquaintance, he'd noticed the shrewd way she looked at the world.

And she got under Travers's skin with incredible speed.

"To what do we owe the pleasure of your company?" Xav asked when Travers remained stubbornly quiet.

"Lady Mallory was kind enough to show me where I might find you. It seems you have forgotten our discussions back in Corlea that led to my being in Tull this summer."

Travers at least had the manners to look ashamed of himself. "I'm sorry," he said.

"Did you ask her to marry you, Trav?" Mallory said.

Travers looked at the ground. "In not so many words."

Mallory gave a divisive snort and folded her thin arms over her chest. Diana kept her head high.

"If I've come all this way for nothing, please just tell me."

"It's not nothing," Travers stammered. "I.. I just can't....you don't understand what's going on."

Xav was exhausted. Truly. How many times would he have to rescue Travers from himself?

"I should like to understand," Diana said, her voice preternaturally calm.

"And I would like to know why you're such a twat," Mallory said with a smile.

"It's better not to get either of you involved," Travers insisted.

"Oh, I think we're past that, Travers," Lady Mallory said. "We've known each other since we were children, and you always get squirrely when you're upset."

Xav did his best not to laugh. Travers was losing ground. "What in the Fairie Hells does that mean?"

"It means you hide things and you try to make everyone else look the other way so no one helps you," the lady said. "So spill it, and why are both you and Lady Passwood being awful to Diana?"

"Maybe Lady Passwood just doesn't like you," Travers suggested to Diana. It was a cruel suggestion, but there was no force behind Travers' words. He was clearly at the end of his line of reasoning.

Diana nodded. "Well, yes, our time in Dunlock made that clear. However, she is a renowned hostess. If word got out…"

"So you've come to blackmail me?"

Xav clapped a hand over Travers's mouth. "Stop talking and let the ladies speak."

"You are a complete utter ass, do you know that?" Lady Mallory said to Travers, with a considerable sigh. Diana reached for her hand in a small gesture of solidarity. They were clearly fast friends.

"I'm going back to the castle," Travers said, jerking away from Xav.

"Don't run away," Lady Mallory said.

He was several yards away when Lady Diana called after him. "What about the Fairies?"

Travers frozen. He turned back, a look of dread on his face.

Xav wondered, briefly, if Diana had somehow been able to work out the covenant, just from a few days in Tull. But no, that was all but impossible. She was an intelligent woman, but she wasn't gifted with clairvoyance.

Travers was back, hurrying back toward them. He grabbed Diana by the arm. "What do you know about them?"

Diana shook off his grip. "It strikes me there's something odd going on here. Twice in one day, I saw a trio of Fairies walk into buildings. And I suspect that the fire at the Pump Room had something to do with magic. Is that related? Does it have something to do with you?"

It was time to put an end to Travers's evasiveness. "Yes. It does," Xav said. "He's in a lot of trouble with the Fairies. And he'd rather sulk and work it out himself than ask for help."

Lady Mallory and Lady Diana traded astonished looks, while Travers looked like he was ready to go on the attack. Xav wasn't sorry. Sometimes, it was better to get everything out in the open.

He hadn't done that in his last relationship, and the lesson was learned hard. He'd kept everything bottled up until it all came falling out of him like an avalanche. If he could keep Travers from imploding that way, Xav felt as if he could pay him back a little for the past few months.

Not the drunken debauchery, but for the rescue. Having someone he could wallow next to had been exactly what he needed when he'd broken up with Bertie.

"What kind of trouble?" Diana asked.

"He owes a debt to the Fairies."

"Shut up, Xav!" Travers hissed.

But Xav wasn't going to shut up. He couldn't help his friend solve this mystery on his own, but he could enlist help.

"What kind of debt?" Mallory asked.

Travers growled and gripped his head in his hands. "They want my territory back. I can't make you a princess, Diana, because I'm not going to be a prince for much longer."

Chapter Twenty-Three

Jordaan

The knight's quarters at Tull Castle overlooked the water. Jordaan had thrown his arm over his face, hoping to block out the sunlight and the smell, but it wasn't helping. Tired as he was, the effects of his potion waning with the afternoon, he couldn't fall asleep. When one of the stablehands came up to the knight's quarters to let him know Lady Diana had requested him, it was almost a relief.

If she was done dealing with the recalcitrant prince, then he could go back to his room at the hotel, burrow under the duvet, and hope Veronica chose to visit him.

"She asked you to meet her outside the stables," said the boy.

Intrigued, Jordaan hurried to get back into his tunic. He left a few coins for the stable master, as visiting knights were supposed to do, and stepped out into the stable yard. He didn't see Diana at first, until he saw a flash of green, set off with blazing red hair, pacing on the far side of the mews, just out of sight of 90% of the castle.

Why was she hiding? That wasn't like her. Which meant... something. Jordaan could only blame whatever part of him absorbed all that chivalry nonsense in his knight's training. A lady didn't summon a knight to a remote location. And Diana was definitely a lady. A smart one.

When she stomped her foot and summoned him with an impatient wave, he knew something was wrong. She'd only been with the prince an hour. How much trouble could she have stirred up in such a short time?

He put his hands in his pockets, slow-walking toward her. He wasn't her child, and he wouldn't be called like one.

"We need to leave," she said. "Right now."

Jordaan didn't pretend to be a genius. He was as ordinary as any man, which meant he was probably dumber than all the women who'd ever existed. But he knew on facing this woman that she was not Lady Diana Yarborough.

It was a good likeness. The creature had mimicked her height and her dress. But the details were all wrong. No little curls were escaping their elaborate hairstyle and framing her face. The freckles on their cheeks appeared to be applied in a repeating pattern as if painted on with a stencil. And the hands were all wrong. Even hidden by the same green gloves Diana favored, the fingers were too long and too thin, the leather sagging around them.

"I think I'd like to stay," he said carefully.

"No, I am a lady and I say we have to go."

There weren't classes on how to deal with shape-shifters. Jordaan wasn't sure he'd ever thought they were anything other than storybook creatures. And he had to admit, if there were such classes, he'd have probably slept through them.

But this Not Diana was very real. Taking up space. Pacing in the small area between the mews and the large stables. And not leaving footprints, despite the fine dirt.

"Has your fiancé chucked you out?"

"I wish to go."

"So you said."

Not-Diana wanted him away from Tull Castle. Why?

"We leave now," said the creature. "Go and get the beasts we ride and take me back to the other place."

Interesting choice of words there. Jordaan shrugged. "Afraid I can't do that."

"We will go now!"

"No, you see, I can't take you anywhere. We haven't been introduced. And even a lowly knight has to know who he is escorting."

"You are the human man who has brought me here and now I will go back to the…"

"Other place, yes, so you've said."

He had no idea where to go with this interaction, but leaving with this thing was out of the question. For one, he'd be leaving the real Diana behind. And for two, he'd rather not be lured away and end up transformed into a bunny rabbit or toad or any kind of wildlife.

"You tell me your name, and I will bow. That's how things are done," he said to Not-Diana.

The creature hesitated. Jordaan hadn't asked a direct question, so it did not have to answer. He tried again.

"What is your name?"

"I am the…" whatever lie they intended to say died on their lips.

Tull Castle wasn't a private place. It was a working castle, and even a hidden-away spot wasn't without other people for long. A group of servants was leading a team of horses from the stables, while others brought one of the elaborate carriages from the mews. And the very distinct sound of female voices and the squeaking of Lady Mallory's wheelchair was quickly approaching.

"Who are you?" Jordaan asked again.

"Needle," The creature said. "I am Needle of the Light Court!"

Jordaan bowed. "A pleasure," he said.

Diana and Mallory were getting closer. He didn't need to see it to know, the panic in Needle's eyes was enough.

The creature howled, a painful, moaning sound that left Jordaan with an uncomfortable urge to shake every bone in his body to dislodge it. In less time than it took to have that thought, Needle disappeared.

***

The young royals had returned from the archery field in a distinctly disquieted mood. They stood in front of the castle entrance, as if reluctant to go inside. Whatever had happened among them, Jordaan wasn't sure he wanted to know. He was still trying to work out why Needle of the Light Court wanted to lure him away. He was certain the shape-shifter wasn't a Fairie. He'd never heard of Fairies who could use a power like that. But it had allegiance to the Light Court, and that meant the Fairies were involved.

Lady Mallory was the most animated among the four, her hands acting out her words in agitated swoops. Jordaan had the stray thought that if someone were to grab her arms and still her movement, no words would come out of her mouth.

"Something must be done. No one can just take the land like that," she was saying.

"I agree, but if there is a covenant, our hands may be tied," the real Diana mused.

Jordaan wondered if there was a time he'd ever look at her again and now check that her freckles remained in their disorganized spatter.

"Stop talking about it like you can fix it," Travers growled. "There have been councilors and scholars talking about it for months."

Prince Xavier put a hand on Travers's shoulder. "The ladies want to help. The least you can do is let them talk."

Help? Jordaan had to ask. "What in the Fairie Hells is going on at this castle?"

All four royals turned to him, all of them suddenly speechless.

"Van Dine this is a private conversation," Travers snapped.

Fairies be, he was a piece of work. Jordaan ignored him and turned to Lady Mallory. He'd taken her measure quickly while they were having tea with Lady Passwood and knew an ally instantly. She wasn't going to suffer a fool. "Is the Idiot Prince in trouble?"

Lady Mallory nodded. "I'll say. In debt to the Fairies."

Diana held up both hands, "Not by his choosing," she added. "But it's bad."

Jordaan didn't want to know. Travers was an ass, and the sooner Diana realized that and gave up on the idea of being a princess, the better. But it wasn't like he had a choice. Not if he was being dragged into this mystery too.

"Anything to do with the Light Court?" he asked. "Because they just sent someone to get me out of the castle."

Diana gasped, her cheeks draining of color. "What do you mean?"

He did his best to explain, but it all seemed so unreal, he wasn't sure he was capturing the full picture.

"A shape-shifter?" Travers scoffed. "Day drinking doesn't become you."

"Day drinking is my middle name, and my best feature," Jordaan shot back. "But I know what I saw. Needle of the Light Court was pretending to be Lady Diana and trying to get me to leave with it."

He only had to wonder briefly if that fact would scare her before Diana burst out, "I knew it, and that's more proof!"

Oh good, not scared, just elated to be right. That was great.

Prince Xavier, however, was visibly scared. "Travers, we have to do something here. This situation could be incredibly dangerous."

Travers shook his head long before the words came out. "What do you expect me to do?" he finally shouted. "Give up my crown? Go be a lowly knight? Let my castle and my territory just rot?"

As the only lowly knight among them, Jordaan was at his limit for dealing with Travers. A handful of moments in his company had always been more than enough to make him want to throw heavy objects at the Prince's head. And seeing the way he was so irrationally angry at the only friend he had, and the two ladies, was pushing the boundaries of Jordaan's slim patience.

"So I ask again, what in the Fairie Hells is going on here?"

His question went unanswered. A loud cracking sound rang through the courtyard, causing all of them to jerk in surprise. A second crack, louder somehow, as if a symphony were only getting started. As they all turned toward the sound, the front facade of Tull Castle crumbled to the stones below.

Chapter Twenty-Four

Diana

A second emergency within a week was too much. Diana surveyed the damage, the piles of blocks and the mortar that should have held them in place were now nothing more than rubble. Every part of her screamed that she was in over her head, and she needed to leave immediately.

But there were people in the castle who needed help. The central stairs, just a few yards from where they'd all been standing, were covered in debris because the facade of the castle had sloughed off like icing from a warm cake. Too many had been caught unaware. Maids on the higher floors, now exposed to the elements, screamed and clung to the furniture. Footmen and upper servants alike were hurrying to gather people and valuables, and looking for the safest way out of the castle.

Diana turned to Travers, who was frozen. Not with fear, she didn't read that from his demeanor, but the kind of inaction that comes from a person not understanding what they're seeing to such a degree that they can't move. He stared into dead space. Xavier tried to shake him, but until there was a third crack, and yet another piece of Tull Castle crumbled, did Travers move, tripping over his own two feet.

"Get out of the courtyard," Jordaan said to them, as he ran back to the castle. He was grabbing fleeing men by the collar and directing them back to the fray to help. Diana had only a heartbeat to appreciate the efficiency of how he'd jumped into action before she had to get moving. She grabbed the handles of Mallory's wheeled chair and urged her to hold on, as the four of them sprinted away from the destruction, Xavier practically dragging Travers with them.

When all of them were far enough away, Xavier turned back. "Be careful," Diana called to him, but whether heard her or not, she couldn't say.

Xavier joined Jordaan. They stood on some of the large piles of rocks, helping those who'd been inside the castle to navigate down to safety.

Mallory turned on Travers. "Are you just going to stand there and let this happen without you?"

"What am I supposed to do?" Travers shouted. His eyes were narrowed at Mallory, sweat on his temples.

"You are an able-bodied man!" Mallory fired back.

"As opposed to you?" Travers said to her with a snarl.

Diana couldn't stop the gasp that came from her mouth at the implicit slur.

Mallory wasn't fazed. "Go. Help. Try to be something other than a jackass for two minutes of your life."

Travers looked as if he were unable to come up with a cutting reply, so Diana took the opportunity to interject. "Your Aunt was in the castle an hour ago. You need to find her."

And that, finally, had Travers turning on his heel and heading toward the danger.

***

There were injuries, but no fatalities. By the time night had stretched and yawned its way over Tull, all of the castle's inhabitants, royal and servant alike, had been accounted for. There was no damage to the outbuildings, and while the main structure had lost its face, the destruction didn't seem to extend to the outer wings of the castle. Still, there was considerable damage, enough that it wouldn't be inhabitable for some time.

Lady Passwood, hale and hearty, had come out of the castle shaken but not harmed. She'd immediately ordered the carriages brought from the mews, and all of the royals taken to the Rutledge hotel. As the outbuildings weren't badly damaged, save a shower of debris, any servants who weren't required by the family and their guests were left to start the cleanup.

Diana hadn't seen if Jordaan returned to the hotel. Lady Passwood had ordered her and Mallory into a carriage. The ride back to the hotel wasn't long, but by the time they'd dragged themselves through the front doors, they were both yawning.

Diana had done what she could. Offering space for the ladies to stay while the hotel sorted out rooms, giving away what things she could spare so that they weren't left in dusty day gowns. And then, finally, when the day threatened never to end, she found herself yawning, so overtired, that it seemed as if she hadn't slept in weeks.

Diana was so worn out, that she felt as if Maryann were moving her about like a puppet. The maid got her out of her dress and into her night things and instructed Alice to brush and braid Diana's hair for her. The younger girl, eyes still red from two days of crying, did so without saying much. She pulled the boar bristle brush through Diana's tangled curls with a trained efficiency. It made Diana miss her mother fiercely. The Countess should be here. She should be the one brushing Diana's hair into submission. None of this would have happened if she had been able to travel. No one, not a Fairie, or a duchess, nor a prince, would dare make this much of a mess of things in the presence of the Countess of Wills.

They wouldn't dare.

After her maids left, Diana stared at the ceiling, unable to relax enough to sleep. Each time her eyes closed, she saw the stonework fall. She saw how close it had come to her and Mallory, Xavier, and Travers.

And Jordaan.

Once again, in the face of danger, he hadn't hesitated. He might be a generally infuriating person, but at his core, the man was a hero. And that was...

That was more trouble than she needed.

She wasn't going to marry Travers. That was clear. There was too much going on, too many confusing things happening in Tull, and Travers was far too emotional.

In comparison, Jordaan was like a breath of fresh air. Courageous. Steady. And so damned good-looking. She had to make herself stop thinking about that last part because she wasn't going to marry him either.

For one, he wasn't royal. Wills needed to align itself with a powerful territory to continue to thrive. And that meant choosing a high-ranking royal. Yes, she would have to live away from her home, but one of her children would inherit County Wills. The Yarborough line wouldn't die out.

Jordaan was just a knight. Indentured to a tiny territory.

Not eligible for marriage.

Rob Lycette wasn't either, her inner voice chimed. *And you had no problem imagining marrying him.*

That was different. She'd known Rob since they were in swaddling clothes, and her infatuation with him hadn't done her any good.

Jordaan saved you from the Pump Room fire.

And then went back inside when you couldn't find Jonah.

Just because those things were true they didn't make Jordaan a potential husband.

You wanted to kiss him more than you ever wanted anything in your life on the side of that road.

Lust wasn't a basis for political and financial stability. Diana had read hundreds of books that made that very point. History was full of very important people making very bad decisions by letting their anatomy rule them.

She was the daughter of the Iron Countess. She was better than that.

Except that she didn't want to be better than that. She wanted Jordaan. She wanted his brawny arms around her. She wanted his beard to tickle her cheek, and to run her fingers through his thick hair.

Comfort.

That's what she wanted.

It wasn't love, it was just the need to feel some comforting distraction.

Diana turned on her side. Her maid had shut the curtains, but light managed to shine through one small gap. It was just enough to show the shape of all her silly trunks lined up along the walls. Left there because there simply wasn't enough closet space for all that she'd brought.

The most light hit the blue trunk, the one with her supplies for her stupid attempt at perfume-making. Why did she ever think she could do that? Just because she'd read a few books?

It was foolish to think just because she'd read something she would be adept enough to do it.

All those books she'd read on the Fairie courts hadn't made her an expert on them, for example. She'd read fifteen different histories of the Light Court, most of them focused on the period before the kingdom was founded, and she never remembered reading about anything like the covenant Travers was facing.

Most of the old tomes were cautionary tales anyway. Foolish old men looking for power and ending up sporting webbed feet, or swallowing a hive's worth of bees. The message was clear. If you're thinking of dealing with the Fairies, don't.

They had so many ways of making life miserable. Using their magic to manipulate the weather, arrange the terms of a contract, or shape-shift.

Wait. Shapeshift. Jordaan had said, right before the castle wall fell that he'd spoken to a shapeshifter. And that name, it was... Needle.

Needle of the Light Court.

Diana threw back her covers, an idea planted in her mind like a splinter under her thumbnail. She knew that name.

It was an old memory, something she'd read a handful of years ago, but she remembered. The Light Court had made a deal with a trio of shapeshifters, several thousand years ago. The shifters had tried to bargain with the Court for the ability to appear more like them, more like the Fairies. But they'd misread the terms of their covenant, and been tricked into eons worth of service.

And Needle had been one of them.

She was almost sure of it.

It was Needle, and Shuttle, and...

The third name escaped her, along with some of the finer points.

Diana pushed back the latches on one of the trunks of books she'd brought.

It took time to find the one she was looking for. It was a tiny book, barely bigger than the palm of her hand. *Mistakes of the Maundry.* Maundry was the collective name of the lesser fae, the beings that were not human or Fairie. If they had ever existed, most of these species had died out a millennium ago and were now relegated to books like this one that was all about bad bargains.

Having found the book, Diana retreated to her bed, tapping on the Zephyr lamp to brighten up to a suitable reading light. She flipped through the pages, eyes straining to see the text. She skimmed the tiny pages. The first stories weren't helpful. Ones about Griffons who willingly gave up their size. Chimera who traded away their strength. Hobgoblins who didn't hob, apparently.

Most of it was nonsense.

But then there it was. Right in the middle of the book.

Needle, Spindle, and Shuttle. The Weavers.

Two out of three, not bad for not having read this particular book in half a dozen years.

The tale began like so many others. Unsatisfied with the life they'd been given, the three Weavers set out for the Fairie Courts. Receiving no welcome at the Dark Court, because they'd called during the day, but unwilling to wait for nightfall, the three changed course and visited the Light Court.

Because the gifts they'd brought were more suitable for the Dark Fairies than Light, the Weavers offended their hosts. And so when the bargain was made, the terms for them to achieve their desire — to appear more like high fae instead of their own, inconsistent forms, were deceptively bad. Unknowingly the Weavers had signed away the rights to the service of the Court, for one inconsistent and vague promise.

Diana turned the last page of the story, hoping to find something more useful, but there was only one final, unhelpful line.

"The Weavers are known to appear to those who find themselves on the cusp of their own terrible bargain."

So if the creature that had tried to get Jordaan away from Tull Castle was the same shapeshifter, what bargain might have he been about to make?

Or, had he already made it?

Chapter Twenty-Five

Mallory

Mallory pulled at the hem of the nightgown she had been given by Diana, tucking her feet under the billows of extra fabric. It was so long that for any practical use, it would need to be hemmed by five or six inches at least. The material was so soft and fine, however, she hated to think of it being chopped up. Likewise, the dresses that Diana assured her would otherwise go unworn.

"My mother over-prepared me for this trip. Or, perhaps she knew additional clothing might come in handy," she'd said as if it were no matter and she handed out gowns made of expensive linens all the time.

That was probably unfair. Diana had looked just as stunned as Mallory felt when they were all hustled into carriages to seek refuge at the Rutledge. She'd let Mallory and Lady Passwood rest in her suite until rooms could be prepared for them and freely gifted them everything they might need until their belongings could be rescued from the castle — stockings wrapped in diaphanous tissue straight from the modiste, stays, corsets and day dresses, even shoes.

All of them were entirely too big for either herself or Lady Passwood and would need tailoring. Diana was taller and curvier; she practically glowed with health and effortless beauty. If she weren't so bloody nice, Mallory would have wanted to hate her on sight. But that was impossible now, seeing as the lady had saved her from being crushed under a pile of rubble.

Lady Passwood wasn't under the same obligation. She was examining all of the seams on the cuffs on her nightgown, looking for flaws. Finding none, she went back to making small, cutting observations about the gifter.

"The Countess of Wills paid too much for this fabric. Zinnj-made crane cloth is always priced too high."

Mallory kept her mouth shut. Questioning Lady P now wasn't going to do any good, and the day had already been so long she wasn't sure she could stay awake much longer.

Besides, it was obvious that the Duchess was trying to ignore the elephant in the room. She was scared. It was evident in small things - the lines on her face, the slight hitch in her breath. Mallory found herself oddly sympathetic toward her guardian. Lady P had just lost her home and was in very real danger of losing her place among the royals of the Known Kingdom. And that had to be terrifying.

"Mallory, darling, sit up straight."

Sympathy was a fleeting emotion. "I'm not sure I can."

"You are a daughter of Vella House. You can do anything you set your mind to do."

Mallory had her doubts. She couldn't get Lady P to let her wear black, nor could she put Tull Castle back together again. And she couldn't figure out why Travers had his head so far up his backside his eyes were brown. Sitting up straight was the least of the tasks and her body wanted to slump down in her chair.

"Mind over matter?" Mallory said, fighting back a yawn.

"It's a skill you'll need for your debut."

"You can't be serious?"

"The castle's loss is a setback," Lady Passwood said, her words rushed. "However, I am determined we will be able to host a lovely event regardless. We need to launch you into society."

Mallory wasn't sure she heard correctly. *Was Lady P serious?* "Your house just exploded!"

"It did not explode. Some brickwork was dislodged."

Mallory was genuinely speechless. The depths of Lady Passwood's delusion were staggering. The front face of the building had slid off like butter from a hot knife.

"Darling," Lady P said, "close your mouth."

Mallory snapped her mouth shut.

"Better. Promise me that during your debut you will not stand about with your mouth gaping open like that."

Polly was going to have a field day when she got Mallory's letter. It was all too easy to imagine her sister cackling like a mad woman when she relayed that her debutante ball would go on with or without a castle to host it, based on Lady P's will alone.

Oh, Fairies be, Polly's dress. If it was damaged, Mallory would have to do some serious groveling to get back in her good graces. With any luck, the dress was still safely in one of her traveling trunks, far away from the rubble.

"There is nothing to worry about," Lady P said, reading her expression but not Mallory's thoughts. "I have the situation in hand."

It was late. The summer sky was already inky black, and Mallory wanted nothing more than to climb into the bed waiting for her on the other side of the suite's little sitting room. The day had worn away her sense of self-preservation, and she couldn't stop herself from biting out, "How?" How do you have any of this under control? Your nephew might lose his throne!"

Lady Passwood was saved from pulling any more bluster out of the air, by the arrival of the man himself. He pushed open the sitting room door with no grace, slamming through the door. Mallory scrambled to cover herself with her robe as Travers's gaze swept over her. For a brief moment, she would have sworn he was surprised to see her, but then any genuine reaction retreated behind his petulant sneer.

"Travers, there are ladies in their night things," Lady P scolded him.

He shrugged and threw himself onto a vacant settee. "I'm not a royal anymore, I don't have to follow those rules."

"Every man is subject to rules," Lady Passwood said. "Even the Prince of Tull."

"Former prince," he said. "I think today proved it's over."

"Nonsense. Now, sit up straight."

Mallory wasn't sure that Travers had ever listened to another human, but to her surprise, Travers pulled himself up to a somewhat more respectable position.

"Better," Lady P said. "Now, we were just discussing Mallory's debut."

Travers scoffed.

Lady Passwood fixed him with a hard glare. Mallory wrapped her robe tighter around her, sure that the room had just dropped a degree or two in temperature.

"Mallory must be out in society."

"Why?" Travers, despite being a monumental ass, had managed to ask the exact question Mallory also wanted to know.

"Because a woman cannot be married before she is presented. And if we are going to save our territory, you must marry her."

It was Travers's turn to let his mouth hang open. He sputtered, "Why in the Fairie Hells would I do that?"

Mallory had only a moment to feel the slight he'd intended.

She turned to Lady Passwood, who was summoning as much dignity as she could, considering the late hour, her state of dress, and an angry nephew. She'd said too much. Mallory could tell. Polly had the same kind of indignation when she was caught off-guard.

"I'm not marrying him," Mallory said.

"Likewise," Travers shot.

"You will," Lady P said. "You must. Mallory is a Vella."

"What does my name have anything to do with any of this?" Despite being seated in her chair, Mallory felt as if her feet had been kicked out from under her. She'd known Lady Passwood wanted her to marry Travers, but now she was making it out to be as if it were the only choice. As if the one thing standing between ceding Tull back to the Fairies, and keeping the territory, was Mallory herself.

"The Vella family is descended from the Light Court. It's the loophole, Travers. The covenant says you must give the territory back to Fairie control. It is not specific to whom. Marry Mallory. Make her the crown princess, and you keep your throne alongside her."

All her life, Mallory had heard stories about the Vella family's connection to the Fairies. They were nothing more than bits of lore and family history woven together in a loose tapestry. Great-great-great-grand-something could spin yarn into gold. Cousin so-and-so once upon a time had grown a curling tail. Auntie This-or-That could make Zephyr lamps. The family's roots are traced back to the original courts, before the founding of the Known Kingdoms. But it was all nonsense. No one took that seriously.

Except, of course, Lady Passwood.

She was deadly serious.

Travers stared at his aunt for a long time, his dark eyes going stormy. "No," he said. "I'm not hiding behind a woman, especially not one who...."

Lady Passwood drew in a great breath. "Nephew," she said with a frosty edge, "I suggest you not finish that sentence."

Travers shrugged. "The best scholars on the continent have been trying to work out a solution for months. Why do you think none of them have come up with this magical marriage idea? Because it won't work."

"You don't know that," Lady Passwood said with steely determination.

Mallory had a great longing to be anywhere else. This discussion, as much as it was about her, was a family affair. The two of them needed to work out their issues and leave her out of it.

"It's not going to happen. She hates me." Travers pointed at her like she was a trial exhibit.

Mallory had had enough. She released the break on her wheelchair and rolled herself toward her room.

"Mallory, Darling, stay, please," Lady Passwood said to her. "You need to know how important you are to this family."

She turned to look back at the Duchess, sorry when she saw the genuine pain on her guardian's face. Sorry because she wasn't the solution Lady Passwood imagined. She wouldn't marry Travers. She couldn't. "I can't," she said. "He's..."

"I've what?" Travers demanded. His eyes were narrowed at her, but Mallory wouldn't shrink back.

"You've been nothing but cruel to me since we were children," she said, not sure she trusted her voice, but unwilling to let the discussion go any farther. "I don't want to be around you, Travers. I won't marry you because of who you are."

"And who is that, oh wise Lady Mallory?"

Mallory shook her head. She didn't want to hurt Lady P, but she wasn't going to let herself be used by her either. Not if it meant spending any more time with Travers. "You're angry and you're mean. When you're in trouble or you're cornered, you lash out. And by the time you realize what a jackass you've been to everyone around you, you never apologize. You run, and then you drink. I will not tie my life to someone like that."

Lady Passwood's face had lost all color. She clutched her fist over her mouth. Mallory didn't want to make it worse, but she wasn't done. She let the silence build, let the misery sink in just a bit more before adding, "Lady Passwood, you have always been good to me and my family. And there is little any of us wouldn't do for you. But I will not sacrifice myself to save him. He doesn't deserve to rule. Let the Fairies take back Tull. Because they couldn't do a worse job even if they tried."

Chapter Twenty-Six

Diana

Alice brought the breakfast tray, arms shaking as she made her way toward Diana, concentrating on every step. When she finally reached Diana's bedside she carefully placed her burden on the nightstand, sighing with obvious relief.

"I can't believe that it didn't spill," she said.

Diana was pleased to see that the young maid's eyes were considerably brighter than they'd been last night. In the morning sun streaming through the suite's windows, she looked like her normal, cheerful self.

"Maryann says she's sorry, but she's still sick. Bill too. The poor things."

"Please tell them both to stay in bed. I'll ask the hotel to send up meals."

"Oh I can do that, My Lady," Alice said. "I'll talk to the cook when I take your tray back down."

Diana offered her thanks. To her dismay, the coffee in the press wasn't as hot as she would have liked. Alice had taken the slow route from the kitchens after retrieving it. But it was drinkable, and since she didn't have to fetch it herself, she was happy to have it.

"How are you feeling?" she asked Alice, who had begun pulling garments from the wardrobe.

Alice turned back toward her, a massive green day dress clasped in her arms like a security blanket. "I'm awfully sorry," she said, with a cracking voice. "I don't know what came over me. Crying over Jonah Berry like some silly thing."

Afraid the girl would burst into tears again, Diana assured her that she had nothing to be sorry about. "I've been in a similar position. It's very hard when someone you admire doesn't return the sentiment."

Her words didn't have the effect she'd hoped. Tears, fat as freshwater pearls, gathered in Alice's eyes. Absently, she used the hem of the dress she held to wipe them away, only to fumble the lot when she realized what she was doing.

"Pull the periwinkle blue one," Diana said, as kindly as she could. "It seems to be very warm today, and that dress is better in the heat."

Alice nodded. "I'll send this one down to the laundry."

Diana left the girl to her chores lest she say anything else to make her cry again. The Countess would probably have some important guidance about how to deal with servants having emotions. Her mother was a believer in the chin-up method of coping, but Diana didn't have it in her to chide anyone about the way they felt. Alice was young, and she would bounce back. But right now what she felt was real and it was awful.

By the time Alice helped her into her chosen dress, and once again brushed and braided her hair, Diana felt it best to let the matter lie. She would check on Jonah, see if it was necessary to send him back to Wills early, or if he could wait until she arranged passage back home for all of them. And after that, she'd do her best to stay out of the love lives of her employees.

Alice got to work tidying the room, putting books back into their trunks. "Have you read all these, My Lady?" she asked.

"Most of them," Diana answered, before finishing off the last of the pastry on her tray. "Although perhaps I shouldn't have brought so many with me."

"Are they novels?"

Diana shook her head. "Most of them are histories. Novels have never held my interest for very long."

"Fairie history?" Alice said, checking one of the titles.

"I find them endlessly fascinating."

Alice looked skeptical as she gathered the last books Diana had left scattered during her late-night rummage. "My mum says humans and Fairies should never mix. She was glad when the old King decided to break with them. Don't trust anything with magic like that."

Diana knew from all of her reading that remarkable things had come from the Fairies. Art. Philosophy. Great buildings and whole cities. But given everything that had happened lately in the Known Kingdoms, perhaps Alice's mother was on to something. Fairie magic hadn't done Princess Kira much good in her life. And Travers, well, if he wasn't exaggerating, his covenant was nothing but trouble. And if she were right, if Jordaan had been visited by one of the Weavers from the Light Court, that was a whole other area where something might be going horribly wrong.

"Do you want me to put away that one?" Alice asked, pointing to the small copy of *Mistakes of the Maundry* that Diana had on her bed.

"No, this one I want to bring up to Caris Mourne. I'm hoping she'll be able to discuss it with me."

Alice shivered and then made a crude symbol with her hands. It was the kind of gesture one made when trying to stave off evil from Fairies. "Oh My Lady, that one is just the kind my mum would tell you to stay far away from. Magic like that isn't natural."

Diana tucked the small book into her dress pocket. "Superstition is all well and good, Alice, but Caris Mourne has never been anything but kind to me. I'm happy to call her a friend."

Alice didn't look pleased, and less so when Diana mentioned that her first errand of the day would bring her to the witch's tower.

"Be cautious, My Lady," Alice said, gathering up the breakfast tray. "I'll remember to tell the cook about a tray for Bill and Maryann."

When the maid was gone, Diana decided she wouldn't waste any more time before seeking out the witch. If Sir Jordaan was getting himself into trouble, and she could do something to prevent it, she would.

Despite the arrival of the Corvin family and their guests, the hotel was still mostly empty. The halls were quiet as she made her way to the witch's door.

Perhaps that was why the sound carried so much.

She was about to knock, her gloved fist poised to strike the wood when a clear voice said, "I will give my life if it means you survive."

A chill ran down Diana from head to toe.

It was the witch's voice. There might have been an answer to the statement, but Diana couldn't pick up the words. Only that whatever was being said was none of her business.

She stepped back several feet and nearly tripped over the little black kitten that Sir Jordaan seemed to think was akin to perfection.

"Oh, I'm sorry," she said to the cat, and then couldn't fathom why she was apologizing.

Veronica inclined her head, as if accepting.

"You don't happen to know if Sir Jordaan is getting himself into trouble?" She asked, knowing it was a ridiculous question to ask a cat. Having grown up around her mother's pugs, perhaps she'd accepted too easily that the animals were as perceptive as the Countess always insisted.

The kitten meowed and turned. Diana had the strange notion that Veronica expected her to follow. She'd just told herself that was preposterous when the kitten turned back and meowed, in a much louder, more insistent tone.

"Are you off to find him?"

Veronica trotted down the hall, and despite her better judgment, Diana followed, even down to the second floor, where she knew Sir Jordaan was likely to be.

Sure enough, Veronica stopped outside the door to the sitting room, her yellow-green eyes looked far too knowledgeable.

"I can't believe I'm asking this, but do you expect me to go in?"

The cat inclined her head once more.

Diana wasn't sure she'd ever be able to explain this moment to herself. It was reckless and foolish and all the other adjectives she could think of that meant "bad idea!" Fairies be, she was taking orders from an animal barely bigger than the palm of her hand.

Worse, she knew who was on the other side of that door. And she knew it would get her into trouble.

But she went in anyway.

And she did not knock.

Chapter Twenty-Seven

Diana

Fairies be, he was beautiful.

Chapter Twenty-Eight

Jordaan

Jordaan didn't know if all the potions he'd been fed since the sleeping sickness set in were helping, but the dreams were definitely getting better. He'd fallen into a hard sleep after the destruction of Tull Castle. He couldn't have fought his way out of it if he tried. Not this time. Because in this deep sleep, the Fairies didn't offer him the usual nonsense. No crowns, no rich foods, no piles of gold.

Just her.

Slipping into the sitting room, and locking the door behind her.

Coming to the settee where he'd fallen asleep. Tentatively touching his hair.

It was all so real, he could feel the little tingle on his scalp as her fingers ran over his temple.

There was no denying it. Not anymore.

He wanted her.

He couldn't have her. Didn't deserve her. But if the Fairies were trying to tempt him into anything, all they had to offer was Diana, looking at him like she was starving and he was cake.

They should have started with that.

For months and months, he'd been falling asleep where he stood. When he slept the deepest there was always a dream, and in it an offer. A bargain.

The Fairies wanted something he had and would give him anything to get it from him.

Nothing had tempted him like her.

But now in the hazy dream state, it was as if he were standing away from his body watching himself sleep with her beside him. And he wanted that. He wanted her to settle in next to him on the furniture and stroke his hair, of all the asinine things. If he had any clue what the Fairies were after, he'd have gladly signed any covenant just to have her stay. He couldn't give her a royal title, much less a throne. But if she loved him anyway, that was worth whatever in the Fairie Hells was asked of him.

"Wake up, please," she said in a whisper that shot like lightning through him. Her words knocked him back into his body, where the vestiges of the sleep paralysis grabbed hold of his limbs, keeping him still.

"I know you must be tired." Her words were aftershocks. "But please, please wake up."

She touched his hand. He could feel the warmth, even if he couldn't see it. The darkness behind his eyes was a swamp full of pitch.

"Don't be tempted," she said, and there was an urgency to her voice, a little crack at the end.

What was that about?

The real Diana wasn't mooning over him. She'd come to Tull to marry a prince, not a landless knight. She was too good for him, and she damn well knew it. So why did it seem like she was worried about him?

He needed to know.

Fighting off death-like sleep wasn't easy, but Jordaan shook off the sluggishness, to yawn and stretch. His vision was blurry. There was too much light in the sitting room, and he didn't trust the picture before him. Diana's red hair caught the sun and lit up like a bonfire. He couldn't see the contours of her face, but somehow, he could pick up the chaos of her freckles.

"Beautiful," he murmured.

She blushed as his vision came back into focus. "You can't fool me. I know you're talking about the cat," she said.

On cue, Veronica leaped onto the settee, and as he sat up she curled into his lap. "Can you blame me?" he said, his voice hoarse. "Have you ever seen a more lovely creature?"

"I don't think she's a cat," Diana said.

"And what would she be?"

Diana shrugged. "Some kind of sprite, maybe? She's entirely too perceptive."

Jordaan used his palm to rub the crust from his eyes. "Why would a spirit want to hang around a hotel disguised as a cat?"

To his surprise, Diana sat down next to him on the settee, her voluminous blue skirt enveloping them both. It wasn't the proper thing to do. But then again, neither was her being in the room alone with him. And if his sleep vision were to be believed, she'd locked the door. The proper thing could take a long walk off a short pier. If the sleeping sickness claimed him again he was likely to fall into her lush curves. Best case scenario, if he were honest.

"I think she's a spy," Diana said. She reached out and gave the kitten a quick scratch behind the ear.

Veronica looked annoyed, and Diana withdrew her hand. Probably because she realized she was far too close to parts of him than a young lady should be.

"Veronica has never done anything wrong in her entire life, ever. She's not a spy."

The cat shot Diana a dismissive look and then preened under his praise.

The lady was right, the cat was entirely too perceptive.

"I didn't say it was a bad thing, someone has to watch out for you."

Her words were like a paper cut, a small but stinging reminder that he was still damaged goods. "Is there a point to you waking me up, Denise?"

"You've used that one before, Jerry."

"Consider it a freebee for when you called me Gordon."

She rolled her eyes and took a small book from her pocket. "I need to show you something."

The book was smaller than his fist. She flipped it open to a dog-eared page and handed it to him. The print in front of him swam, and he handed the book back. "Read it to me."

She sighed but held up the book to read it anyway. *The three beings known as the Weavers — Needle, Spindle, and Shuttle — indebted themselves to the Light Court before the founding of the Known Kingdoms. Maundry who inhabited the space between Fairie and humans often sought to make themselves over to one or the other and often failed. None lost more spectacularly than the Weavers, who traded their freedom for a vague promise that, as far as this author knows, has never been granted.*

Diana put the book down, a look of expectation on her face. "Do you see?"

Jordaan yawned. "Just tell me what I'm supposed to know."

"You said the creature you spoke to was Needle?"

He nodded, and Diana got that wild look of hers that said she'd latched onto an idea.

"This book says that the Weavers appear when someone is on the verge of making a bad bargain."

Like, say, promise the Fairies whatever they wanted in exchange for a beautiful woman? That was too close. "I haven't...I'm not..." he felt as if she'd reached inside his head and pulled out his secrets. It wasn't a comfortable feeling, and he struggled to find the words.

She exhaled heavily. "So you haven't been offered anything?"

Jordaan got to his feet to get some space between them. Diana jumped up and followed him across the room, the layers of her dress rustling. "If you think the Fairies can save you from the sleeping sickness, please reconsider."

"I'm not."

She was entirely too close. "I was going to speak to Caris Mourne but... well, I think I would have been interrupting something."

"Debbie, I don't need you getting involved in my health."

She was startled, as if it didn't occur to her that she might have galloped over a sensitive topic. "I'm just trying to help."

"Don't," he said, the words harsher than he intended. "Just don't. This is nothing you need to worry about."

"You're my friend."

Were they friends? Jordaan couldn't say.

She sucked in a breath at his silence. "I apologize if I've overstepped, but I'm worried that you might be putting yourself in danger."

He didn't need another reason to be in love with her. He needed less so that it would be easier to watch her go off and marry someone else.

"I'll be fine. Stay out of it, please."

She went somehow paler than usual. "I'm sorry to have bothered you," she said.

If he were a better knight or just a better person, he'd have assured her that she hadn't bothered him. He'd tell her that he was touched by her concern. That it meant a lot to him that she would spend even a single second worried about his miserable existence.

He said nothing.

"I'm sorry, Jordaan. I really am."

He might live another sixty or seventy years and never forget the sound of the door unlocking. It wasn't loud, just the gentle metallic click of the pin falling back into the tumbler, but it was enough to shake him from his head to the soles of his feet.

Chapter Twenty-Nine

Xavier

The Harbormaster didn't know what happened to the schedule of ships. He shrugged, unconcerned at the mess, the piles of paper on his desk, and the stink of the crab traps cluttering the office.

"You have no idea what vessels are coming into your waters?" Xavier asked for the third time.

"No ships are coming in today," said the thin man with a shrug.

"But are there ships due to arrive?"

"Always are." The Harbor Master scratched his head, a shower of dandruff falling on the shoulders of his teal uniform.

Hitting his head against the wall might be more effective in communicating with this man. Xavier had to wonder if being hard-headed was a particularly Tullian trait. "I just need to know which passenger ships are coming into Tull and then going north. Why can't you give me a list?"

"The schedule is none of your business," The man said, drawing himself up to his full five-foot-five. "Transportation for passengers is arranged through individual shipping companies, not the Port."

"All of which would be registered with the Port."

Again, another shrug. The man leaned back in his chair and put his feet up on the desk, sending a stack of papers flying onto Xav's lap. Tide tables, letters addressed to arriving passengers and crew, but nothing like a basic schedule of the ships due to arrive in Tull.

It was time to cut his losses. He stood. "I thank you for your time."

The Harbor Master smirked, "You can see yourself out, Sir."

"It's Your Highness," Xav said, relishing a small surge of pettiness. "I'll be sure to mention you to Prince Travers." He tipped his hat to the man and exited the port office.

The walkway along the waterfront was mostly empty, save the usual suspects — a handful of sailors on leave from their ships, dockworkers lounging on pilings, and a handful of women walking briskly, shopping clutched for dear life. Sunlight touched the tops of the tall buildings facing the wharves, leaving the area along the seawall bathed in shadow. It was significantly cooler in this part of town versus the areas up around the castle and the Rutledge Hotel.

His stomach rumbled, reminding him he hadn't bothered to eat breakfast at the hotel. He'd wanted to come down to the port early, to see if there was any possibility of leaving within the next few days. The path Travers was on was one that Xav couldn't follow. He'd indulged, he'd wallowed, he'd drunk himself silly. Anything to escape his own broken heart. He'd naively assumed Travers was doing the same. But whatever Travers was running from — be it the Fairies or something smaller— Xav couldn't help him. It was time to go home.

He'd go by the pie shop, and see if Mina knew which of the passenger vessels sailed North. He could go as far as the Spire coast, and then hire horses to get himself back to Dunlock. Surely finding postillions couldn't be as hard as finding a ship out of Tull.

Although, with his recent luck, he wasn't so sure.

Workmen were fixing the door to the pie shop, and shining new glass cast rainbows into the interior space. Xav was greeted by the warm scent of savory meat pies, and the sizzle of onions caramelizing on the stove. In the few weeks he'd been in Tull, the pie shop was one of the bright spots.

Of the ones he could remember anyway.

Mina was behind the counter, but she didn't seem to recognize him at first. Probably because he was not wearing last night's clothing or nursing a monstrous hangover.

"My friend and I were here a lot in the last few weeks," he said, as gently as he could.

Realization dawned, and a smile stretched over her wide face. "Well you clean up nice, don't you?" she said. "A couple of pies for you?"

His stomach made a loud affirmative. "You don't happen to know anything about the passenger ships? I need to figure out a way home."

"Where's home?" She put two crusty hand pies on the plate, and Xav took a seat at the counter.

"Dunlock," he said, keeping the details deliberately light. He wasn't a prince here, just another drunk who once rolled in after a bender.

Mina whistled. "Fancy place."

Somehow that made him feel homesick. Mina wasn't to blame. She couldn't know that Dunlock was not fancy. There were no major cities, only a collection of villages spread between the castles of various nobility. And his own home, Dunlock Castle, was at best shabbily elegant. He'd told himself over and over again he hadn't missed it while he and Travers had been gallivanting around the Known Kingdoms. He was rather good at lying to himself.

"I'm hoping to catch a ship as far as Triple City in Spire. I just don't know which ships go in that direction."

Mina thought for a moment, absently plating up additional pies for the customers who'd followed him into the shop. "The Vogel line goes up the coast the farthest. Up around the Northern Territories," she said, excusing herself to drop off pies. "A ship leaves about once a week."

Xav took a small notebook from his pocket and scribbled the name of the shipping company. Once he was done eating he'd walk along the water to their offices and see how soon he could get passage. With any luck, he could find it, before heading up to the castle. He needed to see about getting the rest of his belongings out of the castle. He'd been given rooms in the back half of the castle, so he had every expectation that his things would still be in his suitcase, unharmed. He hadn't been there long enough to unpack, and as far as he could tell only the front section of the castle had fallen.

Mina returned and confirmed that the Vogel line was part of the Galdera Shipping Company, which had an office at the opposite end of the harbor walk. He paid his bill, tipped generously, and was about to leave when the door to the pie shop blew open in a strong wind. It slapped shut with enough force to cause them both to jump.

The three Fairies who'd come into the shop earlier in the week passed by the window. They looked just as out of place as they had the first time, only now they collectively looked tired, or perhaps as if they expected spooks and ghouls to pop out from every alleyway. The two women in particular had deep circles under their eyes.

Mina let out an audible exhale. "I can't get used to them, I swear I can't."

Curiosity poked Xav squarely in the chest. "Are there many Fairies around Tull?"

"No," Mina said, wringing out a soiled cleaning cloth over a small bucket. "Until this year I'd never seen one in my life. I always thought Fairies stayed invisible around humans."

Xav had been taught the same, but that was wrong.

"Just this year?"

The proprietress nodded, absently wiping at one of the tabletops. "First of the year was the first time I ever saw one."

The first of the year was when the Fairies had first been turned away from the audience at Tull Castle, at least according to the story he'd gotten out of Travers. It wouldn't be a coincidence.

"Thanks, Mina."

She smiled, and Xav was almost sure it was a genuine one. "Stop by before you leave. I'll pack up some pies for your journey."

"A dozen, at least," he said. "I've never had better and I doubt I will again."

The compliment brought a flush to Mina's already ruddy cheeks. He gave her a small bow and left the shop.

Clouds had gathered in the area around the wharf, threatening summer rain. He was contemplating going back to the hotel versus finding the shipping office when a flash of bright, bright green caught his eye. It was the male Fairie with the skim milk complexion, coming out of a greengrocer farther down the street.

Which was odd, because Fairies didn't eat.

At least not human food. So what were they doing in a shop like that? Were they still looking for Travers? He wasn't that hard to find. He was sure the entire island knew about the damage to Tull Castle, and that the prince and his aunt had been forced to take rooms at the Rutledge. So why were a trio of Fairies still roaming around town asking questions?

He should go to the shipping office and get his passage worked out. It was the sensible thing to do. Get a ticket, pack his things, and leave Tull far, far behind him.

He turned toward the market.

Maybe it was curiosity, maybe it was just foolishness, but something wasn't right here.

146

Maybe it was curiosity, maybe it was just foolishness, but something wasn't right here.

Chapter Thirty

Mallory

Shame was terrible for sleep and not much better for her appetite. She shouldn't have spoken the way she did to Lady Passwood. Prince Travers could take a long walk off a short pier, but Lady P had always been good to her.

Hadn't she?

Mallory couldn't escape the feeling that she'd been used. All that nonsense about finding her a spouse, when she'd planned all along to marry Mallory off to her idiot of a nephew. And for that matter — how long had she known about this alleged Fairie connection? Had Lady P befriended her parents — who had no particular standing among royals — years and years ago. Was it because she'd been playing a long game?

If so, that was sickening.

Her parents trusted Lady Passwood.

And it all left Mallory with humiliation and just a tiny bit of rage.

Because she'd meant it. Travers wasn't a good person. She did deserve someone who never insulted her, never made her feel small and insignificant and useless. And Travers could do all of those things with one side-eyed glance.

She gave up on breakfast in the dining room, having eaten too little of what the waiter placed in front of her. Everything tasted like sand, and her stomach was too topsy-turvy to hold much of it.

Trudy hovered, a look on her round face of worry. "Ma'am, I'm sure the Duchess would want you to eat more. You need food for strength."

Mallory bit back a sarcastic reply. Minor royal though she might be, she wasn't Travers and she wouldn't lash out at her servants with her frustrations. "I'll eat later," she assured the girl.

Trudy was one heartbeat away from wringing her hands, but she nodded and wheeled Mallory out of the dining room.

"Would you like to return to your suite?" Trudy asked.

As Lady Passwood was still in residence, no Mallory would not. She'd risen early to avoid the woman and the conflicting feelings that she'd failed to sleep off. "I think I could use some time in the gardens. There's a lovely view of the water from there."

And hopefully, enough blooming flowers to mask the fishy smell, but Mallory wasn't that optimistic. Still, a dead fish was better than a duplicitous Fairie godmother.

Trudy wasn't pleased with the idea, but she nonetheless rolled Mallory's chair out of the hotel's back garden and helped Mallory onto one of the hanging swings set up on the edge of the flower beds.

"Should I stay, Miss?" Trudy asked. "Or would you like me to…"

Trudy had only been her maid — and a maid at all — for a handful of months since Mallory came of age. She took direction well — sopping it up like a sponge — but often needed clear directions.

"No, that's not necessary. I'd like to stay here for a while. Please ask Lady Passwood's servants if they have some duties for you this morning."

Trudy nodded eagerly, and then dashed off, leaving Mallory alone. She hadn't been alone much since she left Vella House.

It was nice to be by herself, without the weight of other people's expectations. She took a few only-mildly-fishy deep breaths, trying to expel the dread that sat in her chest.

It almost worked.

She looked at the flowers. Mostly pinks and yellows. Mallory wasn't much for flowers. They were pretty, she supposed, but she had no idea what they meant. Vella cranes were small, with dark blue petals. They were practical rather than pretty because their ropy stems were strong enough to weave into baskets and floor mats and such. Beyond that, she did not know blossoms and had no idea what she was looking at.

The clouds were interesting. Big, puffy tufts floating along in the blue sky.

Nice.

Not great conversationalists.

Mallory kicked at the gravel underneath the swing, only succeeding in dirtying her boot. The swing rocked a bit, but to get more motion she'd have to exert more of her stamina, and she wasn't sure she had it spare.

The hotel was too quiet.

There weren't even enough sea birds circling to be a distraction.

She supposed she could try and summon Trudy back to get her a book or some drawing paper. She'd miscalculated her ability to keep herself entertained.

The subtle crunch of boots on the path was enough to give her something to smile about. More when she saw Lady Diana walking on the garden path that emerged from the lemon grove. Mallory waved eagerly.

Diana was startled, as if she hadn't expected anyone to be out in the public gardens. She cautiously held up a hand in acknowledgment.

"Are you alright?" Mallory couldn't help but ask as the lady approached. Her face was rather pale, even given its generous freckles, and her whole manner seemed dejected. She looked, in short, a lot like Mallory felt.

Diana tried to give an affirmative answer, but her voice cracked as she spoke. "Fine... fine," she began. Her big brown eyes were wet with unshed tears. "I hope you are well?"

An equally insincere "fine" was on Mallory's tongue before she shook her head and said, "I'm miserable, actually. You?"

Diana's laugh was small and shaky. "Me too. I thought taking a walk would help, but it turns out looking at lemon trees is a bit boring."

Mallory gestured to the flowers. "Same."

Diana blew out a breath. "What's making you miserable? Is it interesting?"

She liked Diana, Mallory decided. She'd liked her on first meeting her, and more so when she'd stood up to Lady Passwood, but that was more amusement than anything. She liked Diana in a way that meant they could be real friends. And real friends needed honesty.

"I lost my temper with my guardian," Mallory admitted. "And she might have deserved it, but she's a duchess and my Fairie godmother, so I was raised to feel guilty over questioning her."

Diana took a seat on the swing next to her, gently pushing them into motion with both feet. "Oh, that is bad."

"I did get to tell Travers he was an awful person, so it wasn't all bad."

"I practically threw myself at Sir Jordaan, only for him to tell me to mind my own business and leave him alone."

Mallory made a face. "Harsh."

Diana nodded. She reached into the pocket of her dress and extracted a fat lemon. "I picked a few of the ugly ones and threw them at the trees. Care to try?"

The lemon's peel was bumpy, with bits of dirt rubbed into the surface pits. In Mallory's hand, it had a heft to it, as if it had been left on the branch a season too long. "Did it help at all?"

"It didn't make me feel worse."

If she could hit something, Mallory realized, perhaps the day wouldn't be a total loss. It wouldn't be much of an accomplishment, but it would be something. She tested the weight in her hands against what strength she had in her arms. She could throw it about five, maybe six feet. The garden's kidney-shaped beds were all arranged around a central statue of some old codger in a high-collared robe. "I might need to be closer to hit him," she acknowledged.

"You just need some confidence," Diana said. From her opposite pocket, she took out a curved silver flask. She unscrewed the top and handed it over. "It burns a bit going down but after that, it helps."

Mallory couldn't help her eyes going wide. "It's not even nine in the morning."

Diana shrugged one lushly-clad shoulder. "Miserable, remember? Miserable people can have a little whiskey."

Mallory had never had whiskey. She sniffed at the open flask. The scent was sweet and smoky all at once, and tickled the inside of her nose. "Is this a bad idea?"

Diana gave an enthusiastic nod. "That's part of its appeal."

In that case, Mallory took a small sip, and it did indeed burn her throat the same as it had her nose. She didn't cough, but it was a near thing. Only as the liquid made its way to her stomach did she realize its power. The burn faded, and she felt something like warmth bloom in her chest. A second sip made her limbs feel loose and weightless.

"It's terrible and I love it," Mallory said, after her fourth sip. She passed the flask back, and Diana took a longer drink.

"Bad habit I picked up in Dunlock in the spring."

"During the Festival?"

Diana nodded. A significant chunk of her red hair had fallen from her crown of braids to frame her face. She looked wind-swept and lovely, despite her professed misery, like a painting come to life.

Mallory had heard rumors about the Festival of the Flower, each of them more ridiculous than the last. There were stories that people had seen inanimate objects dancing through the halls of the castle and swore that mythical beasts were roaming around the grounds. Kira, the Princess Royal, was allegedly kidnapped and returned with some silly story of being a highwayman.

"What happened there?"

"Stupid boy broke my stupid heart," Diana said.

"Sir Jordaan?"

Diana shook her head. She took another sip and passed the flask back. "No. Not him. An old friend. I got in my head that we could be... but no."

"You loved him?"

"I thought I did. He didn't see me that way."

"It wasn't Travers, was it?"

Diana looked horrified at the suggestion. "Absolutely not. I only agreed to maybe marry him because my mother wanted the match. *It would be a triumph!'* Diana added flourish to her words, including a waggle of her fingers.

Now that was interesting. Another sip of the rapidly disappearing whiskey produced no burn, only that delicious glowing feeling, spreading through her body. Mallory had to suppose the feeling was why so many people became alcoholics, all of them chasing this feeling of contentment from a bottle.

"To whom?" Mallory asked. She peered into the small opening of the flask, distressed to see the magical happy juice all gone.

Diana hiccuped. "To other royals, I guess. Anyone who cares about who has power and who doesn't."

Both of them had been raised to perpetuate the idea of influence and power; which was a stupid system, so Mallory said so.

Diana agreed. "I might need more whiskey to deal with it."

"Do you have any more in your pocket?"

"No," Diana said, with a sullen downturn to her voice. "We should go inside and find some."

That, as far as Mallory was concerned, was an excellent idea. Diana helped her to her chair, but before they were more than 3 feet from the swing, she stopped. "You didn't throw your lemon!" She said with an excited gasp.

An oversight that needed to be corrected immediately. Mallory picked up the lemon again and reeled back her arm. She felt invincible. She would hit the smug-looking statue, square in its ugly smug stone face.

She let out a guttural scream as she lobbed the lemon. It sailed through the air with glorious purpose, straight for the statue.

And instead hit Prince Xavier, who was rounding the path at the base of the statue, in the middle of the chest. His eyes went wide as the wind was knocked from him.

"Oh my god, Xav!" Diana said, rushing toward the staggering prince.

"Did I kill him?" Mallory asked, guilt rushing back to replace the whiskey's temporary joy.

"What in the Fairie Hells?" said the prince, as he recovered. "What are you two doing?"

Diana drew herself up to her full height, which, Mallory noted with appreciation, was a few inches taller than Prince Xavier. "We're day drinking, obviously," she said. "It's not like you died."

Mallory couldn't stop a snort of laughter that bubbled up. It tumbled out of her like smoke from a cottage chimney. "He is still alive!" she giggled.

Diana's lusty laughter joined her own, and the two of them spurred one another on until Mallory felt her abdomen ache with the effort.

"Yes, obviously," Prince Xavier echoed in a dull, dry manner. "Let's get you ladies some coffee."

"Oh, I love coffee!" Mallory said. Everything seemed ridiculous and wonderful, and she had a suspicion that she might be a little bit intoxicated.

"Me too!" Diana said, with an excited grin.

"Yes, we all love coffee," the prince said. "Let's go find some."

Chapter Thirty-One

Jordaan

The witch held a hand to his forehead, assuring herself that Jordaan had no apparent temperature.

"The perspiration is concerning," she noted with a none-too-subtle sniff of her nose.

He'd feel bad about coming to her looking like he'd just crawled out of a sewer but, he didn't have the wherewithal for shame. He hadn't felt so badly in weeks. "Is there a potion you can give me?"

Caris Mourne snorted. "Not for what you have, Sir Jordaan."

"What does that mean?"

She arched a purple eyebrow at him but said nothing. She turned and rummaged in one of the many drawers of a great cabinet that he was almost sure hadn't been the tower the last time he was here. She sighed and pulled out a small package wrapped which she flicked toward him. Jordaan fumbled but managed to catch it. It was barely bigger than the palm of his hand and smelled strongly of herbs.

"What is this?"

"Soap," she said. "I recommend it."

"I've been sick," he said, feeling like a scolded child.

She tilted her head to the side. "Something is bothering you. Yes, the lingering symptoms of the sleeping sickness, but also a condition far less mysterious."

"What?"

"Don't challenge my belief in your intelligence," she said crisply.

If his feelings were all that obvious, he wished the witch would just tell him what they were. Because he didn't understand them. Not even a little bit. Ever since Diana had left the sitting room a few hours ago, he'd been a mess. His body was stiff and tired, and his mind so jumbled he hadn't been able to hold a consistent thought in his head.

"Sorry, to bother you," he said, getting to his feet and offering her a bow. "I'll see myself out."

She nodded. "When you come back, perhaps we can discuss the dreams you've been having."

It was the second time that day he'd felt as if someone had peeled back his skull and peered inside. "Who said I've been having dreams?"

Her sigh was heavy, her clear eyes full of concern. "You've been falling into fits of enchanted sleep for almost four months. It stands to reason."

"It's nonsense. Nothing important," he said, suddenly feeling the itch of sweat on his skin.

"Sir Jordaan, if I am to continue to help you, I need you to trust me. I will respect your secrets, even the ones you keep from yourself, but if something is happening in your dreams, it may be connected to your illness."

Which sounded like a lot of nonsense to him, but he kept that thought to himself. However, given the witch's perception, he wasn't sure that was entirely possible.

"Go," Caris Mourne said. "Take a bath. Scrub away your melancholy. Shave, perhaps. Then come back and see me."

***

To his everlasting annoyance, he did feel better after a hot bath. Taking it so late in the morning was an odd feeling. One of the weirdest things about suffering from the sleeping sickness was the sense that his days had no structure. As a knight he was expected to rise at the same time each day, to eat with the other knights in the castle dining hall at set hours, and complete his duties when told. Convalescence had made him idle, and to his great shame, he hated it. He needed something to do with his time that wasn't lying around feeling sorry for himself.

Veronica the cat wound around his ankles as he trimmed his beard, and dressed in fresh clothing. Occasionally he reached down and gave her a little scratch on the head, which she permitted with only minimal objection.

"Any idea what I'm supposed to do now?" he asked the cat.

Veronica meowed in annoyance.

"Yeah, I thought so. But I am crap at apologizing."

The cat's yellow-green eyes blinked at him.

Feeling oddly chastised, Jordaan sighed. "Fine."

Veronica followed him out of the room. He wasn't sure where to find Diana at this hour. He knew vaguely where her rooms were located, but it was unlikely that she was there. As it was near lunch, he decided to try the dining room.

The hotel had considerably more guests after the accident at Tull Castle, although it wasn't crowded by any means, which meant the chorus of giggles carrying through the hallway was incongruous. There hadn't been enough people in residence for those kinds of sounds. Further, one of those insistent giggles was Diana.

"Well, that makes things easy," he said to Veronica, who blinked at him again. He scooped her up and let her drape over his shoulder. The cat settled, warm against his neck.

The giggles were emanating from the small library on the first floor. He wasn't sure what he would have expected to find, but it wasn't Prince Xavier trying to wrestle away a bottle of what appeared to be whiskey from Lady Mallory.

"You are no fun!" she accused him, cradling the bottle to her chest.

"Where did you even get that?" Xavier asked. He'd been at this for a while.

His top hat was on the floor and had clearly been stepped on. Jordaan scooped it up and punched out the crumpled portion, placing it on a table. "Am I interrupting?" he asked.

Xavier sighed in relief. "Please tell me you're my reinforcement?"

"I'm afraid I haven't been battle briefed, but I'm good in a tight spot."

"Tight spot!" Lady Mallory howled.

Xavier was at a complete loss. He gestured to the two women, who were curled together on a small sofa. Diana had turned her face into Lady Mallory's arm and was laughing so hard she was barely making noise. "I went to get them coffee and they found more whiskey!"

"Don't be mad," Diana said. "We're upset!" And then she dissolved into hiccupy laughter again.

"You sound devastated, truly," Jordaan drawled.

She pouted her lip at him. "Everyone grieves in their own way," she said. Mallory handed over the bottle, and Diana drank.

Even sloshed she was a goddess. "And what are we grieving?"

"Oh like you don't know, you big dummy," Mallory said. "Oooh, kitty cat!"

She bound up from the sofa and scooped Veronica off his shoulder. "Pretty girl," she cooed at the cat.

"Am I the only sane one here?" Diana asked. "You're not a cat person, are you?" she asked Xavier.

"Never cared for them," the Prince answered, a hand over his eyes in exasperation.

"Your loss," Jordaan said, taking the cat back from Lady Mallory as gently as he could. He put Veronica on the floor. She rubbed against his leg in brief thanks, then bolted from the library. He could only hope she was going straight to Caris Mourne for an elixir.

"Now that we've terrified the cat, what is happening here?" he asked Xavier.

"Day drinking," Diana said.

"I think you're doing it wrong," Jordaan said.

Both women broke down in giggles again, as if this were the funniest thing ever said.

"I don't know what to do," the prince admitted. "I thought maybe Lady Passwood might help, but I don't want to leave them alone."

"Don't get the Duchess," Jordaan said. "That won't end well for either of them."

The whiskey bottle had been discarded on the floor. Jordaan scooped it up and handed it to Xavier. "Get rid of this, would you?"

"Then what?"

Jordaan shrugged. "Go about your day?"

"Seriously, you're going to handle this on your own?"

"I'm good with drunks," Jordaan assured him.

"I'll remember that next time Prince Travers gets snookered," he said. He bowed to the women, who only giggled all the more.

"Don't be so uptight," Mallory called after him. "I don't want to have to hit you with another lemon."

The prince's cheeks briefly flared with color, but he managed to leave the room with much more grace than Jordaan would have.

Jordaan picked up the coffee pot and poured two generous cups. "So you're lobbing fruit at royalty now?" he asked Mallory.

"Not intentionally," she said.

"This time," Diana added, and both women cracked up.

They were pretty far gone. One pot of coffee was not going to do it. He added cream and sugar before handing over a cup to each lady.

"I love coffee," Diana cooed, cradling her cup with both hands. She'd lost one glove somewhere and looked up at him with syrupy eyes and a lazy smile. She was in for a hell of a headache if she didn't sober up quickly.

Mallory too, but he wasn't as worried about her. He wasn't entirely sure, but he suspected her drunkenness was at least partially an act. Diana, however, didn't seem to be able to hold her liquor.

He rang for a maid and asked for a tray to include another pot of coffee, a large carafe of water, and some bread and butter. Something greasy might have been better, but he wasn't going to waste time figuring out what he could get.

By the time the second pot of coffee arrived, Mallory had lost the giggles, and Diana was half-asleep, although still laughing as if even the air around her were funny. When he was reasonably sure that both women had eaten, and had enough water to drown a small horse, he knew he needed to get them back to their rooms.

He summoned a pair of footmen to take Lady Mallory up to her room. The hotel had no lift for her chair, and if she weren't steady on her feet she'd need to be carried.

"Keep quiet about what you're seeing," he cautioned both men, adding a few coins to each of their palms. "The ladies depend on your discretion."

Mallory scoffed but allowed the footmen to escort her.

When they were gone, Jordaan found Diana slumped over on the sofa. "You're a cat person," she said.

"We've established that," he said, helping her to sit up.

"I don't like pets."

"Cats aren't pets, they're our overlords."

Diana laughed and rested her face against his shoulder. "You're ridiculous," she said, yawning.

"I am ridiculous," he agreed. "Let's get you to your room."

"What's there to do there? Be miserable that I've destroyed all of my mother's plans for me? Yea."

"Oh, stop being so maudlin, Desdemona. You're better than that."

He caught Diana as she stumbled, and laughed again. "I think I need a nap."

"Capital idea. Come on."

He opened the door and checked to make sure the coast was clear. Seeing no one, he reached for her ungloved hand.

"Do you think there's something wrong with me?" she asked.

"You're perfect, Dulcie. Bloody perfect," he said, quick-walking her through the sunlit corridor.

She shook her head, "No. Perfect people get the prince. And he's not an ass."

"Well, lucky you, you've dodged that particular cannonball."

She chuckled, but the sound wasn't the same merry laugh she'd been using. "I'm a mess."

She wanted to wallow, and who was he to deny her? He'd done plenty of wallowing himself. They took the stairs two at a time. They were back at the door to her room before anyone spotted them.

"In you go," he said.

Diana fumbled in the pocket of her dress for her key. She gave an excited grin when she managed to pull it out, but then couldn't get it in the lock. He took it from her and unlocked the door.

"Sleep it off," he told her.

Diana lingered in the doorway, leaning against the woodwork. Her eyes hadn't lost their glossiness. She was definitely drunk. He needed to remind himself when she gave a breathy exhale and asked, "Why don't you love me?"

Jordaan froze, just for a moment. Sober that she would never have said anything like that. "I gave all my love to the cat," he said, trying for the breezy tone she expected.

Diana shook her head, and more of the pins holding her braids in place came loose. "No. I just wanted to help you. I wanted to make sure you didn't get in trouble and you were so mean."

"It wasn't personal."

"It's always personal. You should have let me help you. In fact, you should love me. I'm great."

"I thought you said you were a mess?"

"Both things can be true," she said, in a tone that said she was far more in control of her faculties than the drunkenness would lead him to believe.

"Drink some more water," he said.

"You should kiss me," she said.

He wasn't made of stone. He was tempted. It would be nothing to step into her room, shut the door behind him, and take her into his arms. But a gentleman didn't kiss a woman in her state. It would be taking advantage when her defenses were down. He needed to get away from her for his own peace of mind. "Goodnight, Dana."

He was a dozen steps down the hall when she called after him. "I didn't think you were a coward, Jermain!"

Chapter Thirty-Two

Xavier

Someone had been in his room.

Or perhaps they were still in his room?

It wasn't any of the hotel staff, because the bed was unmade, and the bin was full of discarded papers. There were no obvious signs. The sparse furniture wasn't out of place and nothing seemed to be missing. Nonetheless, Xavier felt the intrusion as surely as if he'd walked in to find someone sitting in the room's lone chair.

He'd followed the Fairies for as long as he dared, trying to learn what he could. Sadly, that wasn't much. They wandered in and out of various businesses, stopped the occasional sailor or charwoman, and demanded to see the Prince. And plenty of them had told them exactly where to find Travers, more or less.

But the Fairies didn't seem to hear. And the heavy smell of cinnamon followed.

Which was a blessing, considering he'd spent most of the time following them down by the wharf. It was mysterious, but ultimately fruitless to keep following them, so Xav had reversed course and come back to the hotel.

Only to be hit square in the chest with an old lemon. He'd gone back to his room to change out his lemon-splattered shirt for a fresh one. But, as soon as he unlocked the door, he had the eerie feeling he was being watched. He'd turned to see if there was someone in the hall, but the corridor was empty.

The feeling only intensified when he'd shut the door behind him. It wasn't just that someone had been in his room, someone was in his room.

His room wasn't large. His funds had been running a bit low, and he hadn't wanted to rack up charges on one of the bigger suites like the rest of the royals in residence. There wasn't a place to hide, but just to be sure, Xavier checked the wardrobe and behind the curtains. Empty, but he couldn't shake the idea that someone was there. The scent of wet wool, and a subtle warmth as if a person had stood right behind him.

"Hello?" he said, surprised at the quaver in his voice.

There was no obvious answer, but all of Xav's senses lit up like a room full of Zephyr lamps.

"If someone is here, you may be in the wrong place." He felt foolish but what did one say to an empty room that felt occupied?

Why anyone would want to be in his room, he couldn't fathom. He didn't travel with anything of value. His clothing had once been expensive, but after the last few months of frequenting every seedy tavern in the Known Kingdoms, almost none of it would be worth stealing. If he'd brought along a valet it might have not been so bad, but neither he nor Travers had wanted servants watching their every move.

"The magic fades," said the barest whisper of a voice.

Xavier felt every hair on his head raised. He turned toward the voice, which had come from his bed.

And there, lying among the blankets was a creature about the size of a toddler. It was like someone's idea of a Fairie without ever having seen one — pointed ears, although they stood up from the creature's forehead instead of the sides of his head, and large black orb rather than eyes. It had pinkish skin, sparse hair, and wide, thick lips.

The large black eyes of the creature blinked, but his eyelids did not close so much as the yellow irises momentarily disappeared. Xavier shivered but held himself together. An unknown being might be more powerful than its small stature would suggest. To be sure, he bowed to it, as low as he might to another prince.

"Good afternoon," he said, doing his best to keep his voice steady.

The creature blinked again in that disconcerting way, the upright triangles of his ears wrinkling in time with the motion inside the plum-sized black orbs. "You bow to Shuttle?" it said in a creaky, metallic scratch of a voice.

"I do," Xavier said. "One should always bow to a guest."

The creature sighed. "The magic fades." He leaned back into the pillows on Xav's bed, making his toddler-sized body comfortable.

"I am Prince Xavier Moorelow. Can I be of assistance to you?"

Shuttle's pink-flesh ears wrinkled again, exhaling with a heavy gust. "A prince offers Shuttle assistance?"

"I do," Xavier said. He clasped his hands behind his back to hide the shaking in them. A magical creature appearing in his hotel room wasn't an ordinary afternoon. Although nothing about his time in Tull had been ordinary he wasn't sure what had him so spooked. By now, he should be used to the strange and usual.

"A Weaver is never offered the help of a prince," said Shuttle. He turned his large face into Xavier's pillow and breathed in deeply.

Xavier kept his revulsion to himself. He would have the hotel burn the bedding.

Assuming he lived through this encounter.

"You seem very tired," Xavier said, trying to keep his focus on the present.

"The magic fades."

"Is there something I can do to help with that?"

This time, Shuttle's sigh echoed through the small confines of the room. "I seek the Straw Knight."

Riddles? Lovely. So helpful. Xavier cleared his throat to keep himself from saying something untold, and to dispel the feeling he might vomit from the back of his jaw. Whatever magic had brought this creature here, it came with a powerful dose of magic.

One that was making it hard for him to keep calm. "Who is the Straw Knight?" he asked.

Xavier didn't know what kind of answer he expected. More cryptic nonsense, perhaps. Not a dozen colors of magic sparks to surround the Weaver, or the high-pitched hum of bees to shake and tip the Zephyr lamp, nor for the wardrobe to teeter dangerously close to falling.

Nor for the form of Sir Jordaan to be lying on his bed in the spot where the small creature had just been. "You will find the Straw Knight," said this version of Sir Jordaan. "And bring them to Shuttle?" The metallic voice of the shapeshifter crept upward as if it were still a question.

"Of... of course," Xavier said, every muscle in his body telling him to flee, and every bit of his training as a royal telling him to stay as still as possible. A magical creature wasn't someone to piss off, especially one who could assume the form of another.

The faux-Sir Jordaan exhaled, and the little Weaver, with its dog-like ears and large black eyes, was back in place.

"Please, rest," Xavier said. "I'll go... I'll get your knight for you."

"You do the Weavers a great favor," Shuttle said. Xavier watched as the little being burrowed deeper into the bed covers, and let out a sigh of something like contentment.

Xavier bowed again and did his best to leave as if he weren't in a hurry. He closed the door lightly so as to not disturb the creature, and gave himself only a moment to panic.

What in the Fairie Hells was happening? None of this was normal. Fairies wandering out in the open, Travers all but giving up his throne, and now unknown creatures making themselves comfortable in his bed? He took a couple of deep breaths, trying to work through the feeling of disbelief that made his limbs feel like lead.

He needed to find Sir Jordaan.

And possibly a very stiff drink.

Xav wasn't sure what direction to go — he had no idea where in the hotel Sir Jordaan was staying, but he was saved from indecision by a very clear, drunk shout.

"I didn't think you were a coward, Jermain!"

Diana followed up her statement with a resounding door slam. Well, that answered where to find Jordaan. Diana's suite was on the same floor but on the opposite side of the hotel from his own.

Xavier couldn't hear the reply, but he knew it had to be Sir Jordaan. He'd been successful at getting the ladies out of the library. Xav sprinted toward them, incepting Jordaan as he stalked off, muttering something about "trying to do the right bloody thing."

"Oh what now?" Jordaan said, seeing Xavier skitter to a halt in front of him.

"Trouble," Xavier gasped. "There's a thing, it's very, very weird."

He bent double holding his hands on his knees as he tried to get his breath back. He hadn't run far, but the exertion of magic, stress, and trying to keep from screaming at the top of his lungs had robbed him of basic functions.

"How weird?" Jordaan asked. "And please tell me it is not another beautiful drunk woman, because two is my limit for one day."

"No. No. It's...."

Seeing him struggle, Jordaan put a hand under his arm to keep him upright. "Deep breath, Highness. In and out, come on."

Xav tried to follow the instruction, but he couldn't. He grabbed Jordaan's hand and pulled him down the hall.

"Buy a man dinner first," Jordaan said, eyebrows raised.

"Blonds have never been my taste," Xav snapped. "Just come on."

"I'm a little offended," Jordaan said in a bemused way.

Xav stopped outside his door. "There's something. Just be very quiet for a moment."

Jordaan brought a finger to his lips to indicate his silence, and Xav slowly opened the door. He pointed toward the bed where the Weaver, Shuttle, slumbered.

Jordaan's eyes went nearly the size of the shapeshifters.

Xav closed the door as quietly as he'd opened it. "It is looking for you."

"What in the Fairies is that thing?" Jordaan said in a harsh whisper.

"Shuttle. He's a Weaver."

Jordaan went a shade of white that didn't seem possible on a living man. "Oh, no, no, no, it's not."

"You know what that means?"

Jordaan gritted his teeth, his eyes closing as if in disgust. "Sort of. Not exactly. *Fairies be*, she can't have been right." Jordaan let out a series of whispered, but vehement curses, finally saying. "The shapeshifter who came to me at Tull Castle may have been one of those as well"

"So?"

"There are beings... Maundry, that have something to do with the Light Court of the Fairies. Diana thought they might..."

Xav wasn't sure he was following, but that creature was definitely in his bed, so he couldn't deny it was happening. "So go talk to it. Obviously, something is up."

Jordaan dropped his head into his hands, swore again, and then blew out a breath. "Open the door," he said.

Xavier stood back as Jordaan approached the little Weaver, who shifted, his large eyes blinking rapidly.

"Bow," Xav mouthed to Jordaan, who gave a short, curt bow as if he'd been slapped too hard on the back.

"Sir Jordaan Van Dine of Margate."

"The magic fades," rasped Shuttle.

Jordaan's thick eyebrow arched. He looked to Xav for answers.

"He's fond of saying that," Xav said. "I don't know what it means."

"You hold the thread," Shuttle said, before letting out a great snore, dead asleep.

The room was far too small for two grown men and an unknown magical creature. With no room to make decisions on what in the Fairie Hells to do next.

"We need to take him to the witch," Jordaan said.

Xav wasn't fond of the idea of picking up an unconscious magical creature, but he couldn't very well leave it in his room. He hesitated. "If I sprout a tail because of you, I will have you thrown in my father's dungeon."

Jordaan shrugged. "Not sure I wouldn't deserve it."

Xav made hasty work of arranging the linens around the sleeping Shuttle, swaddling him like a baby, just as he'd done with his little brothers and sisters when they were tiny.

Jordaan looked on, fascinated at the speedy tucks and folds. "Practicing to be a midwife?"

"I have 9 siblings, I know how to do things," he said. He scooped up the Weaver, using a corner of the blanket to cover his head. "You've been to the hotel's witch before?"

Jordaan let out a mirthless laugh. "A few times. Follow me," Jordaan said, holding open the door and starting toward the central staircase in long strides. Xav ran to catch up with the knight's longer stride.

Jordaan took the stairs too at a time and Xav had to scramble to keep up. The Maundry was heavier than he'd have expected, rather like his little sister Violet when she threw a fit and turned her body into a two-and-a-half-foot brick.

When they reached the third floor, Jordaan darted toward the far end. Xav did his best to keep up, holding Shuttle steady.

Xav wasn't sure what he expected, but seeing the distinct oak door with the iron bracketing that graced the Dunlock Witch's Tower wasn't it. Because it was indeed the same door. He'd spent his life climbing the steps to fetch cold remedies for his siblings, or to get patched up for something or other. He was fairly sure the gentle indents in the wood were the direct result of his knocks.

Jordaan wasn't fazed by that. He pulled on his gloves and knocked smartly three times.

Xav shouldn't have been surprised when Caris Mourne answered. After all, when he'd left Dunlock she'd been the witch in residence. He wasn't sure how his father had convinced her to serve his territory, but she'd been in residence since the start of the Festival of the Flower.

So who would be behind the door to the Dunlock Witch's Tower but the Dunlock Witch? It was almost comical if he weren't holding a child-sized magical... something.

Xavier couldn't bow, but he inclined his head. "My Lady, we have..."

Caris Mourne acknowledged him with a slight head tilt. She eyed the bundle he held. "And what have you brought me, Your Highness?" she asked with a kind, spritely curiosity.

Xav pulled back the bit of blanket covering Shuttle's face, and the witch's expression changed to one of considerable concern. He'd seen her up close only once, the day she'd come to the orphanage to help with the children. At the time, she'd seemed youthful, if somewhat allergic to the sun, given her exceptionally pale skin. He had only a moment to notice that she looked wane and sickly now. He'd heard she was very old, but it was always hard to tell with a witch. There were things they could do to hide their true appearance.

"You'd better bring him in," the witch said, ushering them into the tower room.

She pulled out a silver pocket watch, turning the top dial. The room seemed to hum for a moment, and then a large cot let itself into the tower room from the door they'd just entered. It walked on two legs, like a person, only to lay down dutifully in front of the room's massive fireplace. White sheets and blankets sprung from cupboards, making themselves up into a neat little nest. Xav laid Shuttle on the cot and stepped back.

"I must say, this is a most interesting development," Caris Mourne said. "I haven't seen a Maundry in decades."

"What does that mean?" Xav asked.

"Maundry are lesser fae. Most of them died out centuries ago, but some, like this one, still hang out."

"His name is Shuttle," Jordaan said. "And he has a sibling called Needle."

The witch turned her clear gray eyes to the knight. "And you know this because you've encountered one before?"

Jordaan cleared his throat. "Yes, technically."

"And you didn't think this was worth telling me?"

"I ... well, it was..."

The feeling of second-hand embarrassment was so strong, that Xav would have liked to be anywhere else at the moment.

"As we navigate your condition, Sir Jordaan, meetings with magical creatures are definitely something I need to know."

Jordaan muttered something that might have been contrition.

Caris Mourne knelt beside the cot, checking over the Weaver.

"It came to my room, looking for Sir Jordaan," Xav said.

"Yes, Maundry were once notorious for their awful sense of direction." The witch magicked a magnifying glass, checking Shuttle's eyes as if looking for clues. "I suppose that two of them managed to get this close to you is something worth noting."

"Lady Diana suggested," Jordaan began. "She thought they might be coming to me to prevent me from making a bad bargain."

Caris Mourne stood and a crooked smile split her face. "Oh, I knew I liked her. She'd have made an excellent witch."

Jordaan looked like he wanted to say something else, but the Weaver groaned and turned, waking up.

"Good afternoon," Caris Mourne said. "I suspect you know who I am?"

Shuttle nodded. "The magic fades."

"I know. I have been most concerned for some time."

Xav shot Jordaan a look, but the knight could only shrug. They watched as the witch helped the Maundry to sit up.

"The Straw Knight has the thread."

"A literal thread?"

Shuttle shook his large head no.

"But you need the thread back all the same?"

A nod and another disconcerting blink were her answers.

"Very well. Rest. You are safe and welcome here."

Shuttle needed no second assurance. He slumped down and was asleep once more.

Caris Mourne settled him back into the blankets and stood up. She took out her watch once more and turned the dial an additional half-turn. "Gentleman, I require your assistance."

"Anything," Xav answered. He knew better than to refuse a magical person, especially given the oddity of the situation he found himself in.

"Gather all of the jars and beakers you can find," she said. Around the room, various items levitated off shelves and grouped themselves on a large worktop by the open windows. He and Jordaan darted around the room getting any empty vessels they could and bringing them toward the collection of ingredients.

Xav couldn't help but notice that Caris Mourne herself didn't move. She seemed to have been sapped of strength, clutching onto the arm of a chair as they, and all those unseen hands, populated the worktop.

As the flurry of activity died, there was a definitive knock on the tower door.

"Your Highness, I expect you'll want to answer that," Caris Mourne said. She beckoned Sir Jordaan to her side to help her across the room.

Xav was too tired and too confused to question it. He opened the oak door, his mouth going dry as he faced, for the first time in months, his father.

Prince Brandon hadn't changed. Not that Xavier would have expected him to in a dozen weeks. Xav couldn't explain it to himself. Somewhere in the back of his mind, there had been the idea that his father was old, that he would never understand what Xav had felt. And that picture of his father had somehow aged the man. But there was no gray in his father's hair. Barely even a laugh line pulled at his eyes.

Prince Brandon was the same vibrant, relatively young man he'd always been. Xav swallowed, afraid he'd break down if he said anything. His father locked eyes with him, and for a pregnant moment, time seemed to be still. Anything Xav might have said died on his tongue.

From her position across the room, Caris Mourne broke the awkward silence. "Your Highness, I am afraid I will need to reschedule our meeting. As you can see, something of a pressing nature has come up."

His father looked past Xav to the sleeping Maundry. If his eyes understood what he was seeing, the confusion wasn't written on his face. One day Xav would have to ask him how he managed to mask it so well.

Prince Brandon shook himself as if he too were in a kind of trance. "Of course, My Lady. May I be of assistance in any way?"

"I shall send a note down if anything comes to me. Why don't you speak to your son for a moment? I can spare him that long."

Xav felt a heaviness in his limbs but managed to follow his father into the hallway. However unbelievably, he was no longer in the Rutledge Hotel on the island of Tull. He stood with his father on the rickety landing outside the Witch's Tower's door. How Caris Mourne had accomplished such a thing he couldn't say, and it left him uneasy.

"I'm glad to know you're well," his father said, breaking up some of the tension.

Xav didn't know what to say. He had written to his parents after he left Dunlock some months ago, but he never told them he was leaving in the first place. He'd snuck out with Travers the day most of the royals had departed the Festival of the Flower.

"Your mother and I…" Prince Brandon began.

"I'm so sorry, Father…I know you must be so disappointed in me."

"Oh, no that isn't…" His father stepped forward and enveloped him with a crushing hug. "We have missed you."

Xav wasn't sure when the last time his father had held him so long. It was simultaneously the most comforted he'd ever been, and the cause of a new form of tension spooling in his gut. He'd been a terrible son, and his parents deserved better than a man who ran away from home rather than dealing with his problems.

"I miss you too," Xavier said when his father released him.

"I won't keep you if Caris Mourne needs you, but when you are ready, we need to speak."

Xav nodded. "I was trying to arrange my passage home just this morning."

"I'll tell your mother. She'll be overjoyed to know you aren't staying away much longer. You know she doesn't like to let any of you children go."

He felt like a fool. His mother had been with child when he ran away. "Is she okay? The baby?"

"Babies," Prince Brandon beamed. "A final set of twins will round out our family."

Two new siblings? Xavier was temporarily dumbstruck.

His father used the pause to embrace him again. "Go. As much as I want you home, I know I can't keep you. But please, please come home soon."

"I will. I promise."

Prince Brandon added an extra squeeze to the hug and started down the stairs.

Stunned, Xav waited until his father was far enough down the spiral staircase that he could no longer see him. He took a steadying breath and re-entered the witch's tower.

Fresh chaos had erupted in the fleeting minutes he'd been on the other side of the door. The little Weaver was standing on the cot, brandishing a pair of heretofore unseen black claws. Caris Mourne held him back with a stream of blue light that seemed to burst from her palms. It was Sir Jordaan, however, who seemed to be in the biggest pickle. The knight was suspended in midair, encased in a thick orange smoke.

"Ah, Your Highness, an assist please."

Xav was saved from any further contemplation of his own mistakes by a beaker flying into his hands.

"Get as much of the smoke in that as you can," she commanded. "We may just solve this mystery yet."

Chapter Thirty-Three

Jordaan

The little shit had turned on him.

Jordaan looked down at the Maundry through the layer of orange smoke. It had taken on the appearance of something nasty, with dirty, jagged teeth. He tried to speak, to let the thing know that he wasn't intentionally withholding any thread, but his voice failed him. He gestured wildly, trying to get Shuttle to notice. If he could talk, he could get himself out of this insane situation. He'd always been good with words. Sadly, the Weaver was not interested. He was going to get whatever he thought Jordaan was keeping back by force.

Which left Jordaan hanging in the air like a tunic left on a wash line.

Caris Mourne seemed to be holding Shuttle back from doing any more damage to him, but she was failing. She'd looked frail since they'd decamped to Tull, but now she was so thin she might as well be transparent. She also had the prince running around like a lunatic, scooping up orange smoke in jars.

It was only when Xavier filled the third jar that she gestured to one of the large windows. "Throw them all open," she said.

Xavier ran over and threw back the shutters. A strong gust of wind blew through them, breaking up the smoke and dropping him unceremoniously to the ground. Every bone in his body rattled out of place.

He was too young to feel so damn old.

Jordaan picked himself up, groaning.

Caris Mourne had stopped shooting lightning from her hands and used some kind of spell to wrap Shuttle in the curtain panels like a swaddled infant. The minuscule beast bared his pointy teeth but was held fast.

"Are you all right, Sir Jordaan?" the witch asked pertly.

"Oh, fantastic. I always recommend levitation and a fall for one's health."

She gave him a bemused look. Considering how little sense of humor the witch seemed to have with him, he considered that a win.

"I am glad you are unharmed," she said. She turned to the Maundry, her mouth downturned. "Now, Mr. Shuttle, perhaps we can discuss this like adults?"

Shuttle growled.

"Unhelpful," said the witch.

"The magic fades. Time wastes," said Shuttle.

"And everyone in this room is willing to help you. So please cease being unpleasant."

"I don't have any thread," Jordaan said. "I don't know what to tell him."

"You don't have any thread that you know of," Caris Mourne said. "But clearly, you have something."

Xavier raised an eyebrow. "How could he have something he doesn't know he has?"

The witch looked up and blinked at the prince as if she just realized he was in the room. "Lots of people have gifts they don't realize."

"But in this case," Xavier ventured. "It wouldn't be a gift, would it?"

The witch shrugged and turned back to the Maundry. "How did the young man come to have this thread, Mr. Shuttle?"

This earned her another low, rumbling growl. She rolled her eyes. "Really, you are thousands of years old, and a subject of the Light Court of the Fairies. One would think you'd have better manners by now."

Shuttle wriggled and thrashed, but was unable to loosen his bonds. "The Weavers are free! We do not serve!"

"Indelible magic, Sir. You will not be free until I let you go. Get hold of yourself and explain."

Jordaan almost felt sorry for the creature. He knew all too well the witch's censure, which cut like a sharp knife.

"My brothers and I will no longer serve the Light Court."

Caris Mourne bit her lip. Jordaan could practically see the wheels turning in her mind. Her eyes darted about the room as if she needed to locate something. "And yet, your Fairie bargain is not fulfilled."

"The Light deceive."

"Fairie bargains are tricky," she said. "Getting out of them is even trickier. Are we to assume that what you seek has to do with getting out of your deal?"

Shuttle growled, but when the witch turned her pointed gaze on him, he stopped abruptly.

"Much better," she said. "Prince Xavier, if you would be so kind as to retrieve my spectacles from my workbench?"

Xavier picked up a pair of thick-lensed glasses from the table near the open window and brought them over. Whatever they were, they weren't ordinary eyewear. As Caris Mourne donned them, the lenses flashed with a rainbow of color. The thickness of the glass magnified the witch's gray eyes, making them nearly as large as the Maundry's black orbs.

"Sir Jordaan, would you do me a favor and come stand next to our friend here?" She phrased it as a question, but Jordaan had spent enough time around her to know it was not. Reluctantly he moved close to the little traitor.

"Oh, I see, I see," she said.

Which was absurd. Her glasses were enormous. She could probably see the Fairie Halls of Zinnj with those things.

"Ma'am?" Xavier asked. "Is there something you need me to do?"

"I'm afraid so," she said absently, still peering through her odd glasses. "Would you be so good as to come stand on the other side of Mr. Shuttle?"

Xavier shot him a look. Jordaan almost felt bad for the prince, who seemed to have been swept into this drama against his will. Which was very unfair. However, Jordaan was spared additional sympathy when he remembered that Xavier was the heir to crown prince of one of the wealthiest, most prominent territories in the Known Kingdoms. Surely a prince like that could use a few pebbles in his metaphorical shoes.

When Xavier had moved to where the witch directed him, she said with a sigh. "I'm afraid, gentleman, this may sting."

Jordaan didn't have time to be properly afraid. The witch took out her watch, turned the top dial, and snapped her fingers with a deafening click. He felt the snap throughout his body, all of his bones rattled, worse than when he'd fallen to the stone floor.

Xavier wasn't immune either by the yelp he let out, but like his fleeting sympathy, Jordaan didn't have the wherewithal to notice any more of the prince's pain. His own was too great. It felt as if a blazing hot wire were being dragged through his body, slicing him into ribbons.

He clutched at his chest, as if his hands might close around whatever was causing the intense pain.

"The three of you, just hold on another moment. I promise it will end soon."

But her words were meaningless. There was only the agony. Jordaan felt hot and clammy all at once. Heavy sweat broke out all over his body. His stomach tried to leave his body by means of his mouth, and his heartbeat viciously against his breastbone.

The witch snapped again, and the sound sent Jordaan to his knees.

Jordaan pulled himself to his feet. Xavier was lying on the floor, clutching his knees to his chest. And Shuttle was unconscious by the look of him, on his back in a tangle of loose fabric.

Caris Mourne had not escaped whatever torture she'd inflicted on them. Although it seemed impossible that the woman could be any more fragile, she was now completely colorless, despite the reams of shiny purple candy floss hair. "I am sorry," she said, her breath short.

"What did you do?" he asked, though he knew as the words left his mouth that it was a useless question. She had done what she needed to do. He felt as if something had been taken from him, something important. Its absence felt like a space inside of him, small and hollow.

"Both of you go to your rooms and rest. There is no more that can be done today."

Jordaan offered a hand to Xavier, getting the prince to his feet.

"I could sleep for a week," Xavier said, dusting off his coat and trousers.

Oddly, for the first time since the Festival of the Flower, Jordaan didn't feel that way. He was tired, his body exhausted, but the need to sleep was different. It wasn't the cloying, drugged feeling that had robbed him of consciousness at all hours of the day.

"My Lady, do you need help?"

She shook her head. "My spouse will be here with the sunset. They shall care for me."

"What about him?" Jordaan asked of the Maundry.

"I suspect one of Shuttle's brothers will come to collect him now that they have what they want in sight."

Jordaan was unclear exactly what had been given. Perhaps it was whatever inhabited the now-empty space in him. If so, that was likely for the best.

Chapter Thirty-Four

Diana

Alice was pale, her hands clutched with enough tension to break a diamond. She hovered at the edge of Diana's bed, eyes darting back and forth. She'd been shaking when she brought in the breakfast tray, hesitating as if she needed — desperately — to speak before she burst like an overstuffed goose.

Diana wanted to ignore the girl. Her headache was fierce, and she was groggy enough that she wasn't entirely sure she was still alive. But Alice was agitated, it was her duty to ask.

"What bothers you, Alice?"

"Oh, My Lady, it's... it is so awful."

Alice was young and prone to dramatics, but her tone made Diana sit up straighter and put down her coffee cup. "Has something happened?"

Alice nodded, hands flexing as if she were fighting the urge to throw them in the air. "I don't know how to tell you," she said. "It's just that... well... I..."

"Is anyone hurt? Is it Jonah?"

"No, no, the healer has cleared him to return to work, but...it's not that..."

Diana tried to steady herself so she didn't lose her patience. She paused and tried again. "Are you well?"

Alice gave an affirmative nod. "It's Bill and Maryann."

"Have their illnesses gotten worse?"

Alice shook her head. "No… they're gone, My Lady."

Diana felt a spurt of horror. Had she been so wrapped up in her drama that two of her servants had died right under her nose? "Gone how?"

Alice withdrew a folded note from her pocket and held it out with a shaking hand. It wasn't a proper letter. No greeting to Alice, or remarks about the weather. And it was only a few lines long, although they had been read multiple times by the creases in the paper and the slightly smudged ink.

The text, written in what she knew as Maryann's tight, neat handwriting, wasn't long.

I fear it is no longer possible to hide my condition. Bill and I would be married at home, but it may be that we have the ceremony done long before we arrive back in Wills. I would not want to disappoint the Lady, but what choice might we have?

And that was it. No salutations, no begging for forgiveness, as if she'd run out of time or words before properly finishing.

Diana sat back into her pillows, relieved that no one was harmed. An elopement wasn't fatal, just foolish. But if she were reading it right, Maryann was going to have a child. Diana could only hope they did make it back to Wills so that Maryann would get her wedding by the crane flowers before the flowers dropped their petals at the end of summer.

"I don't know what to do," Alice confessed. "She was gone from our room by the time I woke up this morning. And… and…"

"There's nothing to do, Alice," Diana said as gently as she could. "We'll be returning home as soon as I can arrange passage back. Our time in Tull is over."

"But, you were to marry the prince?" Alice said with fresh horror.

"Well, that was always in doubt," she answered. "It is best if we go back to Wills before any decisions are made."

Alice's mouth hung open as if she were unsure of what to say next. Diana asked her to pull her blue day gown and instructed her to take the breakfast tray back to the kitchens. She hadn't much of an appetite for pastry.

"I don't know why she didn't leave you a note, My Lady. You were always so close," Alice said.

Maryann had done what she had to do. Diana almost couldn't blame her. Everything since their arrival had been a disaster. She supposed Maryann had simply taken control of her destiny.

Something Diana would have to do as well.

"Sometimes it is hard to write to a person so close," Diana said, thinking of her reluctance to write to her mother as things had begun to go wrong on her visit.

Diana groaned and got out of bed. Before Alice took the breakfast tray back, Diana asked her to arrange for bathwater brought to the suite. She always thought better after a warm soak, and there was much to think about it.

She would go home as soon as possible. There was no reason now to stay in Tull. There was no welcome here, and clearly, an engagement to Prince Travers wasn't in her future.

It was also extremely unwise to stay around Sir Jordaan. Not when she was halfway in love with him, and he had the better sense to keep his distance.

Diana was restless by the time the hotel's footman had brought up the water. She scrubbed until she was raw, but was too wound up to sit still and let the bath cool around her. Although washing made her feel a bit more human, she couldn't enjoy it. She had Alice help her dress and then declared her intention to visit the gardens.

Although, this time she did not tuck the silver flask into her pocket. The blue day gown's pockets barely had room for her coin purse, saving her from herself. She took a pencil and some paper down to the garden with her, determined to draft her long-overdue letter to the Countess.

"Can I bring you anything?" Alice asked.

"If Jonah is back to work, can you send him to me? I'd like him to run some errands in town."

Alice curtsied and hurried to inform the footman.

Diana took herself down to the hotel's back garden, choosing a small bistro table set among the flower beds with a view of the cliffs.

From this spot, it was easy to see the beauty of Tull, the one that her guidebook had raved about. Tull was beautiful in the summer. All brilliant blue skies, dramatic vistas, and light, tickling breezes. She could hear the sea in the distance even if the vantage point from the gardens didn't show her the waves breaking over the beaches.

If it weren't for the strong smell of dead fish, she would almost miss it when she returned home. Wills was lovely in the summer, green and temperate and lush. But it was never warm. There was no sea bathing in the rough Northern waters. The views were to be admired, just not touched.

Diana heard footsteps on the gravel path, assuming Jonah had found her. She glanced up, the approaching figure darkened by the sun at his back. "Hello, Jonah," she said. "I have a list of…"

Prince Traver's distinct voice cut her off. "I'm no servant," he said, sitting himself down uninvited at her table.

"My apologies," she said.

He shrugged. "I might be a footman. Since I am no longer a prince."

"You are still a prince. No one has taken Tull from you yet."

Another disinterested shrug. He stretched his legs out, leaning back in the wrought-iron garden chair as if he were reclining on a stuffed divan. "Maybe I've decided to give it up. Take my chances in the world."

"I suppose you could. Although frankly, that seems exceedingly stupid."

Travers's mouth quirked into an unhappy smile. "Do you know why I picked you, Lady Diana?"

"At this point, I cannot imagine," she said truthfully.

"From the day we met, you weren't afraid to speak the truth to me. Miserable wretch that I am, I thought that was what I needed."

Diana let that comment pass. There was nothing kind she could say in response. Despite Travers's belief in her blunt honesty, there were things that one did not say to a man in a public setting.

"I want to apologize," he said. "I should have been in Tull to greet you when you arrived. Honestly, I have no good excuse for myself."

Diana was glad for the words, as much as she resented that they had to be said at all. "We have also not had any time to talk since I arrived. You've done an excellent job of avoiding me."

He yawned, wrapping his arms across his chest. "I am sorry about that too. Will you forgive me?"

Diana's first instinct was to tell him no. He didn't deserve it. He'd done nothing so far to make up for her ill-treatment. But she was going home anyway. There was no reason to carry a grudge, and potentially make Wills an enemy of one of the most powerful territories in the Known Kingdoms. Whatever uncertainty it faced. "I do," she said. "I've decided to return home. Clearly, you are in no position to contract an engagement."

"No," he agreed. "Although if my aunt has anything to do with it, I'll be married to Lady Mallory before the sunsets."

He spoke with a dismissive tone that rankled Diana's nerves. "You should be so lucky. Mallory is a wonderful person."

Travers wasn't swayed. "She's hated me since we were children. I don't think she's ever said one kind thing to me."

"Are you blind?" Diana asked, throwing her pencil at the prince. It bounced off his shoulder, and startled him but did no damage. "What reason have you ever given her to be kind to you? I heard what you said to her when we met on the archery range. You threw the first insult. And it was ugly and cruel."

Travers had no good response. He looked shaken by that as if his actions had never been subject to scrutiny before. All of Diana's good intentions to keep the peace had vanished. She would not see her friend disparaged, no matter the brevity of their acquaintance.

"She is smart and she is beautiful, and I am happy to call her my friend," Diana said.

"The implication being you don't consider yourself my friend?" he asked, leaning over the small table between them.

"You have previously expressed no interest, so I don't see how that is relevant."

"I want to know," he said, still very much an arrogant royal, despite his earlier statements.

"No, you are not my friend, Travers. You don't deserve me."

The words hung between them until Travers leaned back, and let out an ugly bellow of laughter. "She said the same thing, can you believe it?"

"Is what bothers you so much that you know she is right?" Diana asked. She gathered up the paper she'd brought with her, the unfinished letter to her mother forgotten.

Travers shrugged again, and Diana had had enough. "Well, whatever happens, I hope you have the kind of luck you deserve, Travers."

With as much dignity as she could muster, Diana bobbed a quick curtsy and left the garden.

***

Diana had intended to send Jonah to the post office, but feeling the need for exercise, she decided to walk with him accompanying her instead. The mile walk to town passed through some extremely potent pockets of fishy-death smell, but she would have gladly endured that than run into the prince again.

She clutched a Wills perfume-scented handkerchief to her nose as she and Jonah walked the path through the lemon grove and joined the main road. It was hot, the heat shimmering through the vegetation. Jonah tugged at the collar of his livery as if it were too tight and too hot for the summer weather. She was on the point of wondering if she should have let him rest another day when he spoke.

"Ma'am, I wanted to say…"

Diana stopped to let the footman have his say.

He continued, cautiously. "I know you'll dismiss me once you find a replacement for Bill."

Diana tried to think of why, temporarily at a loss. Jonah took her silence as permission to continue, which gave her the space to remember the Pump Room fire, and Jonah being found in a compromising place.

"But I appreciate all you did to let me heal up the last few days."

"I hope this walk isn't too much for you now?"

He shook his head. "No, My Lady. I just wanted you to know that I… I'm well aware if you had any other choice you'd have dismissed me already."

Honestly, all of that felt as if it had happened lifetimes ago, but as it was first on Jonah's mind, Diana took the conversation seriously.

"I have no plans to dismiss you, Jonah. Not because you are the only choice, but because you have always done your job well. I will not penalize you for one mistake." Diana paused and then added. "So long as it remains one mistake."

Jonah nodded, and that seemed to bring an end to the conversation. They were not quite to town when thick clouds seemed to roll in above them, deep and dark.

"Storm coming," Jonah noted. "We need to get to a shelter."

There were a few buildings in the distance, cottages that sat at the edge of downtown. The sky darkened so much so quickly, that Diana could hardly see. When the rain began, heavy and so unexpectedly cold, they both dashed for the nearest of the cottages, a small stone building with a thick thatched roof.

Jonah pounded on the door. At first, there was no answer, and they considered darting down the road to the next cottage. Finally, though, the oak door swung outward.

Because of the sudden nature of the storm, no Zephyr lamps or candles had been yet lit and Diana stumbled into the cottage blind.

"Thank you," she gasped, trying to wipe the rain from her face. "I'm not sure what we would have done if you hadn't admitted us."

A lamp flared to life, and the faces of three people came into focus.

Three tall, willowy begins with distinctly pointed ears. The same ones she'd seen before, the trio who'd been in the Goose and Grouse and later speaking to the hotel clerk.

Drenched, and more than a little confused, Diana did her best to curtsy, lest she be unintentionally rude to a group of Fairies.

Jonah looked confused but bowed quickly. He stepped forward as if to protect Diana from the Fairies, but she gave a subtle shake of her head to warn him off, less the action implied insult.

"Welcome, Lady Diana Yarborough," said the male Fairie. "We have long wanted to know you."

"Me?" Diana "I can't imagine why."

"You spend time with the Prince," said one of the Fairie women standing on either side of the man.

Well, that was debatable, considering the way she'd just left him not an hour ago. "The Prince is not with me. This is my footman, Jonah Berry."

"Ah, he is irrelevant," said the man.

"You may leave," said the pink-haired Fairie on the right said to Jonah, who made no move to leave despite his obvious discomfort.

"It storms, my dear," the man said. "He can wait until the thunder passes."

"We will both be out of your hair when the storm ends," Diana said carefully as a great crack of thunder seemed to break the very air around them.

The male smiled. In the wan light, she could see the outline of large wings on his back. The woman had similar, though slightly smaller wings. Winged Fairies weren't unheard of, but they were rare. That explained why they'd had heavy coats on the first day she'd seen them. It was probably easier to meet with humans if they weren't distracted by giant wings.

"I am afraid not," said the man. "You will stay. Your servant will go."

Diana wasn't sure why, but she was almost sure the Fairies had summoned the storm. She didn't know if such a thing was possible. What could happen if Fairies had that kind of power? "I am afraid I don't have the pleasure of your acquaintance. I can't possibly visit without an introduction."

The pink-haired woman on the left scoffed, showing off her pointed teeth. "Humans," she said dismissively.

"I am called Smit," said the male. "And my spouses, Bell and Candle," he said, indicating the women on the right and the left in turn.

Despite her fears, Diana remembered her manners. "A pleasure," she said, bending her knees low.

Lightning lit up the interior of the cottage, showing far more of the Fairies than Diana ever thought to see. Her face burned with embarrassment, but she kept herself steady. Being afraid was no excuse to be an idiot. Especially around magical creatures.

"I serve My Lady," Jonah said.

"Leave when you are given leave," warned Smit. "I would suggest going to find Prince Travers and bring him here. Your employer will come to no harm while you are gone."

Jonah looked to her for guidance, but Diana had none to give. She was at a loss. She did not want to get on the bad side of Fairies, but she did not want to be left alone with them in a dark, deserted cottage.

As quickly as it had come, the storm outside rolled away. Sunlight flooded the room, showing not much in the way of furniture, save a small chair by a cold hearth.

There was a flicker of some kind of pink spark, and the oak door burst open. "Go," said Bell.

"Now," said Candle.

"My Lady?" Jonah said.

"Do as they ask," she said, trying her best to keep calm despite a rising tide of panic in her chest. "Go back to the hotel and tell Prince Travers where I am. And when that doesn't work, tell Prince Xavier. He's more likely to listen."

Jonah nodded, promising that he could fetch help. In no time he was gone, darting back down the road.

Diana looked to the three Fairies, who seemed pleased with themselves for the trap they'd laid.

"I don't suppose you have any tea?" she asked, for lack of anything better to say.

Chapter Thirty-Five

Mallory

Lady Passwood handed her a cup and saucer, fragrant with tea. "It will help with the headache," she said, with more kindness than Mallory would have expected.

Indeed, the brew did help. Her scalp tingled as the drink took effect, easing some of the tension that she'd carried since dawn. It eased the brilliant sunshine streaming through the suite windows that threatened to blind her as well.

"We owe one another a conversation," said the Duchess.

Mallory nodded, not entirely trusting herself to speak.

"And let me apologize first. I should have been honest with you from the start."

Mallory was careful to put her tea down, afraid her shock would cause her to spill. She'd never expected Lady Passwood to say such a thing. Ever.

"Thank you," she said. "And I owe you one as well. I am sorry about how I spoke to you the other night. It was badly done."

Lady Passwood took a seat on the settee opposite her. "I appreciate that. I will say that while what you said did hurt me, I know it was not unwarranted. I should have told you and your parents of the difficulty my family has found itself in."

Mallory could empathize. "I suppose it isn't easy to go about saying such a thing."

Lady Passwood gave an affirmative nod. "Travers did not make the conversation any easier. I have been very blind when it comes to that boy."

A twenty-three-year-old man was hardly a boy, but Mallory let that go. Lady Passwood had raised Travers all of his life, his mother having died in childbirth. She was to be forgiven for giving her surrogate son such leeway. "You love him. Despite his faults."

"I do. I want only the best for him. Which is why I wanted you for him. I have always meant my praise of you. I have adored you since the moment we met when you were two weeks old."

"I'm fairly certain I was an unimpressive baby," Mallory said, embarrassed.

"You were beautiful, and one of the daughters of my dearest friends. Nothing will convince me that you aren't entirely perfect."

Mallory groaned. "Don't tell me that! My ego will swell, and then I'll be insufferable to even myself."

Lady Passwood chuckled.

"Did you know you were the first infant I ever saw tell a joke?"

"How?" Mallory said, raising a skeptical eyebrow.

"I was visiting Vella House when you were about six months old. Your mother and I were having tea, and she had you in a little bouncing seat on the table. I forget exactly what we were discussing, something silly perhaps, but your mother made a comment that if our conversation were to get too boring perhaps you'd fall asleep for once. And instead, you smiled as big as any baby I had ever seen and chose violence. You reached your little hand down and pulled up the tablecloth under our teacups, spilling everything. And you laughed and laughed at your cleverness."

"That sounds less like a joke and more like the beginning of my destructive path through life."

Lady Passwood reached out, patting her hand. "Perhaps it was only funny in context, but your mother and I laughed for a good hour."

"So you are truly her friend. You didn't just befriend them because you knew about the whole Fairie thing?"

"Your parents have been my best friends since I was younger than you are now. I would not be where I am if they had not introduced me to my late husband."

Mallory had forgotten that Lady Passwood was a widow. For most of her life, it had only been the Duchess visiting alone. She supposed there must have been a Lord Passwood at some point, but she'd never thought too much about it.

"I'm worried that you… I don't know if it is fair to say, but I was worried that you'd only befriended them to save Travers' throne."

"That would make me incredibly more clever than I am."

"You are the smartest person I know," Mallory said. "I can't imagine you not knowing."

Lady Passwood laughed. "Oh my dearest, you are too kind to me."

They lapsed into a much more comfortable silence, for which Mallory was grateful. It was nice, just to sit with her Fairie godmother, and let the day dwindle. She wished Polly were here, to see how mature she was about spending time with Lady P. Mallory couldn't help but think she'd be proud.

When the tea had run cold Lady Passwood stood up to ring for a fresh pot. In no time, there was an insistent knocking on the suite door.

Mallory raised her eyebrows. Servants knew the protocol. A scratch was preferable to a light knock, and a loud rap was completely unacceptable. But apparently, no one had told the staff of the Rutledge Hotel.

Lady P opened the door, and a disheveled, young man breathing heavily practically fell over the threshold. "Lady Passwood, Ma'am. Do you know where to find Prince Travers?"

"The Prince has his own suite," Lady Passwood said sharply.

"He… he has to come. Lady Diana is in trouble. And they, and they… they have her," he gasped and clapped a hand over his mouth as if to hold the last of his breath inside.

"What's wrong with Diana?" Mallory asked.

"The Fairies have her. They won't let her leave unless Prince Travers comes to them."

Mallory watched all of the colors leach out of Lady Passwood. "Fairies?" she gasped.

"They're keeping her in a cottage on the main road."

"What do we do?" Mallory asked.

"We find my nephew, and then we get some help," Lady Passwood said. "What is your name?"

"Jonah Berry, My Lady," he said, bowing clumsily. "I'm one of the Wills footmen."

"Mr. Berry, catch your breath," Lady Passwood commanded.

Mallory had to admit she was impressed with her Fairie godmother's ability to speak and will things to be so. The footman's breathing was regular after a few deep breaths.

"The Fairies won't let her go until the prince goes to see them."

"I see." Lady Passwood said. "I don't believe my nephew is currently at the hotel, but Prince Xavier may know where he's gone. They've been thick as thieves the last few months."

She dismissed Jonah to try to find both men and then turned to Mallory, a look of steely determination on her face. 'Get your shoes, Darling. "

"Where are we going?"

Lady Passwood sighed. "Tull Castle."

"Why?"

"Because I believe I know where my nephew is, and he's going to need more persuading than I can give."

Mallory bit her lip. "Does that mean you want me to yell at him again?"

Lady Passwood pursed her lips, inhaling through her nose before speaking. "If it comes to that," she said.

Chapter Thirty-Six

Jordaan

He wasn't tired.

Which was perfectly normal, but after months of waking up from marathons of slumber enmeshed in lucid dreams, he was used to waking with sleep still clinging to him like he'd walked into spider webs.

The midday sun shone in through his windows, illuminating the collection of colored vials on his bedside table. No need to take any of them. With the removal of the Maundry's thread, the sleeping sickness was gone. He was hale and hearty and importantly, he could go back to his life. Visit his parents in Margate, perhaps, before returning to his service on Lower Miser.

Leave Tull, and any thoughts of Diana behind.

For the best, but that was going to sting. He supposed one day he'd hear about her, about whatever glorious marriage she made to cement power and status. He hoped by the time that happened it wouldn't feel like a kick to the teeth, but he doubted it.

He wasn't simply going to forget a woman like her. How could he? From the first day he'd set eyes on her he knew she was special. Not just beautiful, but strong and smart. She could knee a man in the balls and knock back whiskey as easily as she could glide among the elites. She was damn near perfect.

She just wasn't his to love.

Jordaan got up, shaking off his maudlin thoughts. He needed to see Caris Mourne again today to be sure the sleeping sickness was gone. As confident as he was that it was gone, she'd told him that fae-caused maladies often had a spikey tale to them. She wanted to monitor him for another day before giving him the all-clear to travel.

And too, he wanted to make sure she was recovering. It wasn't lost on him that she'd grown steadily more ill all spring and summer. When Shuttle had said, "The magic fades," she'd so easily answered her own concern. There were no coincidences when a powerful witch was involved.

The most powerful witch in the Known Kingdoms was ill.

Jordaan washed up and donned fresh clothing. He would need to send his clothes down the laundry earlier than usual so that everything was fresh for his journey. It would take a week to reach Spire, where he'd disembark for the overland trip to Margate, which itself would take another week. He had no wish to spend two weeks with increasingly filthy clothing. Jordaan wouldn't consider himself vain, but he was not unconscious of his hygiene.

Besides, being good-looking and well-groomed opened more doors than being a wretch with stained shirts.

When he was dressed, he made his way down to the hotel dining room. He had only made breakfast a handful of times in his weeks-long tenure, on account of the sleeping sickness, and lunch only slightly more. Having slept so late, he was hungry. Ravenous as if he needed to make up for all the meals he'd missed in the last months.

Everything around him looked good, even if the portions were too small for the gnawing in his gut.

Jordaan ordered three dishes and told the waiter to leave the menu. He tore his way through a plate of roast beef with a flavorful garlic gravy, a mountain of fresh greens, and a buttery pile of biscuits, all washed down with a carafe of chilled wine. He was about to order more, much to the waiter's obvious dismay when he saw a face he recognized run past the opening dining room.

It was one of Diana's footmen, the one he'd pulled from the fire. The man was frantic, his head whipping around like his neck was being pummeled by a gale-force wind. He was sweaty, pale, and panicked. That couldn't be good for a man recovering from smoke inhalation. Besides, Diana was too practical to hire melodramatic servants. Something had to be wrong.

"Charge the bill to my room," Jordaan told the waiter, abandoning his meal.

He caught up to the footman in the lobby. The look of worry on his face hadn't lessened. "You're Jonah, aren't you? In Lady Diana's employ?"

Startled at being stopped, the man vibrated like a frightened rabbit. "You pulled me from the fire."

Jordaan nodded. "What's wrong?"

"My Lady, she's... the Fairies have her."

Fairies? Jordaan's every instinct lit like a Zephyr lamp. "Is Diana unharmed?"

"I think so. They have her in a cottage. They won't let her go until Prince Travers goes to see them, but I can't find him. I've been all over the hotel, even to the Duchess's suite, but he's not here."

A surge of anger bolted through him. It was a good thing Prince Travers wasn't around, but he'd never wanted to hit him more. As if his general air of being an ass wasn't enough — as if he hadn't insulted her enough — now his predicament with the Fairies had come down on Diana.

Jordaan grabbed the footman's arm to keep him from bolting. "Tell me every detail."

***

Xavier wasn't pleased to see him. Jordaan couldn't blame him. The prince had taken the brunt of their last encounter, and he looked the worse for wear. Jordaan had had to pound on the door to his room to get him to answer. Like himself, Xavier had clearly slept most of the day away. His normally neatly combed hair was matted and stood up at various angles, and Jordaan was sure he could hear his stomach growling.

"I don't know where Travers is, I haven't seen him in days," said the Prince with a yawn.

"Do you have any idea where he might be?"

Xavier shrugged. "I found him face down in a puddle last time. So I can't say where he might be."

Jordaan rubbed his palms over his eyes. It didn't make anything clearer. "Come again?"

"Travers and I had," he paused, as if he weren't sure of his words, "an interesting spring?"

There was no time to unpack that. Diana was being held by Fairies, and who knew what they intended? That was more important than Travers' recent dissolute history.

Jordaan had hated to ask for help. He knew if Prince Xavier had woken up anything like himself he was still feeling the effects of whatever Caris Mourne had done to free the Maundry's thread from him. A second favor, to involve himself in this new drama, was asking a lot. Xavier didn't seem to mind the ask, but so far he wasn't much help.

"Any haunts he might be? I need to find him."

"We spent the most time at the Goose and Grouse down by the wharf, but I don't think Travers has any particular attachment to it. He could have gone back to Tull Castle."

Which was currently uninhabitable.

"Would he go there?"

"He might. Why do you need to find him?"

"It's Diana. Her footman said she's being held by three Fairies in a cottage by the high street until Prince Travers shows up to talk to them."

Prince Xavier's tan face drained of color. Jordaan knew they were old friends, but he suspected that the prince was showing more than concern."

"What do you know?"

Xavier rubbed his hands over his face, "I followed three Fairies the other day. They were going all over town looking for Travers. But the thing is people told them where they could find him. Everyone on the island knows about the castle, and that Travers is here. I think there's some magic that's preventing them from getting to him."

Jordaan wasn't sure what to do with that information. His immediate concern was Diana. If she were hurt, he'd never forgive himself. Not that he could have done much, but… she was everything.

"What can I do?" Xavier asked.

"We have to find Travers and bring him to the cottage."

Xavier pulled on his coat. "I'll ride to Tull Castle. You try the tavern and if he's not there, go to Diana."

Jordaan hastily replicated the crude map Jonah had made for him with the location of the cottage. "Either way, we meet there. She doesn't deserve to be in danger because he's a fool. This has to end."

"Agreed," Xavier said, grabbing his hat.

Chapter Thirty-Seven

Diana

One thing was very clear — Fairies were lousy hosts.

Diana had ascertained that much by the time Jonah had disappeared down the high street. For several, long, awkward moments, they'd simply stared at her as if they expected her to burst into song or explode into confetti.

"I'll just take the chair, shall I?" she said, hurrying past the three Fairies to the lone seat in front of the cottage's hearth.

"Your Prince will come," said Smit, with an entirely unearned confidence.

"He may well turn up," Diana said, arranging her skirts around her as she sat, "but he is not mine."

"The town humans say otherwise," said Bell, who was distinguishable from Candle by the sharp points of her teeth. Candle was much easier to look at, having neither the filed teeth nor the look of mania that her twin seemed to hold.

None of the books she had ever read about Fairies had prepared her to be with three of them at once. Knowing that humans who petitioned the Fairie Courts sometimes went away feeling ill at ease, or even sick in their stomachs, did not mean she was at all comfortable with the wave of nausea that hit her when she was cooped up in a dark cottage with them. Their presence was simply discomforting, as if they weren't meant for so humble a space, nor such close confines.

"So that's a no on tea, then?" Diana asked. At first, she'd asked to fill the silence, but in the intervening minutes her throat had gone dry and she was desperate to do something with her hands.

"Do you wish to bargain?" said Bell, her light eyes narrowing in on Diana.

"For tea? No. I'm not so fickle."

"Is there anything you want?" Smit asked. "We are in the business of bargains."

"I'll pass, but thank you for the offer."

"Pity," said Smit. "Humans are usually keen to make a deal."

That wasn't entirely true, although Diana supposed it might be true to the Fairies themselves. People who sought out Fairies, the ones who left generous offerings in the chapels, and offered incantations and prayers to them did want something. Desperately. To the point where magical intervention was the only way they could see forward.

Those were the people Fairies saw. Not ordinary humans with ordinary wants. One did not bargain when their concerns were trivial. After all, the stories of people who brokered deals with Fairies were all cautionary tales. No use of magic ever seemed to end well for the humans involved.

Diana could only imagine how mortified her mother would be if she ended up cursed for wanting a cup of tea. She'd never live it down.

"You must want something," Candle said. Her voice was softer than Bell's, more melodic. She probably had some fantastical gift, like the ability to lull unsuspecting travelers in with a song. Diana tried to keep that in mind. Yes, she was less intimidating than the other woman, but softness sometimes held a lot of fury.

"No," Diana said firmly. "I am content."

Smit laughed, an ugly, forced sound. "Everyone wants something. Imagine something. Anything. Power? Money? Beauty…"

He spoke the last word with a disparaging glance at her. Diana's cheeks burned, but she kept her mouth shut. There were plenty of people who thought she was beautiful. Maybe not loads of people, but Sir Jordaan thought so. That was… unhelpful but not insignificant. She certainly didn't need some Fairie curse that would leave her with a dog's tail or whatever ridiculous idea of what these three thought was pretty.

"I have an idea," Bell said, a nasty smile curling outward. "Let's play a game."

Diana's heartbeat increased. She folded her arms over her chest. "No thank you. I do not play games of chance."

"To not play would be rude to your host," Smit said. "You haven't even heard what the game will be."

"I do not play games and I do not bargain," Diana said, trying to keep a tremble out of her voice.

Bell moved closer, leaning her face down to Diana. Up close she smelled like sugar and vanilla, as if she were made of nothing more than the candy floss that gave her a hair color. "We will tell your fortune. All young women want to know if they will meet their true love."

"Have you?" Diana said.

Bell reared back at the rudeness of the question. "Insolent child!"

"Fairies do not marry without true love," Smit said. "Unlike humans."

"That sounds exhausting." The words slipped out of Diana before she could stop them, but only because they were true. Her own bumblings into love had already left her tired. She couldn't imagine waiting what must surely be decades — even centuries — in the life of a Fairie, waiting for true love.

"Love is never easy," said Candle. "But it is worth it."

She took her sister's place, entirely too close for comfort. The Fairie grabbed Diana's hand, tugging off her glove. She seemed to take great interest in the plain of Diana's palm.

"What do her lines say?" Bell asked. "Will she die as an old maid?"

Candle hummed, turning Diana's hand toward the light coming in through the cottage windows. "I see a marriage."

"I am from a royal household, and the sole inheritor to my father's title. It is unlikely that I wouldn't marry," Diana said.

She wasn't scared, exactly. Fairies might be strange and unusual to her, but they were flesh and blood. And so far she hadn't really been threatened or harmed, only mildly creeped out by the whole experience. Candle's touch, as she ran her long, stick-like fingers over the lines in Diana's palm was unpleasant, that was all. As long as she remained practical, and didn't let any of them bother her too much, she would be fine until Jonah came back with help.

"I see fortune," Candle crooned.

"I am already an heiress so that is also not surprising."

"I see a cat."

A cat? No, that was highly unlikely. Cats and dogs were not for her. "I don't much care for animals," Diana said.

"That will change."

Diana couldn't help but roll her eyes. Her mother had been trying to get her to like dogs since she was a baby. Three Fairies with little sense of personal space weren't likely to make any better headway when it came to pets.

"What of her stars?" Smit said. "Something extraordinary must be in store for the bride of a prince?"

Candle frowned. "There are many to choose from."

Bell stepped forward, taking Diana's hand with a rough grab. She stared down into Diana's upturned palm, her eyes mere slits as if the fine details were hard to read. Whatever she was or wasn't seeing, after a tense moment, she dropped Diana's hand unceremoniously.

"Surely it cannot be that bad?" Smit said. He took his turn looking at Diana's palm lines, frowning as deeply as his spouses. He took her other hand, disposing of her glove with a flick of his fingers. He stood too close for Diana to see where it landed.

"Her moon is here," Smit said, his pointed nail scratching at the mound of flesh below her left thumb. Diana held in a hiss.

"Her moon is cloudy," Bell said. "It will show you nothing."

Smit let go of her hands, stepping back just far enough that she felt as if his piercing stare was encompassing all of her. "I suppose you must be curious about what we're speaking of," he said.

Diana shook her head, tucking her hands into the pockets of her dress. "I would rather not know."

"All humans want knowledge of the future. We've seen yours," Candle said.

"And we know your secrets," Bell said. "Bargain for them."

Not this again.

Diana wasn't a fool. She kept her words, and her curiosity, firmly behind her lips. Of course, she wanted to know her future — at least the important bits. Health, happiness, and how many books she might read. But no. She would keep her wits about her.

"A shame," Smit said. He gathered his spouses in his arms, and the three of them huddled with their heads together. Although she couldn't make out words, they murmured in a way that suggested intimacy to which Diana had no business being privy.

She needed to make a plan. Even if Jonah found Travers, there was no guarantee he would come. Especially after the way she'd spoken to him in the hotel garden. Jonah was smart enough to find someone else to help, but how long would that take?

The cottage held nothing, as far as she could tell. The chair where she sat. The coats they'd worn in town were on pegs by the front door. A heap of cold ash in the fireplace. The Fairies had moved out a foot or so away from her, but still stood between her and an escape. So nothing that was immediately clear as a means to get her out.

Her pockets didn't hold much. The letter she had written to her mother that she'd meant to post. A small purse of coins for shopping. These weren't things that made for great weapons.

Caris Mourne had said she was clever, but Diana didn't feel that way. If she were such a great thinker she might know a way out. Instead, she stayed in her uncomfortable chair while a trio of Fairies tried to push her into a bargain. Likely because they were bored.

She could end up with hooves just because they wanted distraction.

A glimmer of a spark ignited in Diana's brain.

They had asked her to make a bargain. Not the other way around. And that meant...something.

Oh, she had no idea, but it had to be to her advantage, didn't it? She just needed to figure out what to ask for, in such a way she could gain something from it. Her freedom, certainly, but maybe more.

Sir Jordaan and his mysterious illness came to mind. Of course, he'd told her to butt out, but she would help him, if she could, after all he'd done for her. What she needed was information. And seeing as there were no books about it, she was going to have to get it from the people in front of her.

Diana cleared her throat.

That did nothing to break up the cozy huddle of Smit, Bell, and Candle.

"I am curious about something," she ventured.

After what seemed like an agonizing interval, Smit spoke. "And what is it you wish to know, Lady Diana?"

"I was wondering what your plan was, once Prince Travers arrives. Will I be free to go?"

Bell sneered, and Candle continued to look bored. Smit steepled his long fingers together, their jagged tips clicking against one another. It took a great deal of willpower for Diana to remain neutral. The sound made all the hair on the back of her neck raise.

"We will negotiate with the Prince."

"For the territory of Tull?"

Smit's smooth brow furrowed. "We have no interest in the territory."

Well, that was either a lie or a very interesting bit of information. Diana forged onward. "That is not what I heard."

"Gossipy human," Bell said. "We are not interested in your stories."

"You said you wanted to see the Prince. Why?"

"Our ways are not for your kind," Candle said in what Diana now heard as her eerie voice.

"I suppose that's true, but, if you are going to take back the territory from the Corvin family, you will have to understand human ways. And we do ask a lot of questions."

The three Fairies looked confused. Which vastly improved Bell's face, if nothing else. "As I have said, we have no interest."

"But you said so. To the Prince. At the new year?" Diana could only hope Travers hadn't lied to them all about what happened when they'd made their demands. It would make things infinitely more complicated.

"We have only just arrived," said Bell.

"But you were here before," Diana said.

"Imposters," Candle hissed.

Diana could feel the air in the cottage change as if it had been filled with a kind of invisible smoke. She coughed, as the cloying scent of cinnamon and clove filled her nostrils. "Prince Travers has been avoiding you because he believes you've come to take over Tull."

"The Weavers plan is bigger than anticipated," Smit said.

The name of the Maundry registered, but Diana had no chance to gloat over figuring out their involvement. Her chest spasmed and her lungs were suddenly desperate for fresh air. She needed to get out before the magic in the air choked her.

"Cease your noise!" Bell said.

Diana was in no position to comply. She stood, unsteady on her feet, and lurched toward the door. It wasn't a matter of not offending the Fairies. She needed to get outside.

Chapter Thirty-Eight

Mallory

Travers tipped his head back, draining the last liquid from a rather large bottle. "Sorry, I haven't any more to offer," he said, without much sincerity.

Mallory shrugged. "I think I have given up whiskey. The headache isn't worth it."

Travers's short, barking laugh echoed through the empty library. The built-in shelves had been cleared of books and all of the furniture was removed for the upcoming repairs. Without anything in it, and with the front wall missing altogether, the room was a cavern.

Travers sat on the floor, his legs hanging over the side of what had once been Tull Castle's front facade. The wind blew in from the direction of the beach, blowing his loose black hair into tangled clumps. His skin was pasty, and dark circles pressed into the skin under his eyes, making them appear sunken. He had both hands on the empty bottle, and if Mallory's eyes weren't playing tricks on her, they were shaking slightly.

"If you're not here to drink, why did you come?" he asked.

"Just my luck I found you first," she said honestly. A few dozen people were looking for Travers. Lady Passwood had organized every footman, stablehand, cook, gardener, and person passing by on the road to help with the search.

Mallory leaned against the wall nearest him, preserving a little of her strength. Her body was cooperating enough today to go without her chair, but she couldn't be sure it wouldn't give out. And she had no wish to give Travers more ammunition.

"You're not going to jump, are you?" she asked.

"Wouldn't that be a fitting end?" he said with a heavy sigh.

Mallory's heart sped up to a faster beat. She'd spoken in jest, but perhaps Travers was so broken he'd consider ending his life? She didn't know. As long as she'd known him, she had no insight into his head. "It would be a messy end," she said. "You'd set Lady P's renovation plans back by at least a day."

He snorted something that might have been a laugh but was too bitter to assuage her that he wasn't serious.

He turned his head, his dark eyes looking at her. "May I be resigned to the Fairie Hells if I get in the way of the great lady's plans."

"She'd be completely devastated at your death and probably bring down all of the Known Kingdoms in her grief."

"Only second," he said with a sneer, "to how much she'd mourn you."

He never failed to miss the point. *Ever.* How he'd grown into such an obtuse man, Mallory couldn't say. "I don't want you to jump. Does that change your mind at all?"

He rolled his eyes. "Lovely. My greatest detractor cares."

Mallory couldn't stop a sign of disgust. "Stop it, Travers. This isn't something to joke about."

He relented, but not before hurling the empty liquor bottle into the courtyard below. It shattered with a pitch so loud, that Mallory could feel it down her spine. "I was never going to kill myself. I'm just indulging in being miserable, okay? At least for now, I'm a prince. It is my prerogative to be miserable from time to time."

"Yes, but it is so unhelpful," Mallory said. "You are a prince, even if you've never deserved it. You could spend your time doing so many more wonderful things."

"Why?"

"What do you mean *'why?'* It should be obvious. You could help people. You could fund charities, build roads, even fund an exploration of the Unknown Kingdoms for Fairie's sake."

He scoffed. "But why would I want to do any of those great things? What's in it for me?"

Mallory had no answer to that. She hoped that he was just trying to bait her, to get her to be the worst version of herself, so that he wasn't alone in the metaphorical mud. "If you can't figure it out, that's on you. I am here for a reason. You disappeared at a very inconvenient time."

"Is it something I am supposed to care about? I assume as the voice of my missing conscience you'll tell me."

"Lady Diana has been kidnapped. The Fairies holding her are demanding to see you."

That declaration did nothing to the slumped set of Travers's shoulders. If he hadn't heard her perfectly for the entirety of their conversation, despite the roar of the sea breeze, she might have almost thought her words had been lost to the noise.

"No reaction, Travers? Nothing? Fairies be, do something. Diana is in trouble."

"She's not going to marry me," he said finally.

"And for that, she deserves to be held prisoner?"

"They'll figure it out eventually. She's not beholden to me, so they'll let her go."

She couldn't stay still any longer. Mallory pushed herself off the wall. With the entire front of the castle open to the elements, and no railings she might cling to, it wasn't the safest plan. But what she wanted to say could only be said right in front of his face, so there was no chance he could avoid the lecture.

Without much grace, but also without imminent death in the courtyard below, she sat down next to him.

"Miss me?" he drawled.

There were days when her hands could barely hold a spoon. Days when she couldn't turn the wheels of her chair. But no matter how weak she was, Mallory was sure there would always be that little reserve to slap the smile off Travers's face. The sudden smack knocked him back. He had to roll away to keep his balance so he didn't fall out of the front of the castle. Mallory nursed her stinging hand, glad she'd left at least a temporary imprint on his smug face.

"What in the..." he said, wincing.

"Be better, Travers. For your own sake if nothing else."

"Go away, Mallory," he said, now lying flat on his back. "Just leave me alone."

Mallory struggled to get to her feet. Her right arm was like a wet noodle after the slap, which didn't help, nor did the layers of skirt and petticoat settle around her. "Believe it or not, I am trying to help you. I don't know why you're being such a jerk."

She fumbled, falling back down.

Travers's head tilted up, watching her struggle. "Again. *Why?*"

Mallory took a deep breath in through her nose, realizing she might not be able to get back up from the floor. Not without help. It was a humiliating proposition. She was going to have to ask Travers for help. And if he wouldn't help her, she was going to have to stay where she was until Lady Passwood or someone else thought to look into the old library for the missing prince.

"Maybe because we've known each other since we were babies. Or even because you were my first crush? Or simply that my Fairie godmother loves you and I love her. Pick a reason, and get yourself together."

Travers got to his feet, far too easily. He stood over Mallory, a hand extended. "I was your first crush?"

"Leave it to you to pick the most ridiculous thing I've said." He took her hand, giving her a boost. It wasn't quite enough, and he put a hand at the small of her back, helping her to regain her footing.

Upright, Mallory froze. He should let her go, but for some unknown reason, he simply stayed there, hand possessively around her waist, hand entwined with her own.

"Tell me more about this crush," he said.

"My friend is in danger. I do not have time."

Every instinct screamed at Mallory to move away, but she didn't trust her legs to carry her.

Or maybe it was that she'd never been held like that before.

Oh, she'd been carried plenty of times before — she couldn't walk some days and had to be hauled around like a piece of furniture — but somehow, Travers wasn't holding her like she was a burden. Maybe it was a delusion, but in that instant, she might almost believe that he wanted to hold her. It was weirdly intimate, considering how much they despised one another on a minute-by-minute basis. Odder still that she didn't hate it. He radiated warmth, and the touch of his hand was firm as if he would never let her fall. She hated this man, but she couldn't stop herself from noticing that while she could smell the whiskey on his breath, there was also something nice about his natural scent, it was fresh, likely newly mown hay.

"If I kissed you right now, would you slap me again?" he asked, his voice taking on a husky quality.

"Without a doubt," she said, shocked that her voice suddenly registered lower. *Where had that come from?* The whole situation was confusing. Diana might be hurt, or scared at least, and what was she doing? Looking at her greatest enemy's lips like they held some secret.

Mallory took a step back, suppressing a shiver from the loss of Travers's heat. "I'm going to tell Lady P where you are. If you won't go on your own, I'm sure she'll have a footman or two hogtie you."

Travers laughed. "I wouldn't put it past her."

Thank the Fairies she was never going to marry him. His emotional upheaval was too much to handle. One moment he was morose, wallowing in self-pity, only to shift at the slightest hint of a compliment. His self-absorption knew no bounds.

"Well, lead the way, if you're so determined I should go," he said. "Although I would suspect you'd like to see me tied up."

"Don't make me regret being nice to you," Mallory said. "Please."

"I'm the one who got slapped," he said. "What do you have to complain about?"

"Just get moving," she said, doing her damnedest to walk as quickly out of the library as possible.

Chapter Thirty-Nine

Jordaan

The proprietor of the Goose and Grouse wasn't any help.

"Ain't seen any prince around here," said the stubby old man. Jordaan found himself wanting on his natural charm. He told himself that he was still in recovery from his illness, but knew it was all about his preoccupation with Diana. If one red hair on her head had been harmed, he'd tear Travers apart with his bare hands.

He tried again with the bar owner. "Young man. Black hair, just a few inches shorter than me. Drinks heavily."

"Got lots of those around here," the man said with a laugh.

"He mentioned to me he stayed here a few days. With a friend."

"That chap? A prince? Owes me money!"

Okay, that was something. "So he hasn't been back?"

"I was going to stay, he's not welcome back, but if he's a bloody prince I'm not sure I can keep him out of the Goose."

Travers wasn't here then. It was a dead end. Jordaan looked around the dark interior. The Goose and Grouse was full of dark wood and semi-private booths. He doubted that the other patrons were any more cognizant of the fact that the crown prince of Tull had been among them. Too busy drinking the sour ale.

Diana had said she'd waited here while her servants had fetched a carriage, but it was hard to picture someone as vibrant as her in this dark, sad little place.

That sparked something. Jordaan tried again. "I had heard that some Fairies visited this place a few days back?"

The man made a phlegmy sound of agreement. "Yeah, yeah. Three of them. Pink hair one of those ladies had. You see that in pictures, at the Fairie chapels, and the like, but in person? Whoo boy, it's shocking in person! We don't get actual living Fairies around here much."

A male and two Fairie women had come into the Rutledge just before he fainted. What were the chances of more than one trio of Fairies going around Tull? "What did they want, if you don't mind my asking."

"Carpets," said the man.

"Come again?"

"Yeah, I thought it was weird too. Come into a bar asking about how to find a carpet weaver. What do I know about carpets? You don't put down a carpet where beer gets spilled."

The Weavers. The Fairies had been asking about the Weavers. He felt like an even bigger fool for dismissing Diana's theory. The Weavers had wanted something from him, and now they had it. The Fairies wanted to find the Weavers.

"Did they ask about anything else? The prince, perhaps?"

The barman shook his head. "I told'em he was probably up at the castle. Didn't make a difference."

If there was anything more to learn here, Jordaan couldn't discern it. He thanked the man for his time, tipped him a generous bit of coin for his trouble, and tipped his hat.

The recent rain that had torn through Tull had churned up more dead fish and seaweed from the depths of the harbor. The rotting stew floated between the ships at berth, along with a good deal of refuse that had made its way to the water. Brilliant sunshine reflected off large puddles on the boardwalk, making Jordaan grateful for his good boots. He untethered his horse from the bar's hitching post.

He'd taken the shortcut to town through the lemon grove, but he'd taken the high street to find the cottage. Diana's footman hadn't had an address. He'd simply said small, thatched cottage by the fork in the road. Which, if he remembered correctly from his previous walks to town, narrowed it down to about a dozen. The small neighborhood of cottages at the edge of the town wasn't hard to find, but it was easy to waste time knocking on the wrong door.

He arrived at the crossroads in a few moments. He'd been wrong. There weren't half a dozen cottages. There were ten, all alike down to the Tull Exa cranes growing in their front gardens.

If it weren't for the redheaded woman in the blue day gown walking along the road, he might not have known where to look first. A weight he didn't know he'd shouldered lifted. Diana was okay. She was whole and healthy, and decidedly not being held against her will.

Jordaan dismounted his horse beside her, dropping the reins to let the job horse graze a bit. "You are supposed to be kidnapped," he said.

"I decided not to be," Diana said. "It was quite awkward."

"I had plans to rescue you."

She cast a skeptical glance at him. "Did you?"

"Yes, but here all my effort seems to be wasted. You're.... you are well, aren't you?" Diana blew out a breath like she was trying to will herself to calm down. "I am."

He wanted to hold her, to run his hands over her to make sure none of her bones were broken. Propriety be damned, he'd been worried about her. "You're the most remarkable woman I've ever met," he admitted.

Diana's cheeks colored. "You told me to leave you alone."

"I'm an ass. You know that."

She sighed, with a shake of her head that let some of the magnificent red hair loose around her face. "Thank you for coming to rescue me, even if it wasn't necessary."

He reached for her, folding her into his arms. "Next time don't scare me like that," he said, leaning his forehead against hers. It was too public a space to kiss her, to tell her anything like what he was feeling at that moment. Even this amount of touch was too forward, but he would allow himself this indulgence for as long as she would allow it.

"It wasn't my choice to be detained by Fairies," she said.

"I know," he said, taking one of her hands and bringing it to his lips. He placed a gentle kiss on her bare knuckle. "What happened to your gloves?"

"Does it matter?"

"Just want to know if I have someone to thank," he said, turning her palm upward. There were several deep scratches on her palm. "Or to kill," he said, lightly tracing the lines.

"That's nothing," she said, taking her hand from his, and stepped ever so slightly back to create room for good sense between them. "They tried to read my palm."

"What did they find?"

Diana shrugged. She was so infinitely beautiful that even that gesture was elegant. On anyone else, it would be a frustrating, non-answer. For Jordaan, it just made it easier to imagine her shoulders bare, her long hair loose, and caressing her soft skin.

"Nothing unusual. Wealth, marriage. They wanted me to bargain with them for its secrets."

He reached for her hand again. "Did you?"

"I may be the biggest fool to ever step foot in Tull, but I'm not an idiot."

She was far from it. Fairies be. He was going to be infatuated with her until he was an ancient old man. "I'm glad you're unhurt," he said. He wanted to say more, but there was a clatter of hoof beats coming, and they weren't going to be alone for long. Reluctantly he put more space between them so that when the carriage pulled up, he wouldn't impinge upon her honor.

One of Lady Passwood's elaborately painted carriages came to a halt mere feet from them. Prince Xavier was the first to get out of the carriage, then an obviously inebriated Travers. Lady Passwood and Lady Mallory followed.

"I told you they'd let her go," Travers said, seeing Diana.

"I left, there's a difference," she said.

"Regardless, we can go back to the hotel."

"No, we can't," Xavier said. He put a hand on Diana's arm. "Are you alright, Di?"

"I'm fine," she assured the prince. "Just shaken."

"See?" Travers said. "No harm done."

"Oh enough," Lady Mallory said. "Have you heard nothing? Please, just pretend to care about someone else. Just for a moment."

Jordaan decided that his original opinion on Lady Mallory stood. She was fantastic. Not a Diana-level goddess, but a solid human all around.

To his surprise, Travers sighed, as if he'd been reminded of his manners and felt slightly ashamed. "What do you want me to do now?"

"I suggest seeing the Fairies currently hold up in that cottage," Diana said, pointing to the closest cottage. "They have some very interesting information for you."

"I don't want to hear anything they have to say," Travers said. "Everything can wait until after they take my territory."

Diana folded her arms across her chest. "How about the fact that they don't want your territory?"

Lady Passwood, who had until then been hanging back from the younger royals, stepped closer. "I was there when they showed us the documents. The deal with the Light Court..."

"I'm sure it exists," Diana said. "But the Light Court doesn't want Tull. I believe those three would rather be anywhere but here at present."

"The Weavers," Jordaan chimed in, the pieces of the puzzle clicking into place. "They're lesser fae. Shapeshifters. It was them."

"Like that little bugger yesterday?" Xavier asked.

Jordaan nodded. "Yes."

Lady Passwood looked relieved, but if Jordaan were a betting man, he'd say Prince Travers looked sick to his stomach. Although perhaps that was the whisky he'd imbibed.

"You need to speak to the Fairies," Diana said. "Because avoiding them hasn't worked."

"What am I supposed to do, just march in there?" Travers asked.

Xavier nodded. "Yes. The ladies can accompany Diana back to the Rutledge. Jordaan and I will go with you to even up the numbers."

Jordaan wasn't sure he liked the idea of accompanying Travers anywhere, but Diana was the priority. If he could ensure that she was safe, he'd walk through hot coals.

"That is an excellent idea," Lady Passwood said. "Come, Mallory, Diana."

Diana didn't look like she wanted to anywhere near Lady Passwood's carriage, but she wasn't given the choice. She was swept up into the cab and in no time, the driver was headed back to the hotel.

"No time like the present," Xavier said. "Come on, Trav."

Chapter Forty

Xavier

It was all very civilized, this conversation with the trio of winged Fairies, save for the fact the person they were speaking to reeked of spirits. It was lucky that the stone cottage had the cloying stench of magic. It provided a certain amount of cover for Travers, although it made the dim interior of the cottage suffocating.

The male Fairie sat in the cottage's sole chair, the two women standing on either side of him. By necessity, Xavier and Jordaan had arranged themselves likewise behind Travers as a show of support.

"You came to my audience at the new year," Travers said. "I spoke to the three of you."

"Lies!" hissed one of the women. Xav couldn't say if it was Bell or Candle, because of the dim light. "We had not set foot on this crumbling island until last week."

"Then you were impersonated," Jordaan said. "By people who knew about the old Covenant."

"It would seem so," said Smit, the male. "Although how you could confuse some other creature for a Fairie, I don't know. You must not be able to see very clearly."

Xav put a hand on Travers's shoulder to remind him not to lash out. Whatever magic these people held, the prince didn't need to be on the wrong side of it.

"Shapeshifters are very good at fooling people," Jordaan said. "The Weavers, for instance."

The name caused a visible reaction among the three Fairies. The woman with the sharpened teeth growled, and Smit shifted in his seat.

"What are the Weavers?" Travers asked.

"The Weavers are indentured to the Light Court. They should have no business here."

"And yet, they are here," Jordaan answered. "Funny how that happens. Why have you been trying to force the prince into a meeting?"

"I can speak for myself," Travers said, but Jordaan plowed ahead. Xav tried to give him a nonverbal warning to keep his mouth shut, lest he offend the Fairies, but Jordaan was too busy staring down Smit as if he were contemplating ways to tear the man limb from limb. Not good. Cooler heads needed to prevail.

"I think what Sir Jordaan is asking is that you be clearer with us what you are trying to accomplish. We are not enemies, but allies." Xav had no idea if this was true, but it felt like the right thing to say. His father had always told him that politeness was better than aggression when it came to tense situations. Prince Brandon had faults, but knowing how to lead wasn't one of them.

"We don't have to explain anything to you," said sharp teeth.

"No," Xav agreed. "No, Fairie ways are Fairie ways, everyone in this room understands that. What we are asking is that you help us understand so that we might help you."

Travers shot him a look, but as the tension in the room seemed to have dissipated, Xav carried on. "You wanted to speak to the Prince, who was under the impression you've already spoken. And that conversation upset him very, very much."

Travers full-on scowled at him but said nothing. That was as much encouragement as Xav needed.

"And so you have avoided us. Put a spell on us to keep us from finding you," said the quieter woman, the one with the normal teeth. "We had to interact with that nosy cow to get you to come to us."

"Candle is very good at discovering where magic has been used," Smit said, gazing adoringly at her. It was good that he was distracted because Xav was pretty sure Jordaan was going to vault over Travers and tear the woman limb from limb for insulting Diana.

He didn't miss that part of being in love, that guttural instinct to lash out.

"I have no spells on me," Travers said. "The witch we employ at Tull Castle is there for minor magic, and she's currently vacationing in Noola. I haven't gotten more than a cold remedy from her in years."

"Untrue," said the nastier one, Bell. "My sister has read of the spell in the stars. It has kept us from finding your direction."

Jordaan spoke again, barely containing the tension in his voice. "Just putting it out there, but perhaps the Weavers used a spell to keep you from finding Travers? Considering they've been impersonating you?"

"Trying to take my territory," Travers added. "So what would these Weavers want with my lands?"

The three Fairies again exchanged a worried look. "The Weavers are in service to the Light Court."

"We've established that," Jordaan said, fist clenched.

"They wanted to be high fae. But stewardship of the land is a requirement for our kind."

Xav's head swam. If he was hearing this all right, the little monster who'd been in his room and then subsequently attacked Jordaan had been trying to swindle Travers out of his territory in order to become more like the Fairies they served.

"Got tired of waiting for you, did they?" Jordaan said.

"It would seem so," said Smit.

"You are the prince of this territory," Bell said to Travers. Xav shivered a bit on his behalf. It was either the teeth or the sneer, but he wouldn't want to be sized up by the Fairie. "You must tell us where the Weavers are."

"How would I know?" Travers said. "I've never seen them."

"One is currently in the Witch's Tower at the Rutledge," Jordaan said, cutting him off. "I suggest you start there."

Bell fixed Jordaan in her sights. She nudged Candle, who sighed.

"Remove your glove," she said to Jordaan.

"What?"

"Remove your glove," Candle said in an eerie calm that made Xavier shiver.

He watched as Jordaan, although confused, pulled off one of his gloves. Candle stepped forward and took his hand, drawing one of her talons over the lines on Jordaan's palm.

"What do you see, my Darling?" Smit asked.

Candle gave an impatient snort, dropping Jordaan's palm. "A cat."

"What does that have to do with anything?" Travers asked. "Are we or are we not serious here?"

Xavier was thankful that the Fairies were too distracted by the notion of Jordaan's future cats to care about the disrespect dripping from Traver's voice.

"Specific or general?"

"Neither," said Candle, pointing into a dim corner. "I see a cat."

The cat in question, a small black kitten no bigger than a melon, gave a loud "meow." Jordaan smiled and scooped up the cat. "Veronica, you naughty girl. Why are you following me?"

The cat gave another meow and then yawned as if it couldn't be bothered to answer. Odd as it was, the upside was that Jordaan was no longer a pile of scalding rage.

"That is more than a cat," Smit said. "I would suggest you use caution."

Jordaan ignored him, giving the kitten a scratch and a kiss.

"Can we stop talking about cats?" Travers said. "I have a territory to save and you've got devious little monsters to stop."

All three Fairies looked wary of the small black beast, snoozing contentedly on Jordaan's shoulder, but agreed to return with them to the Rutledge.

Chapter Forty-One

Diana

The witch's hair had turned bright white. Diana had to keep herself from staring. Caris Mourne was known for her long, deep-purple hair. The change was startling, although she had to admit the witch looked healthier than she had for the last two weeks. Unlike the glamor she'd put on herself when they'd had tea, there was a genuine brightness about her skin and eyes.

"I thought you would want to know what's happening," Diana said, shaking herself. As much as she'd wanted to crawl into her bed and let the whole day disappear, she knew that it would be important to tell Caris Mourne about the Fairies.

"I appreciate your candor," Caris Mourne said. "Are you well?"

Diana wasn't so sure. The whole afternoon had left her feeling off-kilter. "Physically, I am. The rest, I can't say."

Caris Mourne gave her a sympathetic smile. "That is understandable."

The windows in the Witch's Tower brought in a cool breeze, making the room more comfortable than any other room in the hotel, and likely Tull in general. Diana wasn't sure how the witch lived with such large windows open all the time, but she had to admit the cool air did make her feel better. A little like being home in Wills, when a balmy day required a light jacket.

"I expect this will be the next place the Fairies visit," Caris Mourne said. "They will want to see my guest."

Diana hadn't noticed the small creature bundled up like a baby at first, so distracted by the change in the witch, but there was indeed an unconscious figure at rest on a small cot near the hearth.

"Is that? Is it one of the Maundry?"

Caris Mourne nodded. "Yes, You were very astute to suss out their involvement for Sir Jordaan. He is quite cured now."

Diana was ill at ease with the compliment. She felt nothing but silly and uneducated. "His sleeping sickness is gone?"

"Thankfully, yes, and so we move on to the next mystery."

"I'm not sure I have any mysteries left in me," Diana admitted. "I fear I would make a poor witch after all."

The witch fixed her with her kind and sympathetic gaze, "You are stronger than you think, Lady Diana. No rule says you must run at the top level all the time. You can slow down, you can take a deep breath."

Diana tried to imagine that, not striving to achieve all of her goals at once. She had to admit she didn't know what that would be. She had been prepared by her parents for greatness. To be great on behalf of County Wills. That meant marrying well and securing the succession of the title.

"I may not have a choice," she said. "My erstwhile engagement is no longer, and I... I seem to keep getting infatuated with entirely the wrong person."

"Ah," said the witch. "Well, the heart is a fickle player."

Diana felt that from head to foot. "May I ask you a personal question?" she ventured.

"Hm?"

"In the spring, you said that your spouse was your great love. How did you know?"

Caris Mourne's face brightened, and Diana was almost sure her now-white hair took on an iridescent sheen. "We met during a great upheaval in my life. Everything I thought I knew seemed to be crumbling around me. At the time, I was sure I would never be capable of loving anyone. Yet when I was at my lowest, they were always my bright spot. They were the person to whom I always wanted to tell my troubles and my triumphs. And I began to see that I was the same for them. I won't claim that it was any one action or romantic gesture, although there were plenty of those in the course of it. It was simply that I did not want to have anything good or anything bad happen to me without them."

Diana felt a pang of envy, sharp as a knife. What Caris Mourne described sounded like all of the Fairie Heavens coming together all at once. "That does sound nice," she admitted.

"May I ask you a personal question? This current infatuation, what makes it so unsuitable?"

Embarrassment burned through Diana. Her face might as well have been on fire. "I seem to have... I seem to be fixated on yet another... he has no land. No title of his own. All of the things I have been told are important."

"But what about this man catches your eye? If I remember the last time, it was an old friendship and a good deal of beauty. What of Sir Jordaan?"

Of course, she knew. Diana could hardly have supposed otherwise. Caris Mourne was the most powerful witch in the Known Kingdoms. Diana's secrets were hardly any match for that kind of knowledge. "He's impossible. Silly. He takes nothing seriously, except of course his cat."

The witch had a cheeky smile. "Animals can be very perceptive."

"He dotes on that cat as if she were a queen."

"She may be. Veronica is not 100% a cat."

Diana laughed. "If she's not a cat, what is she?"

Caris Mourne didn't know. "Magic takes odd forms," she said with a shrug.

"Yes, well, Jordaan likely won't care. He's smitten. He's going to surround himself with cats, like an old hag in a storybook."

Caris Mourne's laugh was slight and rusty, but it was there all the same. She got up from the chairs where they sat, dismissing the tea that had long gone cold with a turn of her watch dial and a snap of her fingers. She tapped the watch face with her finger, frowning. "My time runs short I'm afraid," she said.

"Oh, I should... I should go."

The witch tucked the silver watch back into her trouser pocket. "One more thing. If you would do a favor for me, Lady Diana?"

It took a great deal of restraint not to over-promise her idol any number of favors. "What can I do?"

Caris Mourne went to a lectern set up near one of the open windows and opened the heavy box from which the wizard, William, had appeared. "I'd like you to meet with my friend. Talk to him. Explore what it might mean to work with magic. You have such potential." Caris Mourne summoned a quill and ink, opened the box, and slipped in a hastily penned note inside.

Diana felt more hopeful than she had in days. "Do you believe I could have been a witch?"

"Oh, I still do. I do not bestow my praise where it is not earned. I've asked him to meet you tomorrow morning in the hotel garden. I believe a little time with him may make some things clearer to you."

Diana wished that were true. She watched as the box opened of its own accord, and the paper flew out again. The response was short and to the point. "Promptly at 10."

"I'll be there," Diana said.

"Just one more thing? If you see my traitorous cat, please tell her to stop leaving the hotel grounds."

Diana chuckled and bobbed a curtsey. "I'll do my best," she promised.

***

Alice was pacing in the hall outside Diana's suite, looking like she was about to expire on the spot.

"Why are you in the hallway?" Diana asked.

Alice didn't seem to have the words. She shook her head, her hands twisting together like taffy.

Diana reached into her pocket for her key but Alice snapped it from her hand. "It's awful, Miss. Awful," she whispered.

In the course of the day, Diana had been kidnapped, forced into a carriage with Lady Passwood, and had a very confusing interaction with Sir Jordaan. All she wanted to do was put her head down on a stack of pillows, burrow under the covers, and consider the day done. Except that fear was painted across Alice's face, and that she couldn't ignore.

"What is wrong, Alice?"

"It's...it's Bill and Maryann."

"They've returned?"

"Not exactly," Alice said. She took the key, but before she could get it into the lock, the door opened, and a flood of light poured into the hallway.

For the briefest moment, Diana saw two blurry figures in her suite, going about cleaning her room as if they'd never left.

"Hello Lady," said Not-Maryann, waving with a seven-fingered hand.

"Greetings," said most definitely not Bill, who was holding the broom the wrong way round, poking it into the ceiling.

"So lovely to have you back," Diana said. "If you will excuse us just a moment. I just need to give Alice a bit more instruction."

Neither Not-Bill nor Not-Maryann seemed to find the statement as odd or awkward as they sounded to Diana. Not-Maryann shut the door in a way the real Maryann wouldn't dream.

"What do we do?" Alice asked, her voice breaking.

"Go find Jonah, and stay near him until I send for you."

"What are you going to do, My Lady?" Alice asked, biting her lip.

"I don't know, But I will figure it out."

Chapter Forty-Two

Jordaan

How he'd ended up embroiled in Travers' mess, Jordaan wasn't entirely sure. By the time they'd all returned to the Rutledge — all three Fairies, both princes and his sorry self — Jordaan realized that regardless of his confusion, there was no getting out of it. There was too much he didn't know about what had happened to him, and how it tied into the larger mystery. He couldn't duck away and pretend he was innocent of all involvement. The Weavers had wanted something from him as much as they wanted something from Travers.

But he was going to need a drink before too long.

They had tramped into the hotel, heading straight for the Witch's Tower. And apparently, she'd known they were coming, because the space had been cleared, with chairs available for all of them.

Caris Mourne had taken one look at the Smit, Bell, and Candle, and said. "You will sit and listen," she said

"How dare you," Smit began to say. "You have no right to command the Fairie folk."

"I am well-versed in your ways, Smit," Caris Mourne answered without hesitation. "And you must obey the rules of equal magical beings."

"You assume too much if you believe that we are equal," said Bell.

Jordaan would be very glad to never see that particular Fairie ever again. She was rather like one of the snapping turtles who lived in the river beside Margate House. The ones that used to bite his fingers when he tried to move them out of the carriage path so they weren't crushed to death under horse hooves.

The witch wasn't intimidated in the least. She smiled and said in a peppy, sing-song voice. "Do not test my power, Bell Geis of the Light Court."

For a woman who wasn't above five feet tall, Caris Mourne towered large. Bell glared at her, but Jordaan would bet his best boots that the Fairie woman was a little bit afraid of her. He'd learned a few key things about the witch in the months that she'd been treating him - and the primary one was that under no circumstances should you ever underestimate her.

The Fairie trio could learn the easy way or the hard way, but either way, they were about to learn.

"Your Highness, perhaps you had better start the tale of what brings us all today," Caris Mourne said, turning her attention to Travers.

Before Travers could speak, there was a frantic knock at the Tower door.

The interruption caused everyone in the room to exchange looks. It was a bad time for someone from either Dunlock or the Rutledge to come asking for a cold remedy.

"I'm sorry to interrupt," Lady Diana said through the door. "But it is urgent."

Caris Mourne turned her watch dial, and the giant oak door swung open. Jordaan wanted to rush over and enclose her in his arms, but he held back. He had no right to soothe the obvious worry on her face, as much as he wanted to do.

"I'm so sorry," Diana said, "But I believe you are missing two of the Weavers."

"Do you know where they are, Lady Diana?" Caris Mourne asked in a decidedly kinder voice than she'd used with any of them so far.

"They are currently in my suite, masquerading as two of my staff."

"Oh, I see," Caris Mourne said. "Let's get them up here, shall we?"

She turned the dial on her watch and tapped the face twice. There was a great rush of wind and a snap like overhead thunder. The room filled with the heavy scent of clove and cinnamon shortly before two people, a man and a woman in the pale pink and gray uniforms of Wills appeared in the center of the room.

It was obvious they weren't human. The details were all wrong. The man's face seemed to be sliding toward the floor, and the woman had entirely too many fingers on each hand.

"Welcome," Caris Mourne said. "Rather interesting disguise you've chosen."

She might as well have taken a match to dry paper for how quickly the two reacted, orange light bursting from their palms. Just as quickly, however, Caris Mourne had them encased in what looked to be a giant soap bubble. They were no longer in the guise of Diana's maid and footman but rather had reverted to the same small creature that was currently in his own bubble by the fireplace.

"Ladies and Gentleman, meet Spindle and Needle. Their brother Shuttle sleeps by the fire. They are very old, very crafty, and very much indebted to the Light Court."

The trio of Fairies seemed neither impressed nor ashamed of holding their indenture.

With the Weavers secure, Caris Mourne pulled a glass vial from her pocket. "And they very much want this object right here."

That got the Fairies' attention. The witch held up the vial to the light. Inside was a single, sparkling thread. "I believe you may be missing something?" she said to Smit.

Jordaan glanced around the room to see how the royals were taking this revelation, but it didn't seem to mean anything to them. If the thread hadn't come from him, he might not have understood the significance.

"My Lady," Jordaan ventured. "Didn't you say the thread was not actually a thread?"

"I did, yes," she said. "But sometimes we use magic to make the invisible just a bit visible so that we can better understand our problems."

Jordaan had no idea what that was supposed to mean. He felt thick as a bowl of stew. He looked at Diana. He could practically see the gears turning in her mind. She was drawing connections, referencing that delightful brain of hers to put the pieces together faster than anyone else in the room. Thankfully, both Travers and Xavier looked as dumbfounded as he felt, so he wasn't alone in not having any idea what was going on.

"Where did that come from?" Diana asked.

"Sir Jordaan had been carrying it around for some time."

"That was the cause of his sickness?" she asked, although it seemed clear she already knew the answer to that. "But how did he get it?"

"That was stolen from the Light Court. We hold the Weaver's thread as part of our bargain," said Smit.

Caris Mourne chuckled and tucked the vial back into her trouser pocket. "But you lost it. Because the Weavers finally outsmarted you. They took back the Thread they used to weave together time, hoping it would free them from their indenture."

"I believe Sir Jordaan may have inadvertently interrupted the Weavers' first attempt to use the Thread while he was helping search for Princess Kira last spring."

Jordaan had no memory of that search. He remembered setting out from Corlea Palace with his friend, Sir Robert. He remembered them hitting a storm that had sprung up so suddenly it spooked the horses and caused them to bolt.

After that, it had all gone black. He'd woken up in the Knight's Quarters in Dunlock, unable to keep his eyes open for more than a few minutes at a time.

"What the hell does any of that have to do with my throne?" Travers asked.

"Because it isn't enough for the Weavers to sever their obligation," the Fairie, Candle, said, her voice crawling down his spine like a spider. "They want to be high fae. And to do that they need stewardship of land."

Caris Mourne beamed at her like a proud mother. "And so they pretended to be Fairies from the Light Court, coming back to claim land they'd abandoned centuries ago."

Inside their bubble prisons, the three Weavers snarled and snapped, desperate to escape. But the witch was having none of it. "I think it is time to send the three of them home, don't you?" she asked Smit.

"Return them to the Light Court and hand over the Thread," he said.

"One out of two," she said with a smile. "You know as well as I that the Thread of Time no longer belongs to you."

"You claim it?"

A wide smile and a doe-eyed expression were the only answers he got.

"I don't give a damn about a thread," Travers said. "What about my territory?"

Jordaan was sure Bell would have attacked had her sister not held her back.

"We assume you wish to renew the deal with the Light Court," Candle said. "A thousand years?"

"What would I have to do?" Travers asked.

Both Diana and Xavier looked like they wanted to object, but Travers plowed ahead.

"You must venerate our kind," Smit said. "Fairies must never go out of favor with the court of Tull and the Corvin family."

Jordaan cringed internally at Travers's answering, "Deal." He held out his hand to Smit to shake, but the Fairie ignored the gesture. "Our business here is done. A covenant will be sent to you."

And with that, all three Fairies disappeared within a blink. Caris Mourne let no dust settle and used her watch to banish the three Weavers.

"Now then," she said. "I believe that is all the mysteries we have to deal with for today."

Which was a very polite way of telling them all to get out of her tower.

Jordaan was more than happy to oblige.

Chapter Forty-Three

Diana

Diana had woken up feeling a sense of hope that made her jittery. Today she would know whether or not she was meant for magic. She'd prepared for her meeting with the wizard, William, by putting on one of her best day dresses and making sure Alice did her hair in a coronet of braids to show that she was practical. When William had joined her in the hotel garden, she did her best not to fidget or appear overeager.

She needn't have worried. The first test of magical ability wasn't anything like she imagined. The wizard handed her a stick.

"Now let's see what you can do," he said with a friendly smile.

Diana turned the stick over, hoping it would reveal some clue about what she was supposed to do with it. Sadly, it didn't include instructions. It looked like something picked up off the ground in the lemon grove. "Is it magic?"

William shrugged. "It is if you want it to be."

When she was a child playing witches and wizards, a stick was essential. Find a good one, call it a magic wand, and swish it about like an orchestra conductor.

Magic was fickle, so perhaps it was that easy?

She and her friend Robby Lycette had made up a little ritual to begin their games, and taken it very seriously. For lack of any other idea, she laid the stick on the palm of her hand and ran her other hand flat over the length of it. She felt nothing in particular here, but forged ahead with her made-up enchantment. "I call upon the Fairies to give me magic," she said, waving her hand back and forth over the stick.

William raised one fluffy eyebrow. "What are you doing?"

Diana blushed and handed back the stick. "Truthfully, I have no idea," she said. "It was just something I used to do when I was young."

William considered this for a moment. "Admirable, but not helpful."

He shrugged and tossed the stick into the air, where it promptly vanished. "I don't believe natural magic is your gift."

"Is magic a gift?"

"Depends on the practitioner," he said cryptically. "So, let's try something else." From the voluminous sleeve of his royal blue robe, he pulled a silver bell. "Can you make it ring?"

Diana took the bell and gave it a little shake. It was surprisingly loud for such a small object, the silver tone echoing through the garden.

William took the bell back. "I meant without touching it," he said.

"Can you tell me how that is done? Do you have a book I could read?"

William chuckled. "Books on magic? Now there's a scary thought. No, I keep nothing so cursed in my possession."

"How then did you learn magic?"

The question seemed to delight the old wizard, whose smile grew bigger. "Trial and error. One day I thought I might turn my neighbor, Mr. Hawley, into a newt. So you might say it started from sheer determination. I had a few tricks to learn first before the big transformational magic, but low and behold, twenty-five years later, I finally managed it."

"You learned magic for spite?"

"There are few more powerful motivations."

Diana didn't have spite in her, and could only hope there was some other motivation that made a decent witch. "Did you ever turn him back?"

William sighed heavily, "Sadly, yes. His wife lodged a complaint with the coven. Horrible people, both of them."

"Perhaps you should have turned them both into lizards?"

"I thought about it, but not knowing how fast they produce offspring, I worried I'd be overrun with baby newts."

Diana laughed, although she wasn't entirely sure that she should be laughing. "I suppose that would be a concern," she gasped, trying to reign in her mirth.

"You are good at conversation, Lady Diana. I see why Caris Mourne admires you."

Diana's cheeks flared with color. "I have admired her my entire life. It is so odd to me that she knows who I am, let alone has any idea of me being worthy."

"In my experience, Caris is stingy with her praise. Take the compliment and run."

William produced a scroll of paper from the same sleeve he'd pulled the bell, unrolling it. To Diana it appeared blank, though the wizard's eyes moved across the page as if he were reading. When he seemed to reach the bottom, he handed it to her. "Anything, Lady Diana?"

She took the blank page, which wasn't in the mood to reveal its secrets. She blew across the surface. Words appeared and disappeared as fast as a blink. "It wants to keep its secrets."

"That is an excellent assessment," he said. "So many people just assume it is blank. Well done."

He took back the scroll and it, and like the twig and the bell before it, it vanished into thin air. He rummaged in his sleeve once more, and asked in a distracted manner. "Ever tried to do any magic? Redirect the wind, mix a potion, stop time, perhaps?"

He stuck his head into his sleeve to look for whatever object he had in mind.

"Um, well, I recently tried to make a perfume. I understand that might be considered a potion."

William emerged from the sleeve, a small green bottle in his hand. "Any luck?'

"No, it smelled awful, no matter what order I mixed the ingredients."

"What were you trying to create, in terms of a perfume?"

It seemed so silly, when Diana thought of it now. But there was no point in trying to hide the truth, not from a magical being. "I thought having a signature scent that I invented might make me stand out. I would be something other than the prince's rich bride."

"So something to give you place, status, is that it?"

Diana nodded. "I hoped, certainly."

William seemed to consider this a moment. He held out the bottle. "What would you do with this?"

Diana held the bottle up to the light, trying to get an idea of what was inside. By the way the light hit, it was clearly liquid, but only just so. Whatever it was, the stuff was thick. She flicked the side of the bottle, but it made no discernible sound, nor did the contents splash. She supposed there was only so much she could learn without seeing the liquid herself. Diana took out the cork, and sniffed. Its smell was surprisingly sweet, probably made with honey or some kind of sugar syrup. Diana stripped off her glove, and dabbed a bit of the mixture on the tip of her finger. It didn't produce any reaction on her skin, even as she rubbed it into her fingertip. She had the sense that the liquid was likely something to be consumed, but rather than risk instant death from being too hasty, she placed the smallest drop she could manage on her tongue. It was indeed sweet. So sweet, Diana felt lightheaded.

She handed the bottle back to William. "It is quite strong."

"That was remarkable," he said. "You used all of your senses. Sight, touch, taste, smell, and sound. You would not believe how many senseless people try to swallow it all without understanding what's inside."

Well, how else was she supposed to learn about something when there were no books available? "Is it something dangerous?" she asked out of belated curiosity.

William was noncommittal. "Isn't everything dangerous?"

"I suppose so," Diana said.

None of what they'd done or discussed so far had told Diana anything about her own potential to practice magic, except perhaps the maxim "Don't be an idiot." She was about to ask, when William set off across the garden with long, striding steps. Diana was forced to run a bit to catch up with the wizard, who seemed to be measuring the garden with the length of his own stride.

"Sir, is there something I should be doing?" she asked, trying to keep pace with him.

"No, no, I am enjoying this interlude. I rarely leave my box. Sometimes I forget that the land has the most remarkable attributes. Soil. Flowers. Sunshine! The sun is horrible for my skin but I do enjoy it on occasion."

Diana stopped trying to follow him, instead letting him take his laps, realizing that perhaps magic wasn't for her. As excited as she'd been just an hour ago, she felt nothing now. She couldn't imagine rarely leaving a witch's tower, or committing herself into living in a traveling truck. It seemed rather lonely. And the way she felt now, missing her parents, her home, and even her mother's silly little dogs, told her she wasn't meant for a solitary life.

"When I was very young," William called from across the garden. "I so enjoyed walking outside. Did you, Lady Diana?"

"Yes, I suppose so. I was often out of doors when I could be," she said. The lightheadedness from the liquid seemed to grow worse. Her head felt as if it were swimming. "I especially enjoyed going down to the beaches. I've always loved watching the waves."

"I suspected as much," he said, turning back toward her. "Your spirit is very connected to the water."

Perhaps it was the potion, stripping back her inhibitions, but Diana was sure that bit was nonsense. A watery spirit? What good was that going to do her? She was the heir to a royal house. She was meant to marry well and help her home stay strong and powerful. And that mattered. It was on the tip of her tongue to tell William that she was sorry for wasting his time, when one of the hotel's footmen appeared in the garden. He stopped in front of her, bowing. "Lady Diana Yarborough?"

"Yes, that's me," she affirmed.

The servant held out a stack of letters. "These arrived for you today."

Diana took the letters, all of which bore her father's neat, square handwriting. Father was not a frequent writer. That he'd written five different times made Diana sick with dread.

She thanked the servant, and took the letters to one of the small bistro tables set among the flower beds.

The letters had all been written in the first weeks of her departure. He'd written when she couldn't possibly get the letters. She would have still been onboard the Princess Vogel, sailing toward Tull, full of her own importance. She arranged them hastily in date order, tearing open the wax seal.

Each missive was short. *"Diana, I fear your mother is much more gravely ill than she acknowledges. I know you have not yet reached Tull, and this letter is unlikely to reach you in a timely fashion, However, I must ask that when you do read these words you make arrangements to return to Wills. Your mother will forgive me for taking you away from your suitor, because I know nothing will give her as much comfort as your presence. –Your Loving Father.*

"The healers have recommended we bring in a witch to make a more powerful potion…"

"I fear that we can do no more..."

Diana held back a sob. How could she have been so thoughtless? Her mother had been ill when she left home, and Diana had barely given her mother a thought since she arrived. She was a horrible daughter, and now her mother was so gravely ill Diana might never see her again.

William had finished making his exaggerated steps and came to a halt in front of her table.

"Ah, so the truth reveals itself," he said, eyeing the letters.

Aghast, Diana broke out into tears, "What? What does that mean? Did you know my mother was..." Diana couldn't bring herself to mention the word dying.

The wizard colored. "No, no my dear. That is not... Oh, I've bunged it up."

Diana was beyond caring if she kept herself composed. "The letters are out of date, what if... what if...?"

"Be easy, Lady Diana. Do not invite trouble."

Diana wiped away tears, realizing she'd never put her glove back on. "My mother needs me and I must go home."

"Yes, yes. That is best. What is magic when a family is in peril?"

The ability to work magic had been something that fascinated Diana her entire life. As a little girl she'd dreamed of the spells she could make if she were a powerful witch. Not that she had any pretensions to power, but it had been a story she'd told herself again and again. A version of her that wasn't awkward or lonely, but one who could instead conjure incredible things to delight everyone.

She'd been foolish.

She stood and bobbed a curtsey. "I must go. Thank you for your time."

Chapter Forty-Four

Jordaan

He needed to pack. He had passage on a ship leaving the day after tomorrow, and no sailing vessel worth her salt was waiting for a knight who was dragging his feet. But his shirts and his tunics were going unfolded. Instead, he watched Diana as she followed the wizard in the blue robes around the garden. The view from his window was the perfect vantage point to indulge his obsession.

Which was all that it could be, this preoccupation with her. All the innuendos and strong hints implying he was in love with her — couldn't, wouldn't change a key fact. He wasn't royal. Diana needed to marry into another royal family to secure her family line and protect her home territory.

His term of service to the Duke of Lower Miser had several years to go. When it was over, he'd carry the designation of Sir for the rest of his life. That was an admirable status, but it did not make him royal. And in all likelihood, by the time he finished standing guard on the Lower Miser crenellations, Diana would likely have been married for years.

He watched the footman approach Diana, who had drifted away from the wizard. The man handed off what looked to be a small package or a bundle of letters. In seconds, he watched her face change, the bemused expression crumbling into something of restrained misery.

Abandoning his pretense of packing, Jordaan sprinted out of his room and down the hotel's central staircase, taking the steps two at a time. Whatever had caused Diana to cry, it had to be critical. She wasn't weepy by nature.

He encountered her in the lobby. He wasn't made of stone. Seeing her so visibly upset, her eyes brimming with tears, it took all of his reserve not to fold her into his arms right in the middle of the *very* public lobby.

"What's wrong?" he asked.

Diana shook her head. "I can't talk. I have to go." She moved as if to leave, but Jordaan could see she was in agony. He took her hand, threading his fingers through hers. Although the hotel had more guests than at any time during his stay, the library was one space that was always empty.

"I have to go," she said, her voice cracking. "I have to get home as soon as I can."

Jordaan pressed a handkerchief to her cheek. "Bad news?"

Her lip wobbled and she nodded, rather than speak.

"One of your parents?"

"Yes," she croaked. She took the handkerchief, dabbing at her rapidly shedding tears. "My mother. She took a turn after I left, and I've just now received all of my father's letters."

"The next departing ship going north leaves tomorrow," he said. "Let me arrange your passage."

"I have... staff, and..."

"It would be my honor to help you."

Her breath caught. "Why?"

"Oh, Delilah, you know why."

Jordaan took the opportunity to step closer, just to breathe the same air. She was so remarkable, he wondered if she was even a little bit aware of it. Well, how could she not? She was a smart woman, as well as beautiful.

"You could tell me," she said, her voice low. "You could say the words."

Jordaan felt the punch to the gut but summoned up some of his usual bravado. "And ruin you for all others? I'm a gentleman."

Despite her tears, she let out a small laugh. "You are a good man, Sir Jordaan."

He shook his head. "I'm a miserable wretch. But I am excellent at booking space on ships. Just tell me how many you need."

"Three, myself, a maid, and one footman."

She dabbed at her tears again and held out the damp handkerchief. He waved it off. "Keep it. Clutch it to your breast when you think of me."

"Oh you are ridiculous," she said, pressing the material into his hand.

He stuffed the handkerchief into his pocket and stepped back to bow. "I'll send word through the hotel."

***

Jordaan had to give up his berth to get enough space for Diana and her staff on the ship on which he was due to leave. He was sorry not to get to travel with her, but it would only be prolonging the inevitable. He dashed off a note to Diana, and one to the Duke of Lower Miser to revise his date of return.

His glorious purpose as a knight errant done, Jordaan found himself at a loss. He still had to pack, but he very much wanted a drink. He found himself in a tavern by the harbor, a miserably lit place that had only bitter ale on tap.

The first swallow was awful. The second was an experience he wouldn't care to repeat. But he did because the alternative was thinking about what an ass he'd made of himself in the last weeks.

"It doesn't get better," Xavier said, taking a seat in the booth across from him. He hadn't seen the prince enter the bar, but he wasn't unhappy with the company. At least he wasn't drinking alone.

"Oh goody, I was hoping it would stay disgusting."

Xavier snorted and took a long drink of his ale. "So you're indulging in a little misery drinking?"

Jordaan raised his glass and knocked it lightly against Xavier's own. "I deserve it. You?"

"Just the usual," Xavier said. "Putting off going home."

"What is there to stay for? You don't want to keep hanging around Travers?"

Xavier shrugged. "He's not that bad. He was a friend to me when I needed it. I just don't think I can stay and watch him deteriorate anymore."

"He's not losing his throne, what else does he have to make him miserable?"

Xavier didn't know. "I think if he knew he'd ignore it."

Jordaan didn't have much brain space for that. He wasn't fond of Travers, although he knew that was because of Diana. He hated that such an unrelenting ass had ever had a chance of marrying her, simply because he was a prince. But if Xavier was right and Travers was falling apart, he felt something like pity. He raised his glass again. "Well, here's to him."

Xavier clinked his glass again before going up to the bar to get another round. He was back all too soon, dropping a glass in front of Jordaan. "Excellent news, they had plenty more ale."

"I should have been more discerning in my drinking establishments."

Xavier smirked. "Oh, the Goose isn't so bad. Charming decor, really," he said, gesturing to the dark timbers and sticky collection of tables. "So what have you got to be miserable about? You didn't fess up."

Jordaan wasn't sure he had it in him to say. He choked back a taste of it and wiped his mouth on his sleeve.

Xavier leaned across the table. "Can I guess?"

"Do you have to?"

Xavier snorted. "I think you're here because of a certain redheaded heiress."

"Are you well, Xavier? Feverish perhaps?"

The prince shook off a laugh, drowning it in his ale. "What is your hesitation? Diana is wonderful."

Jordaan swallowed a spurt of irritation. Like the bitter ale, it went down hard. "As you said, she's an heiress. She has to marry someone for the good of her territory."

A momentarily confused look crossed Xavier's face. "Aren't you a Van Dine?"

"Yes, but I'm the fifth son. Non-royal."

"Sorry, just bear with me a moment. Am I wrong in thinking your family has more money and influence in the crane flower trade than any other family in the Known Kingdoms?"

That was technically true, although there were other considerations. "It is more complicated than that."

"Rob Lycette is the third son. His family has so little it's criminal, and yet there's a very good chance he's going to marry Princess Kira."

"I'm not Rob. He's so upstanding I don't think he knows how to sit down. And let's face it, the Princess isn't exactly known for her judgment."

Xavier raised his eyebrows. "Insults to my friends aside, do you have any reason to believe Diana might have feelings for you?"

"No."

"Because you're lying to yourself, or because you haven't asked her?"

"I'm sorry, do you not have something more princely to do than gossip like an old woman?" His outburst only made the prince laugh.

"Not today."

"It doesn't matter anyway. Diana is leaving tomorrow. Her mother is sick, and she's leaving with the next ship out of the harbor."

A dark shadow crossed Xavier's previously bemused expression. "The Countess?"

Jordaan nodded. "Diana got word earlier today. Lady Wills got very sick soon after she left."

"Then she needs to get back there. Diana and her mother are extremely close."

"I arranged for a berth on a ship going north tomorrow."

Xavier shook his head and down the rest of his second glass of ale. "That'll take too long to get her home."

"Well, what other choice is there?"

"For Fairie's Sake, Jordaan, we know one of the most powerful witches in the world! And after she used me as a human pin cushion, she owes me a favor. Diana can go through the portal she has to Dunlock, and be home in three days. I'll escort her myself."

A dual feeling of being an idiot for not thinking of that himself, and being annoyed that what little service he could render to Diana was being taken from him played out in Jordaan's chest like a brass band. "I didn't think of that."

"Too busy drowning your imaginary sorrows," Xavier quipped.

***

The hotel was a hive of activity, a drastic change from most of his time in Tull. Staff in the teal and black trimmed uniforms adorned with the Corvin family crest were busy moving furniture and trunks both into and out of the hotel amid a chorus of shouting. The front drive was lined with carriages, each of them more burdened with household goods than the last, forcing him to hand off his horse at the end of the drive, instead of at the front steps.

Jordaan watched as a young man in the pale gray and pink livery of Wills brought out a truck with brass fittings. No sooner had he deposited the trunk among a pile of suitcases, than a man in a fussy, old-fashioned wig was bearing down on them.

"That goes in, what are you bringing it back out for?"

"Orders, Sir," the footmen answered.

"I'm the one who gives orders, and I don't remember asking anything to be piled up in the driveway!"

A young maid in a soft pink uniform came flying down the hotel's front steps. "Jonah, you know that must go in the pile!" the girl shouted at him. Jordaan recognized the man he'd once help rescue from the Pump Room fire.

The wigged man didn't take lightly to his enterprise being interrupted. "Get out the way, Girl. We've got a whole castle's worth of goods to bring in."

Time to intercede. Jordaan stepped up, holding up both hands. "My good man, if I may be of help."

All three of the servants involved in the scuffle over the trunk looked at him as if he'd suddenly grown an extra head.

"I think you're at cross purposes here," he said, as gently as he could.

"I've been entrusted by the Duchess herself to get everything from Tull Castle into this hotel and that I intend to do," said the man indignantly.

"Yes, and you're doing an excellent job at organizing all these things. But I believe these two are trying to get their mistress's things out, so that you may have room for all of these items."

For a moment the old man froze as if the information didn't sink into his head. Then he glared at the young maid. "Well, why didn't you say that?" the man asked.

"I tried," said the maid. "You wouldn't listen!" She turned to Jordaan as if to confirm her astonishment. "Every time we brought out Lady Diana's trunks he ordered someone to take them back in!" Sweat had gathered at her temples and across her upper lip from the heat of the day. He had no doubt based on her pinched expression that the young woman was in over her head.

"No harm done. You're doing admirably. It is Alice, isn't it?"

Surprised that he knew her name, she bobbed her head. "Yes, yes Sir."

"Do you have a cart or a carriage for all of Lady Diana's luggage?"

"The hotel manager asked us to leave it all on the front steps," Jonah answered. "There's a cart coming back from town for us."

Jordaan did his best to take control of the situation, directing the Wills staff to take the current pile to the far end of the drive, and to have the wigged man inform everyone hustling the mountain of boxes and end tables inside, to steer clear of the spot.

By the time he was back in the hotel, he was exhausted. He intended to slip back into his room and sleep until his ship left tomorrow. However, before he could make it to the stairs, Lady Mallory, who was sitting in her wheelchair in the hotel lobby, waved him over.

He bowed quickly. "Good to see you," he said, stifling a yawn. "Are you waiting for someone?"

"No," she said, "I am doing my best to stay out of the way. Lady Passwood is determined to get this hotel refurbished in the style she believes her precious nephew deserves."

"Did she really have everything brought from the castle?"

Mallory nodded. "The witch who is overseeing the reconstruction told her that it would be a few more weeks before anyone could move back in, so she rented the hotel for the rest of the summer."

Jordaan came from wealth. He knew that the easiest way of solving a problem often involved large sums of coin. However, the Rutledge was not an inexpensive hotel, as evidenced by the exceptionally large bill he'd paid off before venturing out this morning, and he'd only had one of the smallest rooms. He whistled. "The entire hotel?"

"Yeah, she's afraid Travers won't have enough room to do whatever drunken wastrels do."

Jordaan smirked. "How long have you and the prince been mortal enemies, exactly?"

Mallory lifted one slim shoulder. "He knows what he did."

"Fair enough," he said.

"Are you leaving us too?" she asked, her dark eyes a bit too focused on him for his liking.

"I am. I just need to pack my bags."

"I hope we meet again," she said, adding a sly, "Have you said goodbye to Diana yet?"

"Not yet," he admitted.

"And might you, oh, say a few more things to her." Her eyes sparkled with mischief. If he weren't the subject of her mirth, Jordaan would have appreciated her teasing, but he couldn't summon up the energy. Perhaps it was the day drinking but he felt more drained than he had when he was still under the pall of the sleeping sickness.

"I will wish her a safe journey," he said.

"Hm. Nothing else? Maybe a declaration of your undying love for her."

"I'll do that when you admit you are madly in love with Travers," he said with a smile.

"You are a sick man," she said, rolling her eyes.

"Not sick, just tired. Goodbye, Lady Mallory. I do hope we meet again."

She inclined her head, and Jordaan headed for the stairs. He was on the second step when she called after him.

"A blind man could see she's in love with you!"

He turned and bowed at her. There was nothing else he could say. Even if Diana were in love with him, they both at least knew it was hopeless.

Chapter Forty-Five

Diana

Diana apologized to Alice for the 10th time since they'd begun packing.

"I'm so sorry to put you in this position. I know the journey will be hard for you."

Alice, who seemed to have matured a decade in the last hours, was all calm assurance. "I will be fine, My Lady. The Prince's plan is a good one. Both Jonah and I want to see you get home as quickly as you can."

Leaving Alice to sail back with Jonah, who had so recently spurned her affections seemed a cruel casualty of her own expedited journey home. While it was comforting to know she would be back in Wills before the week was done, she hated to abandon her young maid. "I am sorry to leave you behind."

Alice gently pried a crumpled nightgown from Diana's tense hands. "Don't trouble yourself, Lady Diana. Leave the packing to me. Perhaps you should go say your goodbyes to your friends."

Diana recognized a dismissal when she heard one. "I did want to say goodbye to Lady Mallory."

The plan had come together so quickly, that Diana wasn't sure she would have time to meet with anyone. By the time she'd been informed of the plan, all she could think of was the mountain of trunks stacked up in her suite. Most of them had never been unpacked, like the gifts she was to bring to Tull Castle and her library of books, but still, there was much to arrange. The plan was for Xav to accompany her through Caris Mourne's secret door to Dunlock, and for them to travel by carriage to Wills. Alice and Jonah would go by ship with all of her trunks, save what she needed for a few days' journey.

"Go ahead and pay your visit," Alice said, seeing her out of the suite door.

At a loss as to what to do next, Diana composed herself and made her way to Mallory and Lady Passwood's suite. She ought to have sent a note, but there hadn't been time. She was leaving in a few hours.

One of Lady Passwood's maids admitted her to the grand suite, which put her own room to shame. The Duchess knew how to request the best rooms in a hotel because while her room had a comfortable elegance, this series of rooms was downright opulent, all velvet furnishings and extra plush carpet.

Mallory emerged from her room, using a walking stick. "Finally, someone with sense."

Diana laughed uneasily. "I think you're giving me far more credit than I deserve."

"Are you all right, Diana?" Mallory asked, her voice dropping down to a low tone of concern.

Diana shook her head. "I'm leaving Tull today. My mother is ill, and I need to get home as soon as possible."

"Oh my." Mallory reached for her, hugging her tight. For a young woman who looked frail, she had a surprisingly strong embrace. "Is there anything I can do?"

"No, but if you will write to me. I have enjoyed being your friend."

Mallory released her, and they sat together on one of the plush settees clustered in the middle of the room. "You cannot lose me, don't worry. I'm like a tick. I latch on and don't let go."

Diana smiled, trying to fight back tears once again. If nothing else had come of this wretched visit to Tull, she had made a good friend, and she would be forever grateful for that. She filled Mallory in on what was happening, including her folly trying to learn magic.

"I don't think it was in vain," Mallory pointed out. She had called for tea, for which Diana was grateful. Holding a teacup gave her something to do with her hands.

"I was meeting with a powerful magical being," Diana said. "And suddenly it all felt like a giant waste of time."

"But you learned something about yourself. You learned that practicing magic isn't the future for you. That's important."

Diana wasn't sure she was ready to reframe her morning as such, but she allowed Mallory might be right. "I guess I just wish I knew what the future was supposed to be. It was all so clear when I arrived, and now, I feel like I've been through a dozen potential lifetimes."

Mallory could sympathize, but she remained practical. "I don't think any of us are supposed to know what's in our future. That is a recipe for disaster."

"True," Diana admitted.

"And now that you know that, maybe you can start to see your future including a certain knight of our acquaintance?"

Mallory couldn't quite wipe the devilish little smile off her face.

"I cannot imagine who you mean," Diana said, keeping her expression vacant.

Mallory rolled her eyes. Diana was sure there was a clever retort on her tongue, but she was saved from it by Lady Passwood entering the suite.

Diana stood and curtsied, and to her surprise, Lady Passwood curtsied in return. She wasn't sure that had ever happened before. She glanced at Mallory and saw confirmation of her surprise.

"Lady Diana, I heard you will be leaving us," said the Duchess.

"Yes," Diana said, taking her seat once again, "in just a few hours."

"I am glad to see you before you depart. I wanted to apologize for my conduct. I should have been in Tull when you arrived, I cannot excuse my own conduct and I want you to know that I am ashamed of it."

Shock was too calm of a word for what Diana felt, hearing the apology. She opened her mouth to respond, but the right combination of words didn't seem to want to come out. It took several excruciating seconds for her tongue to move again. "That is kind of you to say."

"Consider it an old woman's folly, I was so eager to match my nephew with my ward, that I failed to see how I was conducting myself where you were concerned."

The day had been so emotional that Diana wasn't sure she could absorb the apology, although she knew it was unlikely to be repeated. Lady Passwood was, in temperament, so much like her own mother that she knew such statements were rare indeed. "Thank you," she said, unable to say more.

"I hope we will see you at the Palace this winter."

"I have no plans to be there in the coming months," Diana said. "Until I know more about my mother's health, I will not be traveling."

"You must not have received the news. The Queen Regent has announced that there will be an official presentation at the Palace. All eligible young men and women in the Kingdom may choose to make an official debut. If I know your mother she will rally for just such an occasion." She passed Diana an official scroll, bearing the seal of the Vineland family, the two crossed crane flowers.

The heavy paper proclaimed that in honor of the twenty-first birthday of the Princess Royal, Kira Sabrina Stephanie, the crown would hold an official Presentation ceremony. Any family in the Known Kingdoms was welcome to submit their son or daughter's name for presentation to the Queen Regent and the Princess. All applicants would receive a date and time to appear at the Palace.

It was exactly the kind of event that her mother would love. Lots of pomp and circumstance, elaborate gowns, and likely a hundred society events surrounding the actual days of Presentation.

Diana would gladly attend a thousand of them if it meant her mother was healthy. "I think you're right. When I made my debut my mother lamented the lack of a formal presentation. It must be twenty years since one took place."

"At least," Lady Passwood agreed. "The late king ended so many of our rituals. I'm curious to see how the Queen Regent will handle it all."

Mallory smiled. "What she means is that she is eager to see all the drama surrounding it and if the Queen is up to the task."

Lady Passwood shot her ward an exasperated glare. "I meant only what I said, Dearest."

Diana stifled a laugh, not sure her fragile peace with Lady Passwood was strong enough to withstand it.

Mallory ignored her guardian's censure and turned to Diana. "I hope you will come. It would be lovely to have you at my official entry to society."

Lady Passwood looked concerned at that comment, but her face relaxed, and she summoned up a smile. "Please make sure your mother knows you will both be our honored guests at Mallory's debut ball."

"I will."

"Now you've promised, so be warned, if I have to wheel you in on my lap, you're coming," Mallory insisted. "Now go home and make your mother better."

Diana could make no promises, but she was able to leave Tull knowing she had at least made a final, positive impression.

Chapter Forty-Six

Jordaan

Having finally fit all his belongings into his traveling case, Jordaan was left with only one more errand to complete before he left Tull for good the next morning. A box of empty vials, the last remnants of their elixirs still clinging to the glass, rattled in the too-large box Jordaan had thrown them in for the short trip back to the Witch's Tower. Veronica, perhaps conscious that he was carrying potentially breakable items, refrained from winding around his feet as he took the stairs. He supposed he would have to return her as well. Technically she wasn't his cat, and ever-much as he wanted to tuck her into his traveling case, she belonged to Caris Mourne.

He knocked softly on the giant oak door, not expecting it to open so quickly. Involuntarily, he started at the unexpected face in front of him. The Fairie, Jacobee, clad in the gold-trimmed ceremonial robes of the Dark Court, scrutinized him. "The hour is late," they said.

Although their voice was calm, Jordaan couldn't help but feel he was intruding. He bowed. "My apologies for arriving unannounced, I came to return these." He held out the box.

Jacobee stepped back and admitted him to the tower. "Place them over there," they said, pointing to a worktable. "I'm sorry, but Caris is not here to wish you safe travels."

Jordaan couldn't escape the feeling that something was wrong. He thought back to what he'd heard days ago. All summer, Caris Mourne had looked almost colorless, the final straw being the white hair that had replaced the brilliant purple that was her calling card.

"I did want to thank her for all she's done for me. Is she well?"

Jacobee's eyebrows raised. "I would not say that."

"I'm sorry to hear that," he said, knowing the words were ineffectual.

Veronica, as if not to be excluded from the conversation, meowed. Jordaan reached down and scooped her for one last cuddle before he was forced to hand her over.

Jacobee leaned toward the cat, giving her a scratch on the head with their long fingers. "I see you have an admirer."

"She tolerates me. Which is the best we can hope for from a cat, isn't it?"

Jacobee smiled. "She is not a cat."

Jordaan held up the black kitten, looking into her yellow-green eyes. Diana had said much the same, but there was still nothing in the animal's demeanor that said anything other than *Cat*. "You could have fooled me."

"Humans are easily fooled," the Fairie said. They didn't shrug, but Jordaan took that as the implication.

"She's been a good companion, regardless."

"I would have thought Lady Diana would have been more to your taste," Jacobee said, taking the not-cat. "You were rather infatuated from what I remember."

"Cats don't have to marry well," Jordaan admitted, fighting a flush of embarrassment. He'd rather not be reminded that his penchant for Diana was obvious to everyone he'd met in Tull. "Anyhow, I guess I'll go. Please tell your spouse I am sorry to have missed her."

He bowed and the Fairie inclined their head. Jordaan turned to go, but something nagged at him. Another gift from Diana — her endless curiosity. "Just one more thing. Caris Mourne's condition, is related to the business with the Maundry?"

Jacobee raised their eyebrows. "Why do you ask?"

"Spindle kept saying the "The Magic Fades." And she agreed that it was important. I don't know what it means, but it seems like it might be connected?"

The Fairie's piercing gaze made Jordaan regret asking, but he supposed that was the legacy of Diana's influence. She would have asked the question, and so he asked the question.

After an excruciating pause, Jacobee inclined their head once again. "Yes. Her particular variety of magic relies on a natural life force. My kind has seen it fading for years."

"What is that? Is it something in nature?"

"In a way, yes," Jacobee answered. Veronica was still curled in their arms, but alert, eyeing Jordaan with a stare that matched the Fairie's. "Magic is energy. And this particular kind of energy is waning. Caris is feeling the effects. But do not worry about her. She has more tricks up her sleeves than even I can comprehend."

Before he could ask more, the Fairie held up the cat once more, looking in her eyes. "Well, if you insist."

Jacobee held out Veronica. "She wants to go with you."

Jordaan didn't hesitate to accept. "Cat or not, she has excellent taste." He kissed Veronica on top of her head, and gave her a good scratch behind the ears.

"Goodbye, Sir Jordaan," Jacobee said, signaling the end of their interaction.

Jordaan bowed once more and left before they could change their mind about keeping Veronica.

***

Jordaan slept badly during his last night at the Rutledge, which was ironic considering how often he'd fallen asleep at inconvenient times and places all over the building. Even with Veronica curled into his stomach like a purring hot water bottle, he was restless. He found himself staring at the ceiling for long stretches of time. It didn't get any more interesting as the night wore on.

Maybe because Diana was gone, and he hadn't been there to see her leave. She was a few thousand miles away, and he was still in Tull, feeling a little sorry for himself.

He'd done what was right. She was looking for a spouse with power and influence. He couldn't give her those things.

True, yes, Xavier hadn't been mistaken. His family was rich, and they had their own kind of influence. But money wasn't everything. He had four more years of service to the Duke of Lower Miser.

He couldn't ask her to wait that long.

Could he?

Lady Mallory's assertion that Diana was in love with him lodged in an uncomfortable space in his head.

She was definitely not in love with him. It wasn't possible. She knew better. She was to inherit the County of Wills, one of the most strategically important territories in the Known Kingdoms. Her future husband would need to be just as powerful if not more so. Diana was too smart to downgrade from a prince to landless knight. When she'd implored him to speak, to tell her that he loved her, that wasn't because she felt the same. She'd just wanted the words for her vanity.

Well, no, that wasn't it. Diana was not vain. She was confident in herself, but never vain. That confidence — entirely earned — was part of what made her so damn sexy.

He sighed, and turned rather violently, dislodging Veronica, who screeched at him.

"My apologies," he murmured to the cat.

He sat up, leaning against the headboard, and gathered Veronica in his arms. "I need to get back to work. Idleness is making me an idiot."

Jordaan had always had cats as a child. Chubby tabbies, elegant snow-white cats who shed whole sweaters worth of fur, and even scrawny barn cats who preferred the company of cows. But never, in all of life had he had a cat like Veronica. She turned with her yellow-green eyes, opened her mouth, and spoke. "Go to her. Tell her you love her. Now let me get some sleep."

"I guess I will?" Jordaan wasn't sure if he was awake, or if Veronica's smokey rumble of voice had come from some deep part of his unconscious brain. Either way, he decided, if he was at the point where a cat was actually speaking to him, that made two things abundantly clear. One, he would never tell anyone what just happened. And two, he would be making a stop in Wills before returning to Lower Miser.

Chapter Forty-Seven

Diana

In the weeks she'd been home, Diana had walked every inch of the land around Wills Castle. Summer was fading into an early autumn, as it did every year. While the southern territories continued to sweat, the north turned cooler. The crane fields were in their final flowering, the palest phase that produced the sweet and subtle perfume Wills was known to make.

Oftentimes she walked for hours as a way of not thinking about her mother, whose illness continued to linger. Her father, who was eager to show her all about being the steward of the Wills territory, had decided that her walks were an excellent time to instruct her on what she'd need to know when she took over the territory.

Diana would have liked to tell him that she preferred to keep her walks solitary, so that she could dwell on the bruised state of her heart, but she supposed the Earl of Wills needed distraction too. The love of his life was in fragile shape, and talking about the rotation of the crops and the other things that their tenant farmers grew in the leagues of fields in Wills was his main way of keeping his mind busy.

"Our farmers trust us to make fair decisions. To use our resources in the best interest of the land."

Her father waxed on about the importance of purchasing needed equipment, and getting the best price for the cranes. Diana's mind wandered back to Tull. She didn't miss it. Not the heat, nor the unrelenting sunshine, and especially not the smell of dead fish.

She supposed she missed the friends she had there, and the sense of independence. Jordaan calling her everything but her own name.

She would need to know all the information her father was sharing one day, but that was so far off. Her father was hale and hearty and he wasn't dying anytime soon. She wouldn't allow it. Besides, she knew her father was keeping up his constant stream of words to distract himself from the Countess's illness.

Mother's cough had settled so deeply in her chest that she was often at the point of full-body spasms. None of the healers and witches who had been to call at the castle could explain why she wasn't getting better.

Weeks of illness had left her mother drawn and weak. During the hours of the day that she was able to see either Diana or her husband, speaking was difficult. She kept to her room with her army of pugs.

Diana had written to Caris Mourne, apologizing for asking for yet another favor so soon after she had made it possible for her to return home easily, but unable to think of anything else to help her mother. She could only hope that the witch had some remedy that hadn't yet been tried and that her answer arrived swiftly.

Father stopped at the edge of the crane field, where a row of dying blossoms were drooping in the late afternoon sun. "These have sat too long," he said, pointing to the damaged petals. "We won't be able to harvest these so late in the summer."

Diana knelt down and plucked a few of the undamaged petals from a group of flowers. They gave off a sweet, fragrant aroma, despite the fact that they curled at the edges. She couldn't escape the notion that there was life left in them yet. She tucked a good handful into the pocket of her dress. She'd put them with the sad remains of her attempts to make perfume in Tull. After all, even damaged they couldn't produce anything that smelled as bad as the concoctions she'd tried to make.

"I'll have to speak to the land manager," the Earl said. "He should have made sure this field was plowed."

Most of the field had been plowed under. There was only a twenty-foot-wide strip here at the field's edge where the flowers remained. Her father wasn't usually so prickly about issues like one small area not being part of the harvest.

"He likely had a reason," Diana reminded him as gently as possible. "Have you been in to see Mother today?"

The Earl green eyes turned toward her, a sheepish expression written in the set of his mouth. "Are you trying to change the subject, Diana?"

"Yes," she said, giving him a small smile. "You've always trusted your managers. If you're finding fault with one small area, I know it isn't because you're upset over a few hundred flowers."

He sighed, his shoulders slumping under the neat line of his tweed coat. "You are too smart for your own good," he said. He leaned toward her, and kissed the top of her head. Although Diana was often taller than most people, her father made her feel like a dainty, protected girl.

"You should be the one to visit your mother today. Tell her again about the Presentation at the Palace. That always makes her want to get better."

"Yes, but when she gets too agitated, her dogs get antsy. And then they bark and *lick*." Diana shuttered. Dog slobber would forever be disgusting.

"Fine, then I shall go visit her and tell her all about how I'll be looking for a new manager."

Diana decided to return with him. The castle grounds were beautiful, but if she were to keep walking before too long she was going to wear out the soles of her boots. Besides, with the sun fading and the wind picking up, the day was no longer distracting her. All the traversing the property she'd done thus far she hadn't been able to shake the belief that she failed the Countess. As silly as it was to imagine that her lack of social triumph had anything to do with her mother's illness, the idea lingered foremost in her thoughts. She hadn't made a glorious match, hadn't secured the admiration of either the prince of Tull or its people. How could her mother not be disappointed? That was what she'd trained Diana to do. And thus so forlorn, she just wasn't getting better.

As they took the path from the far fields up toward the castle grounds, Diana fell silent. Although she had spent plenty of hours by her mother's side since returning, most of that had been while the Countess slept.

"You are too quiet, my dear," the Earl said. "Tell me why."

It was her first instinct to say nothing, to promise her father that all was well, but the closer they got to the great gray stone edifice of Wills Castle, the more the feeling of inadequacy lingered.

"I know this is unlikely, but....do you think Mother is so disappointed that I'm not going to marry Prince Travers that it's making her illness worse?

The Earl's expression shifted to one of concern. He put an arm around her shoulders and hugged her. "Why ever would you think so? Your mother loves you beyond anything. You could never..."

"But she was so happy when we left the Festival of the Flower last year, because I had that invitation to go to Tull. It was her big triumph."

"Oh my girl," the Earl said, taking her hands. "There is one thing I know about your mother, and that's that she wants what is best for you. *You* have always been her triumph."

The words poured out of Diana. She hadn't realized how much she needed to get them out until most of the story was laid out in front of her father.

Not the bits where she'd nearly kissed Sir Jordaan, obviously, but the rest. Her rough start in Tull, and Travers being anything but kind or welcoming. Lady Passwood "forgetting" about her invitation. The fire, the dead fish, and the castle collapse. Losing Maryann and Bill, and having no idea where they'd gone. "I just feel like I messed up every chance I had to make her proud."

Her father's hand squeezed hers. "You aren't responsible for how anyone else feels, Diana Michelle. Not Prince Travers, or Lady Passwood, or even your mother. I know that we sent you to Tull with good sense and good manners, and you made the best of what sounds like a very uncomfortable situation."

Diana wiped away an unexpected tear. She hadn't realized how much she'd been holding in, and when it had come out, she'd released so much she was practically dizzy. Her father kissed the top of her head, as he'd done when she was little. "No matter what, you are still your mother's daughter. And she will want to know all you've just told me because it has been bothering you. Not to blame you or chastise you or put the blame for her illness on you, but simply because she loves you. You'd do best to go see her, and tell her all of what you've just told me."

Diana nodded. She wasn't sure she had a second emotional outburst in her, but she would tell her mother. Perhaps if the Countess knew she had to start strategizing a new plan for Diana's future, she would rally.

They resumed their walk back to the castle and were met with the sight of three carriages, two of which had a tower of trunks strapped to the roof. Mother's pugs all yipped and barked as the servants began unloading.

"What's all of this?" The Earl asked.

Diana recognized a few of the trunks, and soon caught sight of Alice, telling a sheepish-looking Jonah to take some of the smaller suitcases into the castle.

"It would seem my belongings have arrived," Diana said.

Her father eyed the carriages. "Did you really take three carriages worth to Tull?"

"Only two that I remember, but I suppose we didn't pack as efficiently on return."

Her father chuckled as they approached the castle steps. "I can only hope among all of these things you remembered to bring me presents. I do love the lemon candy they make in Tull."

Alice seemed to have the orchestration of unloading Diana's things well in hand, pointing the cadre of footmen from the castle toward each box and case. Diana and her father approached, Diana giving the maid a welcoming smile and her father offering the maid a bow.

Alice curtsied to them both, a smile across her thin face.

"Oh my Lady, I'm so happy to see you."

"I'm glad you're back, Alice. I hope the sea journey wasn't too rough."

"No, not at all. Sir Jordaan got me my own cabin, can you imagine? I had a whole room all to myself, and once a day someone brought me fresh water and changed the linens."

"Sir Jordaan did that?" Diana asked, astonished.

The four pugs, all of whom were overly excited, had gathered at the door to the unladen carriage.

"Yeah," Alice said. "When he saw I only had a bunk among a bunch of sailors, he said I couldn't travel like that, being as I was a lady. Can you imagine? I was so glad he was on the ship with us."

Jordaan had been on the same ship? Diana felt her pulse quicken. "He traveled with you as far as…"

"As here, My Lady. He's just there." Alice pointed to the first carriage. "When he saw Jonah and I struggling to get everything out of the Rutledge and to the port, he stepped in to help, and then came all the way home with us."

"And who is this Sir Jordaan?" her father asked with a raised eyebrow.

Jordaan had climbed out of the front carriage by then, issuing stern commands to the jumping pugs to sit. Diana's eyes grew wide as all four fat, excited animals sat themselves down on the cobblestones.

He was dressed impeccably. Dark trousers, and what hat looked to be a new blue and gold knight's tunic over a crisp white shirt. His long, shaggy blond hair had been trimmed and slicked back into a queue. He'd shaved, much to her disappointment, although she had to admit he looked just as delectable cleaned up. He bowed deeply to her father. The pugs, seeming to understand this was an important guest, dutifully kept a step behind, sitting when he came to a stop in front of Diana and her father.

"Lord Wills, I am Sir Jordaan Van Dine of Margate."

Her father inclined his head and then held out his hand for Jordaan to shake. "An honor Sir Jordaan. Are you related to Baron Van Dine?"

"My father," he answered.

The Earl looked impressed. "And to what do we owe the honor of your visit to us, Sir Jordaan."

Diana's mouth was suddenly dry. She didn't know what she expected Jordaan to say. She wasn't sure that she wasn't dreaming. Jordaan, here in Wills, was something her mind had only conjured up in her dreams, the only space where it was possible he'd followed her through Caris Mourne's enchanted doorway, and declared all those feelings she wanted him to have.

"I've come to pay a call on Lady Diana. Because I wish to court her, and one day marry her, if she'll have me."

***

The Earl had moved their conversation into the castle proper, ringing for drinks to be brought to his private study. Diana was too stunned to speak. Her heart was beating furiously, so that every time she opened her mouth to say something, she thought it would jump right out of her chest.

Jordaan had slipped his hand into hers as they climbed the stairs to the study. Her palm was hot, and sweaty from her walk, but she was grateful for the steady presence of his grip.

"Now, let's get acquainted, shall we?" her father said, eyeing their clasped hands.

"I know this is sudden," Sir Jordaan said. "But I seem to be very much in love with your daughter."

Her father looked as if he would speak, but he turned to her instead. "My dear, is there something you wish to say?"

Diana blew out the breath she'd been holding. She looked up at Jordaan. She had missed him. How was that possible? They'd spent less time together in Tull than it had taken him to accompany her maid and footmen back to Wills. And yet, his face was the only one she wanted to see. "Only that I believe I," she paused, not because she was unsure of the feelings that she had for Jordaan but because they felt too big, too potent to be said out loud. "I love him."

A grin broke out on Jordaan's face, the kind of smile he specialized in, like a cat who'd caught a canary. "You are magnificent. Have I told you that?" he half-whispered.

Diana felt a rush of heat fill her cheeks. Her stomach seemed to be filled with over-excited butterflies, dancing triple-time.

The Earl of Wills cleared his throat in a significant, *'please don't forget I'm her father and standing right here,'* manner. "Well, I can see we have much to discuss. Diana, why don't you go visit your mother while Sir Jordaan and I discuss a few things."

Diana looked at Jordaan, who dared to wink at her. "Please give the Countess my regards. I look forward to meeting her."

Diana reluctantly let go of Jordaan's hand, slipping out of the study. The four pugs all wagged their tails as she entered the hall, tongues out, eager to jump all over her. Diana held up her hands to ward them off, but her furry siblings didn't seem to take commands from her.

"Oh fine," she said, swooping up Fritz, her mother's oldest, quietest pug into her arms. "Let's go visit Mother. But you had all better be on your best behavior."

Although perhaps it would be good to have the little beasts be impossible. That might be easier than explaining to her mother how she was — for the second time this year — practically engaged.

Chapter Forty-Eight

Jordaan

When Jordaan had envisioned this moment, sitting across from Diana's father and confessing his intentions, he'd had the picture of the Earl of Wills all wrong. From every account he'd heard, the Earl was a recluse. He never traveled with his wife and daughter when they visited other royals. And thus, somewhere in Jordaan's mind, that meant the man was old and feeble.

That couldn't be farther from the truth.

Across from him was no frail, white-haired old man, but a red-headed giant who, despite the well-cut tweed suit, looked as if he might rip tree trunks in half. *For fun.*

As soon as Diana had left the study, Jordaan had sensed a shift in the man from a loving father who would give his daughter everything in his power, to a man who was set on protecting his most cherished child. Possibly with those tree trunks.

"Tell me how long you've known my daughter," he said.

Jordaan sipped the whiskey the Earl had given him, glad of its burn. "We met in the spring, at the Festival of the Flower, and then saw each other again in Tull where I was recuperating from an illness."

The Earl nodded as if he might have already known this information. "And what in Fairie Hells makes you think you're good enough for her?"

Now that was a question he'd expected. "Oh, I know I'm not. Have you seen your daughter? She's the most beautiful..."

"I'm well aware my Diana is a treasure. What I want to know about you, Sir Jordaan. You're what, a fourth, maybe fifth son?"

"Fifth," he said. "There's quite an age gap between me and my next-oldest brother."

"Hm," The Earl said. He poured himself another whiskey from the elegant crystal decanter that a servant had brought. He did not offer any more to Jordaan. "And you're a knight. Currently in service, I assume?"

"To the Duke of Lower Miser. I have four years left on my contract, and I intend to fulfill them."

"Four years is a long time to wait to marry a woman you confess to love."

"The fact is I could leave the Duke's service. My parents have set aside a generous income for me, and my father is eager that I join him in working in the crane trade. But I want to see my contract out. I don't believe I would be in any way the kind of man that Diana needs if I were to leave my commitments so easily."

The Earl considered that for a moment. He didn't sit, but paced the wood-paneled study, always keeping an eye on Jordaan. "Having the title of Sir for the rest of your life won't hurt either."

"I can't do anything about being a non-royal fifth son, but I can elevate myself a little by being a knight. And frankly, I enjoy the camaraderie and the work."

"And while you finish out that work, you want to court my little girl?"

Jordaan knew the question was a loaded one. But he loved Diana. He didn't need his talking cat to tell him, or anyone else. His job at that moment was to convince the Earl that he was sincere and his feelings were true. "One of the things I have learned about Diana was how much she loves her home. She would have done marvelous in Tull, had Prince Travers not been such an ass."

He paused for a fraction of a second, hoping that his criticism of the Prince didn't set off any resentment in Diana's father. Seeing only the acceptance that this must be true, he continued. "She was there not because she felt much for Travers but because she loved County Wills. In addition to being intelligent and fascinating in the best ways, she was doing that because she wanted the best for her territory. If I knew nothing else about her, that would be enough to tell me she's the best kind of royal. She wants to be here and she wants to learn everything she can. Frankly, that's sexy as..." he let his words die off. Sexy was possibly not a word to use around a future father-in-law.

The Earl looked a bit embarrassed by that statement, but he brushed it off. "And you know that if you married her, you would one day be royal once I am gone."

"My Lord, you're not planning on dying are you?"

The Earl snorted at his impertinence. "No, I am not. I am, however, going to make sure that while you court my daughter you never, ever disappoint her. I will be watching."

There should be a medal for this moment when the father of the woman he loved accepted his suit. An orchestra should be set up to play, possibly some kind of scientific exhibition set up so people could marvel at how deliriously happy he felt.

"I love Diana, My Lord. I will work every day so that she knows that."

Chapter Forty-Nine

Diana

The Countess of Wills was pale and much diminished from the fevers and coughing spells that had ravaged her body since the summer began. But she sat up in bed, directing her maids to help freshen her up, to get her presentable. Diana had drawn a chair at her bedside but kept having to duck out of the way as gowns, makeup, and other items were all brought to her.

"A Van Dine, you're sure? One of the Baron's sons, not some far-flung relation?"

"Yes, he's the Baron's fifth son."

"With that family, even a fifth son will be well placed in life. The Van Dines have influence in every territory in the Known Kingdoms and a few in the Unknown Kingdoms. They're incredibly powerful."

"I guess I knew that, but Mother, he's more than his family, he's also a knight."

"Admirable, yes, although Lower Miser is not exactly the highest of kingdoms. Still, an association with the Lycettes is never a bad thing. They are one of the oldest of royal families."

"And our friends," Diana reminded her.

"That will make a splendid marriage for you. We must begin planning."

"Mother, it's likely a wedding is a long way off. He has years before he's finished his contract."

Mother's drawn face split into a wide smile. "Oh Diana, my darling, perfect, wonderful daughter."

"Not that I'm allergic to the praise, Mother, but I think you're overdoing it. Sir Jordaan is kind, certainly, but also infuriating. It is so far off that this all might come to nothing."

Her mother had a way of arching her eyebrow that made Diana squirm. She did her best to ignore it, but her mother pressed on. "You love him."

Diana nodded. "He sneaked his way into my heart when everything was going wrong in Tull. He's wonderful. Although he is a cat person, so we may have some trouble there."

Her mother cuddled Fritz, her oldest, dearest, and entirely silent pug close to her chest, stroking his head with determined pets that made the animal's eyes bulge. The other three curled at the end of her mother's bed like little loaves of sourdough bread still heaving in the oven. "I don't mind cats. They're not as intelligent as my pugs, but they are not so bad."

Diana had to wonder if there was a polite way of telling her mother that she knew of a particular black cat who would be very much offended by that statement. She could only too easily imagine Veronica taking one look at her mother's pugs and making them her minions.

"Well, let's go meet this wonderful man, shall we?" Mother said. She rose from the bed she'd been in since Diana had returned home. Although unsteady on her feet, she had two of her maids help her into her dress — a deep, intimidating red that put color in her cheeks and made her look every inch the Iron Countess of Wills.

Diana had to wonder if Jordaan had any idea what awaited him. Because while her father was a mountain of a man not afraid to use his size to intimidate when needed, the Countess of Wills was in a category all her own.

***

"Delores, perhaps we should run away."

Diana grinned, taking his hand. He wore no gloves and his gently calloused palm surrounded hers. "I don't think so, Jackson. You've made some big promises to my parents."

Jordaan groaned. "I have, haven't I? I am so good with parents. I should write a book."

"You're impossible."

"Yes, but I'm yours," he said, pulling her close, and wrapping his arm around her waist. She was pleased to have been right. They were exactly the same height. She could look directly into his eyes. She could close the distance between them with the barest lean forward, and their lips would meet.

They weren't entirely alone in the castle's long gallery. A maid trailed a discreet distance behind them, pretending interest in the portraits lining the walls. She did a decent job of signaling with decreet coughs that her back was turned.

"Do you really want to wait four years?" she asked.

"But not a day more," he said.

"Why?"

Jordaan got uncharacteristically serious. "Because I can't imagine a better life for myself than by your side." He brushed a loose curl back from her temple, his fingers lingering by her ear. "I'll get to watch you be amazing at everything you do."

"No pressure there," she said.

"You'll rise to the occasion," he said.

The maid cleared her throat, and Diana stepped out of Jordaan's hold. She was the colder for it, but priority must be maintained. The gallery opened on the far end to a balcony overlooking the beaches on the far end of Wills, and they stepped outside to look at the stars. The maid stayed indoors, just by the glass doors.

"I'll visit you whenever I'm able. Lower Miser is not so far away."

Diana felt bold as they stepped out into the night air. The autumn-like wind cooled her flushed face. She turned to Jordaan, brushing her hand along his clean-shaven jaw. "I miss the beard."

"It was itchy."

"It made you look distinguished, but I can learn to like this too."

"As it's my face, I hope so," he said, his voice low.

"Perhaps if I look at it a little closer," she said, wrapping her arms around his neck.

"Daria, what are you on about?"

"Oh shut up and kiss me, Jeremy."

Author's Note

I don't know if it is obvious, but I love these characters, especially Diana and Mallory. They are fictional, but I've given them little bits of personality and attributes from some of my best friends, who are smart and beautiful women who are so much fun to be around. Writing parts of this novel was like getting to hang out with them. And we don't get to do that nearly enough.

It was also a no-brainer to use Sleeping Beauty as inspiration. Back in the day when Disney Channel was a paid extra on cable (that we *definitely* didn't have), there used to be "Free Preview Weekends" where we'd burn through a lot of blank VHS tapes. My mom taped Sleeping Beauty for me, and I watched it, with the 1-800-number superimposed over the bottom of the screen, until it broke.

And while we're talking Sleeping Beauty, I apologize to any purists out there (if there is such a thing), but I don't regret making Jordaan my Aurora. Writing his banter with Diana was a joyful experience. I know that dark, brooding, and morally gray heroes are all the rage, but they're exhausting. I'll take a snarky golden retriever any day.

I have two more books in the works for this series. The next is Rebels & Royals, Bertie and Xavier's second-chance love story, with nods to Little Red Riding Hood. Travers and Mallory will get their love story (to be named later) shortly after. And as for what's going on with a certain purple-haired witch, that mystery is purposefully left unsolved for now. I know, and once book four is done, so will you.

Thanks for reading, it is much appreciated. I'd love it if you would leave a review on Amazon or Goodreads. You can find more about this series, and other projects at my website, https://sun-valley-books.com.